FREE STORIES

Pixies, Shades, and tribal Magick—having a baby is hard enough, but having a Magician's baby is in a league all of its own...

Sign up at www.martin-shannon.com to get "Danderous Delivery," the Tales of Weird Florida short story only available to newsletter subscribers.

GATHERING GLOOM

MARTIN SHANNON

To my wife, the Porter to my Gene.

PART I
IN THE GARDEN

1

NIGHT JOBS

Bzzt!

"Dang it," my roommate mumbled, mashing a handful of buttons on the vending machine's aging keypad. "Come on..."

Ed and I huddled just inside the dim halo of a snack dispenser on the second floor of the now closed accounting building somewhere in the bowels of the college of business. The blue display cast just enough light to see our faces reflected in the dusty glass. Behind those patchy beards and messy hair, an angry red exit sign lit the remainder of the empty hallway. The harsh light gave an already unpleasant location a malevolent hue. Small packages of salty snacks hung like expired stockings from narrow metal posts in the machine, their colorful wrappers muted in the gloomy darkness.

My roommate banged on the glass. "It's a simple transaction. I put in a dollar, you give me the crackers," he said, frowning at the truculent machine.

A tiny blue LED display popped up in glowing letters.

NO SALE.

Bzzt!

Ed's dollar rolled back out of the machine like impromptu origami. He sighed and rubbed out the creases. Nothing else stirred on the long vinyl floor, nothing except for my roommate and a persnickety vending machine. Pockmarked with closed doors and the occasional bulletin board, the hall was devoid of all life, just the way you'd expect a haunted building to be on a Friday night.

Ed shoved the dollar in again.

NO SALE.

Bzzt!

"Ed," I whispered, grabbing his shoulder, then checking the hall for signs of ghostly activity yet again. "What are you doing?"

"Getting a snack." My roommate flipped surfer-blond locks out of his eyes and rammed the dollar back into the vending machine yet again. "I never exorcise on an empty stomach."

Bzzt!

You wouldn't know it to look at him, but Ed Lovely was quite the eater. A couple inches taller than me, and lacking my more rounded form, Ed had the body of a distance runner— light on the muscle and heavy on the sinew. Right now, that body was doing its best to hold up a fishing vest of tiny pockets, each one practically bursting at the velcro'd seams with all manner of oddball items.

"Aren't we supposed to be quiet?"

The young man shrugged his thin shoulders. "I doubt it matters much. What time is it?"

"Ten," I said, holding my watch up to catch what little light trickled out of the ancient vending machine. "I think?"

"We got at least thirty minutes, this place has been nothing if not predictable."

"Are you sure?"

Ed nodded and flipped his long bangs out of his face again. "Completely. Besides, you finished the sigil and I've got

Qulvers's Infinite Keys." He patted a lump in one of his vest pockets. "What are you worried about?"

I checked the empty hall again. "I'm not worried. I just think we shouldn't be making a lot of noise, that's all."

Ed smiled. Those dimpled cheeks played well with his girl-friend, but I knew they were just an early warning indicator that almost always meant trouble. "You worry too much, Gene, relax. You're a Magician, you got this."

Do I?

My name is Eugene Law, and I'm a Magician—at least that's what I tell myself. I don't do balloon animals, or kids parties, and I'm not much for card tricks. I deal in real Magick, the cosmic powers of the universe, and all the baggage that comes with them.

Bzzt!

The machine ejected the mangled dollar, forcing Ed to rub the offending bill against the side of the display. "Do you have another dollar? It doesn't like this one."

"I'm not your personal cash machine."

My roommate pointed to the darkened interior. "I think they have peanut-butter crackers."

Ed wasn't a Magician, but he did know how to get me to magic up some dollar bills.

"Fine." I pulled out my wallet. "But I think I gave my last dollar to Morgan."

Ed rolled his eyes. "What on earth for?"

"Because she's my girlfriend and she asked for it?"

Ed Lovely shook his head, his fishing vest of tiny pockets jingling along with it. "You do know just because they ask you for things doesn't mean you have to give it to them, right?"

"I have a five," I said, ignoring his comment. "But I don't want—"

Ed snatched the bill out of my wallet. "Excellent. I'll get you change."

"But I—"

"And peanut-butter crackers."

Sigh.

"Fine."

Bzzt!

My roommate scrunched up his face. "Dang it. Come on, you stupid machine. We have two hungry Demon Hunters out here who need to sustain themselves through the trials and tribulations ahead. Give us your bounty, oh great and holy—" Ed paused to squint at the tiny lettering just above the digital readout—"Apex Food Services Delivery Cash-n-Go. Bestow it upon your supplicants such that we may bask in the life-giving nourishment of preservatives and salt."

"Demon Hunters?"

Ed kicked the machine. "Yeah, I lumped you in with me, just in case the machine was listening. Most of the time these things hate Magicians."

Whrr.

My roommate's eyes lit up. "See, I told you." He pointed to a spot a few feet away, where we'd drawn the Velcurses Conundrum on the vinyl floor in grease pen earlier. "Stand over there, Gene, you're getting Magick on the vending machine."

Demon Hunters...

Ed Lovely wasn't your typical roommate. To say he was eccentric would have been doing a disservice to truly eccentric people. Ed was wholly unique, and for a guy like me that worked out all right.

My roommate had no Magickal power to speak of, his well was dry—bone dry you could say, but I didn't, because neither of us talked about that. What Ed did have was an almost encyclopedic knowledge of all things supernatural. The man was a walking field-guide to everything from Magickal Sigils to Demons, and, as luck would have it, hauntings.

"I'm telling you, Gene, it's a simple Poltergeist. Nothing

major. We could totally handle it in a single evening," my room-mate had said only a few hours earlier.

"I'm not sure... isn't that the accounting building?"

"Right! What's it going to do, spreadsheet us to death? Come on. It'll be good practice for you."

I'd begrudgingly agreed, then helped Ed into his Demon Hunting vest of trinkets and yard sale rejects—more than half of which I knew were Magickal, but had no idea what they did. After all of that I somehow ended up carrying his backpack.

Ed's keys had unlocked the main door, as well as the second-floor hallway. All of which had led us to this rather ornery vending machine. That was how we'd ended up here, in the accounting building, waiting for a ghost my roommate insisted would show up at ten-thirty.

This amorphous haunting is punctual, Gene. I'm sure of it.

"Yahtzee!" Ed cried when the first snack item hit the bottom of the vending machine.

A cool wind kicked up and whistled down the empty hallway.

"Ed..."

"Damn, they're cheese crackers, man. You still want them?"

The exit sign flickered gently, its light popping on and off in rapid-fire succession.

"Ed..."

My roommate dug an arm into the machine and shoved it up to his elbow. "Don't worry, buddy, I got you. I think I can reach them. It's not really stealing if the machine doesn't give you what you ordered."

The distant red glow winked out and left us with only the machine's glowing digital readout to see by.

"Ed!"

"What?" My roommate contorted his body to dig deeper. "Can you just be patient a few more seconds? I've almost got it."

The young Demon Hunter's fingers grazed the edge of a plastic-wrapped stack of crackers.

"Ed, the sign just went out."

"Huh?" My roommate pressed his cheek against the display case.

"And did you feel that breeze?" I asked, trying to find the grease-marked sigil we'd drawn in the machine's dim light.

Ed scrunched up his face and grabbed the lip of the dispenser slot. "Is it ten thirty?"

"I can't see my watch, but—"

"Then we're fine. I told you, this Poltergeist is punctual. It's like clockwork. You could set your watch by it. In fact, my mom always used to say that if you—"

"Ed," I cried, pointing down the hallway, where a pair of red pinpricks glowed in the distant dark. "What's that?"

"I'm betting it's the same thing that has my hand."

Bang!

I spun around to find my roommate's face smashed against the vending machine's glass.

A black-and-shadowy set of clawed fingers inside the glass-covered display case squeezed my roommate's fingers.

"It's got your hand!"

"Tell me something I don't already know." Ed pulled back with his arm only to get his cheek slammed back into the machine a second time. "It's not ten thirty."

Soft whispers echoed in the hallway, hissing and angry as they bounced off the stark walls and hard floor.

"And that's not a Poltergeist," I said, pulling on his shoulder.

"Nope." My roommate used his other hand to pry his face away from the display case. "Those are Shades—"

Bang!

Ed's head hit the glass again. More red eyes twinkled like stars along the edges of the darkened hall. Sharp claws scraped on the hard concrete. "What do we do?"

"You're the Magician. Warm up that Magick while I get my hand out of this damn box."

"Okay, do I power up the Velcurses Conundrum?" I asked, trying to find the sigil in the dark hallway.

"Yeah, wait, you need to—"

Bong!

My roommate's face smacked into the display glass hard enough to leave a mark.

"Ed?"

My only response was the scraping of claws and glow of angry red eyes reflected in the vending machine's dingy glass.

Crap.

2

ROCK ON

I grabbed Ed's shoulder. "What? I need to what?"

The clawed hand holding my roommate captive released its shadowy fingers, instead reaching for me through the dusty glass.

"Ed," I cried, yanking the dazed Demon Hunter free of the vending machine's grasp. "What are Shades?"

My roommate shook his head. "Huh?"

More red eyes lit up the hallway, too many of them to count. They bobbed like angry fireflies, crawling along the walls, the ceiling, and the floor.

I dragged the stunned Demon Hunter into the sigil and tried to make sure I didn't smudge any of the complex lines in the process. "Ed, what do I do?"

My roommate shook his head a few times. "Give me a second."

"We don't *have* a second."

Shadowy claws reached up from the floor, their fingers searching, while all around us bright eyes pressed in closer.

I slammed my palm against the ground and dug deep for the Magick I knew swirled around in my body. Using that power was always a risk. I hadn't mastered much in the way of control —that was what the sigils were for—at least according to Morgan.

God, I wish Morgan was here right now...

My girlfriend would have known what to do. She was a master at these sorts of things. The brilliant gothic angel possessed a Magick that was as delicate as it was precise. She understood the power tucked inside those whorls and lines far better than I did, and even though we'd worked on them for next to forever, I still didn't feel like I'd made any headway. But I did know one thing: a sigil's power is tucked up in its design, and in how it manipulates the Magick you push into it.

Pushing Magick—now that I can do.

I directed that swirling cosmic power into the sigil, sending it racing down the complex lines and dancing between the twisting whorls.

Come on...

A dim glow drifted up from the concentric pattern, like the twinkling of stars at night. The faint light played off Ed's face, as well as the scowling visages of hungry Shades.

"What are you doing?!" Ed cried, suddenly very much awake.

"You said to get the Magick going. That's what I'm doing."

My roommate grabbed my arm. "You don't pour Magick into the Velcurses Conundrum in the presence of Shades!"

"You don't?"

Whispering mouths opened around us, their fleshy, cavernous interiors sucking up the sigil's power like vacuums on overdrive.

Ed shook his head. "No, you don't. What is she teaching you? Crap. You just powered them up."

"I did?"

Shades swelled around us, buoyed by the Magick injected into the Velcurses Conundrum and hungry for more.

"Yes, you did," Ed said, fumbling with one of the many pockets on his jacket. "Shades are creatures of the Gloom."

"Huh?"

My roommate slapped his forehead. "Is she teaching you *anything* beyond how to undo a bra strap?"

Morgan had taught me a lot of things, but it may have been possible my mind had drifted a bit from time to time. Hungry shadows swelled and filled the space around us. Red eyes glittered in the sigil's soft glow.

Ed retrieved a chromed lighter from one of his many pockets. A fierce bald eagle, with claws at the ready, was embossed on the side of it. "Crash course. Here we go. The Gloom is full of terrible and dangerous monsters. It functions like a shadow of this world, and it's stupid cold."

The Shades pressed in on us. Red light poured from their ravenous jaws.

"Is now the time for this?" I asked, backing into my roommate.

"There's never a bad time to learn something."

Black claws raked at my hands and I yanked them aside before I lost those fingers to a famished Gloom beast. "I'm not positive that's always true."

Ed ignored me and flipped open the lighter. "Okay, I need you on Magick and air guitar."

"Huh?"

My roommate held the silvery metal eagle above his head. "You heard me. I need you to funnel some Magick into this rock ballad while I deliver the soul-crushing vocals."

Shades pressed in closer, rows of oddly curved teeth undulating inside their rounded mouths. "Ed—"

"Air guitar, Gene."

"Uh…"

My roommate grabbed my shoulder and aimed me toward

the advancing Shades. "I need you to deliver some solid Gloom-shredding air guitar moves. Think you can do that?"

"I don't—"

Ed slapped my back. "That's the spirit. Here we go, one, two, three!" Ed struck the flint, but all we got was a small dusting of sparks. "Hold on, the Rock God's Reward takes a few tries. I think I got it wet once."

"Ed," I cried, stumbling forward and catching myself just before I fell out of the Velcurses Conundrum. Something was pulling on my Magick, draining it *and* the life force that went with it.

The Shades!

"That's just the Gloom beasts. Try to keep a stiff upper lip and all—Rock Gods don't cry."

"Do they get their souls sucked out?"

Ed struck the lighter a couple more times, frustration becoming evident on his face. "Well, groupies can do that…"

My shoulders fell and my chest ached. "Ed…"

"Right. Come on, you stupid lighter. Hang on there, little buddy. We've got this. Any second now it's going to—"

Whoosh!

The lighter's wick caught a spark, and immediately the hallway filled with its flickering orange glow. Hungry Shades pulled back, but not nearly far enough.

"Okay, time to shred!" Ed's voice echoed in the wide hall as if amplified by an unseen microphone.

"Huh?" I could barely keep my head up, the Shades' soul-sucking cold was too great. "I don't know what to do."

"Gene, pretend to play guitar or we're both toast."

I held up a lone hand like I were cradling the neck of some invisible instrument. "Like this?"

Somewhere behind me, Ed's hand grabbed mine and pulled it up higher. "Come on, man. You are a rockstar, at least try to act like one. Imagine those panties flying up on stage."

The twisting mouths of hungry Shades filled the space around me—women's underwear was about the last thing on my drifting mind.

"Strum, Gene!" Ed cried, the Gloom beasts reaching for us both. "Strum like your life depends on it."

So tired...

"Strum, damn it!"

I dragged my fingers across the air in a loosely guitar-like motion, and much to my surprise the first notes of a soulful power-chord roared out and into the Shade-filled hallway. "Ed?"

"Not now, Gene. Keep strumming and get ready to pump up the Magick volume. It's time to unload a full can of rock ballad badassery on the half-living."

I dug in harder, buoyed by the powerful notes. My hand picked up steam with each burst of righteous sound.

"Yeah, that's the ticket," Ed cried, holding the lighter higher. "We who are about to shred your shadowy asses, salute you!"

It's working?!

My imaginary guitar's chart-topping power-chords cut a path of destruction through the surrounding Shades. Like candles in the wind, their bodies were torn apart in the heavy-metal fury of the crushing chorus, and what I didn't reach, Ed took out with his face-melting vocals.

"We've got them on the run, Gene. Pour it on!"

Yes!

I stood, my legs no longer numb, and strummed that imaginary guitar with everything I had.

"I mean the Magick, Gene."

"Oh, right."

No longer siphoned by the Shades, I pumped my foot against an imaginary Whammy Pedal, sending the Magickal notes roaring. The guitar's powerful notes shook the walls, while Ed's vocals rattled the closed doors and knocked bulletin boards off the wall. Shades melted away by the dozens, unable to stand in the presence of imaginary rock gods.

"Kick ass, Gene," Ed cried, holding the lighter as high as he could. "Maybe bring it down just a little."

My roommate was right. The Magickally enhanced music shook the walls and rattled the doors, but it didn't stop there. It shook *everything*. Overhead lights rattled, snapping free and raining down sharp glass and hazardous chemicals.

"Gene!"

"I'm trying," I shouted, doing all I could to rein in the unruly Magick. "It's not listening."

A window at the far end of the hallway shattered. Glass rained down on the courtyard below.

"Try harder."

I reached deep inside, down to the power that rumbled in my chest.

The remaining Shades surged for the broken window. They spilled out of it like lemmings at the ocean's edge, but still the crushing chords didn't stop.

Boom!

The vending machine toppled over. Its dusty glass shattered and a cornucopia of brightly wrapped candies scattered across the floor.

"Gene!"

I pushed deeper and reached for the source, for that mental off-switch that might stop the soul-shredding sound.

There it is...

"Got it." I tamped the Magick down, then ripped my hand through one last power-chord. Together, Ed and I collapsed against the broken sigil, the scorched lighter falling from his fingers.

"We did it..." I said, still trying to come to grips with exactly what it was we'd done.

"Yeah—" Ed pushed himself up and grabbed a couple of

packages of peanut-butter crackers before collapsing back against the floor—"sure did. To the victor goes the spoils. They aren't women's underwear, but they'll do."

I peeled open the wrapper. "Thanks, Ed."

"Sure thing."

Beep! Beep! Beep!

My roommate's watch alarm ripped off a series of beeps.

"What's that?" I asked between mouthfuls of hard-earned cracker.

Ed pressed a button on his watch. "Oh, that just means it's ten thirty."

3
WORDS OF POWER

*lang!*

"Ed…"

My roommate lay nearby, crunching on crackers. "Yeah."

"Did you hear that?"

"Probably just the junk settling."

"Oh, right." A cool breeze ruffled my shirt. "Ed?"

"It's just the wind, Gene."

I pulled another couple crackers out of the package. "Yeah, that's got to be it. I mean, it wasn't a Poltergeist, right? Just some Shades."

"That's my guess. I wouldn't expect there to still be anything else."

Rustle. Rustle.

My roommate put a hand on my shoulder. "As long as you're digging through the snacks, would you grab me something sweet?"

"I'm not digging through the snacks, Ed."

Rustle. Rustle.

"You aren't?"

"Nope," I said, sitting up alongside my roommate.

Wrapped candies floated gently in the air around us, twisting and turning in stark defiance of gravity.

"Ha!" My roommate snapped a chocolate bar out of the air. "Now *this* is a spirit I can get behind. Maybe we could invite it to the dorm room..."

Pling!

Long shards of vending machine glass joined the gently floating treats.

"Ed," I slowly backpedaled away from a wicked-looking sliver, "maybe we could just leave the ghost here?"

My roommate set his crackers down, then nodded. "Yeah. That sounds like a good plan, a very good plan."

Cling! Cling! Cling!

Thin metal spokes joined the already crowded airspace. Hangers that had once held individually wrapped treats now drifted menacingly, their pointy ends directed at Ed and I.

"So, make a run for it on three?" I asked, slowly getting my feet underneath me.

Ed nodded. "Works for me."

"One..."

I brushed aside razor-sharp glass to clear my path for the exit.

"Two..." Ed got to his knees and slid a floating Gobs-o-nuts bar into his pocket.

"Three," I cried, springing to my feet and making a run for the distant door.

Crash!

The vending machine uprighted itself, and like an expert linebacker it filled the space between me and the only exit that didn't involve jumping out the window. Twisted metal and broken glass wedged the hulking beast in tight.

"Okay." Ed's overburdened fishing vest jingled comically. "Okay, okay, we can handle this. How's the Velcurses Conundrum looking?"

I backed up from the monstrous machine, my feet crunching on the hard floor. "Covered in broken glass and scratched beyond recognition."

"Great," my roommate fumbled with his vest, "I didn't like Velcurses anyway. Never was a fan before, not a fan now. We'll work this the old-fashioned way."

Shards of glass and metal spokes twisted in the faint moonlight.

"Old-fashioned way?" I asked, keeping an eye on what amounted to floating steak knives.

"Totally. Back in the day my mom used to exorcise Poltergeists with a perfectly cooked quiche."

Black metal hangers shifted into an attack pattern, like fighter jets in formation. The sharp spikes oriented themselves at our heads.

"Quiche?!"

My roommate shrugged. "My mom has a lot of talents. I've always been proud to be her son. One of these days I'll have you come with me when I visit her."

The thought of two Lovelys was almost too much to bear. "How about we just focus on this problem right now?"

Ed unzipped his fishing vest and dug into one of the interior pockets. "Sure thing, Gene. Sounds like a plan. Now, with Poltergeists, it's important to not antagonize them. Think of this thing like an obnoxious classroom full of sugared-up kindergarteners. It's just as liable to pee on your shoes in excitement as it is to bite your arm."

Coins tumbled out of a broken hole in the vending machine, only to be sucked up into the air along with everything else before they reached the floor.

"Have you ever actually seen kindergarteners?"

My roommate frowned and took his vest off, his fingers digging into the interior pockets. "No, but I challenge you to refute my argument."

A drifting quarter snapped out of the air and pelted Ed's cheek. "Ow!"

Something yanked on his vest and pulled it out of his hands. The jingling outerwear quickly joined the rest of the gravity-defying flotsam.

"Ed?"

"Okay, now that's a problem."

Clang!

A metal hanger impaled itself in the concrete wall behind us, missing my head by mere inches. "You think?!"

Bulletin boards spun like angry tops.

"Stay frosty, Gene." My roommate gently backed up against me. "Here's the deal. You can't make a quiche. I've seen you cook."

"And you can?" I frowned, having a hard time tearing myself away from the metal hanger that could have ended up in my eye.

"No, but that's besides the point, I'm not a Magician—you are."

I slapped at my neck, only to find a thumbtack embedded in my skin. "Uh, huh. I am, but the sigil is ruined."

Clang!

Another metal shiv shot past us and banged off the opposite wall. I had the distinct impression this was what rubber ducks at the fair felt like—being at the wrong end of a shooting gallery was no fun.

"Gene," Ed said, dodging a small swarm of thumbtacks. "You don't need the sigils. They're just a focusing tool. Think of them like glasses. Powerful Magicians can work their Magick without any of those crutches."

Half a dozen quarters peppered me in the gut and I doubled over. "Really?"

Ed nodded, keeping his eyes on the sharp hangers hovering

in attack formation. "Yes, really. Hasn't Morgan explained that to you?"

Morgan...

She'd taught me so much, but Magick without sigils? That wasn't something we'd covered. Morgan believed in precision, accuracy, and above all else, control. To her, Magick was not an art, it was a rigorous and exacting set of instructions that when followed properly elicited the result you wanted. The steps could not be skipped, lest something truly terrible happen.

"Gene." Ed pointed to the twisting shards of glass. "Now would be a pretty good time to graduate to a little sigil-less Magick."

"What do you want me to do?"

My roommate pointed to his drifting vest. "There's a shoehorn in there. I need it."

"A shoehorn?"

Clang! Clang! Clang!

Metal spikes rocketed at us in rapid-fire succession. I dodged them—Ed didn't. My roommate took one of those shivs across the leg.

"Yes, a shoehorn. Ghandi's Shoehorn, if you must know," Ed said, slapping a hand on his thigh. "That is, unless you want to see what we'd look like run through with snack hangers?"

"On it." I closed my eyes and reached out to the Magick swirling inside me. Cosmic power danced between my mental fingers, playing like a school of unruly fish. I stabbed at it, but the capricious energy slipped through my grasp.

Shatter!

"What was that?" My eyes snapped open to find Ed leaping out of the way of a swinging fluorescent bulb.

"Well, it wasn't your Magick, that's for sure. Come on, Gene, I know you can do this. Get me Ghandi's Shoehorn."

"Did Ghandi even wear shoes?"

"Gene!" Ed ducked a twirling bulletin board.

"Right, it doesn't matter."

Papers spun like frisbees between us, sliding up one wall and down the other.

"Uh, Ed, any suggestions?"

My roommate grabbed a spinning board with his hands and ripped it out of the invisible Poltergeist's grasp. "Use your Magick!"

"I'm trying, I just don't know how…"

Like rubber bullets shot at point blank range, more loose change spewed out of the vending machine. My roommate jumped in front of that barrage, absorbing nickels with his makeshift shield. "Well you'd best figure it out quickly. What about a power word?"

"Power word?"

Ed nodded, his hands directing the corkboard and deflecting anything headed my way. "Morgan has explained power words to you, right?"

Yes…

"Gene," Morgan's sultry voice played in my head, her soft words lilting like a harp's plucked strings. "Sometimes it helps to use words in a language other than your own to direct the Magick where you want it to go."

"That's why you have all these books on Latin." My fingers ran across the tops of both modern and ancient volumes that lined her shelves.

My girlfriend nodded, her bright green hair falling in splendid curves around that heart-shaped face. "One of the many reasons."

She removed a dictionary from the stacks and shoved it in my hands. A crumpled paper fell from the open space it left and I picked it up.

"What's this?" I asked, unfolding the heavily inked sheet in my hands. It contained a complex sigil—one I'd never seen before. This design was nothing like the others. It had darkness to it, a jagged and violent malevolence.

"Research." Morgan snapped the paper out of my hand and tucked it back on the shelf. "It's a little advanced for you, Gene. You need to focus on the simple stuff."

The simple stuff.

"You need to focus, Gene!" Ed's voice shook me from my memory. "Gene!"

Here goes nothing.

"Venit… Uh," I cried, letting the Magick go and directing it toward Ed's floating vest. "Venit shoehornicus?"

Brilliant.

4

VESTED

*E*d's vest spun out of the Poltergeist's control. It unfurled like a cocktail umbrella, its many pockets spilling their contents.

"Shoehornicus?" Ed cried as his valuable collection of Magickal artifacts danced in the air like sugar-plum fairies.

Now largely empty, the vest caught the edge of Ed's shield. The board bounced off his head before knocking the two of us to the ground.

My roommate scrambled to untangle himself from both me and the now empty vest. "What did you do?"

I scraped Ed's head off my chest just before a razor-sharp piece of glass would have done it for me. "Power words. You said to use power words—that's what I did."

My roommate scrambled out of the way of an equally fast-moving metal post. "I didn't say to make up non-sensical words."

"It *might* be a real word." I got to my feet only to have the pointy metal end of a fluorescent bulb rammed into my gut.

"It's not." Ed danced around the swirling junk and ducked a few brightly colored poker chips. "Stay away from those."

I gave the bright red and blue plastic pieces a wide berth. "What are those?"

"Bad debt." Ed yanked me down to avoid another twirling object. It was a novelty-sized chain with two small manacles attached to the ends, neither could have been large enough to hook my pinky finger.

"Damn it, Ed."

"Sorry," my roommate said, dodging more glass and metal. "It's best to stay clear of all of Maxwell's binders."

"I don't even want to—"

A jagged piece of sharp glass cut across my arm, taking with it a chunk of skin and leaving a nice gash in my only jacket. I slapped a hand on it to try and stem the blood. "Ed, where is the shoehorn?"

My roommate skipped around a swarm of angry thumb-tacks. "I don't—wait, there it is!"

The polished metal shoehorn spun past us in the air, its curved surface twirling like a top.

"Great, what do we do with it?"

"What do you think you do with Ganhdi's Shoehorn?" My roommate asked as if this were common knowledge.

"Put on shoes?"

Ed shook his head. "You can do that if you want to. Me, I'm going to use it to calm this Poltergeist." The young Demon Hunter lunged for the spinning twist of metal, but his fingers missed it and he ended up stumbling into the wall.

"I got it." My hand brushed the spinning metal but was unable to come down with it.

"Look out!"

"Huh?"

Smack!

A small roll of black electrical tape clunked into my fore-head. I rubbed at the sore spot between my eyes. "A little sooner next time would really be helpful."

Ed pointed at the now unrolling black ribbon of tape. "Gene, that's Timbo's Terrible Tape!"

"I don't want to know, do I?" I asked, doing my best to avoid another barrage of quarters. The long and sticky end of that black tape clasped itself to my leg and immediately set to work winding its way around my knee.

"Terrible tape, terrible, terrible, tape."

The carnival of gravity-defying items hadn't stopped, but my ability to avoid them sure had. It didn't take long before Timbo's Tape had my leg covered up to the man bits, and from there it seemed all set to make a break for my waist.

"Ed!"

My roommate avoided a smattering of broken glass and unknown trinkets. "You'll be fine, Gene. We've got plenty of time."

The tape twisted around my gut, squeezing me tighter than a belt on Thanksgiving. "We do?"

Ed nodded. "Sure, hasn't even made it to your neck yet. Besides, once I get the shoehorn we can wrap this all up nice—"

Gandhi's Shoehorn shot past Ed on a trajectory that would take it out the far window. "Okay, that might be a problem. I'll be right back!" My roommate took off after it, his feet crunching on the glass-covered floor while the Terrible Tape lived up to its name.

Come on, Gene. You're a Magician—act like one!

The black and sticky tape snaked under my arms and around my chest, then tightened down like an unwanted hug. "Ed!"

"Almost got it, Gene. Think skinny thoughts."

Skinny thoughts? Oh, so help me...

The tape cut across one shoulder and back around the other, while all around me glass and metal spun in a tiny whirlwind of destruction.

"Just about got it, Gene!"

If my roommate didn't hurry, it wouldn't matter whether he

stopped the Poltergeist or not—I'd be lost beneath a Magickal wad of self-directed electrical tape.

Do something, Gene!

There were no sigils for this sort of thing, and I wasn't about to try another power word just yet, but there had to be something. I closed my eyes and reached deep into the power that bubbled up in my chest. The Magick was there, and like a hungry dog, it was excited to do whatever I asked of it, provided I knew what I wanted.

What *did* I want?

The tape cinched its first pass around my neck, and in that moment whatever it was I wanted went right out the window. What I needed was to be free of Timbo's Terrible Tape right the hell now.

"Not out the window," Ed cried, his voice fading against the crushing darkness of asphyxiation.

I let go of my Magick, and instead turned my attention to the tape, trying to find a way to unravel its power, or at least undo the power locked within those plastic strands. The black ribbon pulled tighter, and I abandoned that idea. Unraveling an ancient Magician's Magick was just not in the cards for me at this point in my life—and it might not ever be if I didn't come up with a solution quickly.

I opened my eyes to find the whirling dervish of glass and metal still spinning above me.

Maybe...

I flopped to one side and used a free hand to push myself up just a little.

This is nuts. What am I doing?

The tape squeezed tighter, cutting off the blood to my brain and filling the edges of my vision with stars.

It's this or being taped to death. What's it going to be, Gene?

I reached out with my Magick, I couldn't stop those shards

of razor-sharp glass, but I might be able to push them just enough.

Right, and you also might impale yourself.

When Timbo's Tape reached my chin I decided the pushing strategy was a risk worth taking. I clawed myself up enough to be in the middle of the maelstrom, reaching out with my Magick and tugging at the spirit's uncontrollable power.

What's this?

I'd expected a spirit, but that was not what I found. The power swirling around us was no angry entity, it was unconstrained and chaotic Magick. Out of control and without boundaries, cosmic power like this was often the deleterious side-effect of more traditional efforts gone bad.

Did I do this?

Glass shards shot past, one of them catching the edge of Timbo's Tape, though the edge wasn't enough to cut it completely.

I reached further into the mysterious Magick, doing my best to gently coax anything sharp to glide past the tape. Darkness closed in on the edges of my vision. I didn't know how much longer I could keep this up. Chaotic energy swirled in a whirlpool of unruly force, but something else shifted between the crashing cosmic waves. That dark sigil and its strange design, there was something to it in all of this, something I couldn't put my finger on.

Slice!

A rogue sliver of metal cut across Timbo's tape, drawing blood, but also releasing the Magickal black ribbon's crushing hold on my neck.

"Got it." Ed rushed back into the fray just in time to see my neck get cut and blood trickle down the front of my shirt. "Gene!" Ed dropped to his knees and pulled me back down next to him. He held the shoehorn up to his lips like a microphone.

"Happiness is when what you think, what you say, and what you do are in harmony. Be harmony, Gene."

I clutched at my neck and grunted out an assent.

All around us items dropped from the air. Glass shattered and coins plinked. Ed's vest, and just about everything it had contained covered the floor like an overturned flea market vendor's table.

Timbo's Tape sloughed off, peeling away like wet crepe paper. "Thanks," I said, checking my neck to see just how much blood I'd lost.

Not enough to worry.

"That wasn't a Poltergeist, was it?" Ed scooped up his vest and dusted it off.

"No, that was uncontrolled Magick."

My roommate frowned. "That's no good…"

Beep! Beep! Beep!

Ed's watch rattled off another series of alarming beeps and my stomach dropped. "What's *that* for?"

My roommate tossed me the vest and started collecting artifacts from the floor. "Relax, Gene, that's just the Porter alarm. It means she's working and we might be able to score free drinks. Hop to it!"

5

FREE BEER

 My roommate slid into the booth, still arguing with me about the evening's events. "I'm telling you, that's Gandhi's Shoehorn."

"Ed," I said, grabbing a stack of paper napkins and pressing them to my neck to see if I was still bleeding. "Gandhi wore sandals. If you look at any of the pictures you'll see."

"Uh, huh." The Demon Hunter scooped a menu off the table and flipped it over. His hunched shoulders and disinterested frown were a clear indicator he didn't agree with me. "So you're an expert on the peaceful protests of the Mahatma?"

I held up the napkin—no blood.

Well that's a relief.

Life as a Magician had its advantages—rapid healing being one of the best of them. My neck might still feel sticky from Timbo's Terrible Tape, but at least it wasn't bleeding. I had a feeling even though Ed's girlfriend worked here, they'd have a hard time serving a blood-covered college kid.

"I do not have intimate details, no," I said, wadding the napkin up and shoving it in my pocket. "But if you look at the old footage or pictures you'd see that—"

Ed waved me off with his menu. "Pictures can be faked."

"You're telling me people faked pictures of Gandhi just to hide the fact that he wore shoes and used a shoehorn?"

"That's *exactly* what I'm telling you." Ed slapped the menu down on the table.

"But I don't—"

"Gene," my roommate shook his head slowly, as if he were trying to explain a complex concept to a child, "you're young and inexperienced."

"We're the same age!"

Ed frowned. "I have more wisdom."

"What does that have to do with a metal shoehorn?"

"These artifacts don't exist by happenstance, Gene." Ed pointed to the folded-up vest he'd set next to him in the booth. "Do you think the world is interested in harmony? Or peace, for that matter? Look around you." My roommate gestured to a distant television, where images of an escalating desert conflict played out in vibrant and gruesome color. "Peace isn't profitable. War sells, Gene. War, strife, conflict. That's what the world wants, and that's what it gets."

"I don't—"

"Let me put it another way." The Demon Hunter picked up the saltshaker and poured a small mound of it into his hand. "If there *was* a shoehorn that could bring peace and harmony to the leaders of the world, do you think they'd use it?"

"Well, if it meant less people dying, yes."

Ed tossed the salt over his shoulder, much of it landing in the food of the people in the booth beside ours. "Wrong. It would never make it to them. Evil exists at all the levels, Gene. All the way up the food chain. Gandhi's Shoehorn is too great an artifact, which is exactly why no one knows about it. All the videos and pictures show him wearing sandals for exactly that reason. If anyone knew about the shoehorn, they might try to use it to bring about world peace."

An explosion lit up the distant television, filling the grainy green image with brilliant white light. The Demon Hunter frowned and slid his menu to the end of the table. "And that would ruin the destructive plan they have us barreling headlong into."

"All that from a shoehorn..."

Ed nodded. "Yeah, don't get me started on Kennedy's Yo-Yo."

"Wait, what—"

A cute young girl slid into the booth next to me. Her long brown hair was done up in a half-hearted bun, a lone pencil all that kept those luxurious locks from tumbling down her shoulders. She wore a tight visor around her forehead, just like the rest of the wait staff, except she'd added a few pins to the otherwise simple front. "Oh, please tell me I didn't show up for Kennedy's Yo-Yo?"

"It's an important part of American history that is often—"

The waitress cut him off, twisting around to extend her hand to me. "Hi, I'm Porter. You must be Gene."

Her wide smile and sparkling eyes caught me completely off guard. Ed had tried to explain Porter to me before, but appeared he'd left a few details out.

I shook her hand. "Yeah, it's good to meet you."

"Oh, right. Porter, this is Gene. Gene, this is Porter. Now you've both met."

Ed's girlfriend let go of my hand and slid the menus around on the table to face her. "Well, I take it by the fact you are both alive it went well?"

My stomach dropped.

She knows?!

Ed nodded without skipping a beat. "Oh yeah. You are looking at two premier Demon Hunters and slayers of Shades."

Porter tilted her head and gave us both a once over. Doing her best to feign disappointment, she was clearly hiding a smile beneath those pursed lips. "Shades?"

Ed waved away her pretend concerns. "Shades. Yeah, nega-tive-energy beasts from the Gloom. Listen, it's fine. My boy Gene is a monster on the air guitar."

"Uh, huh," Porter said, giving me a friendly nod. "He is, is he?"

What has Ed told her?

Most people forget about Magick the second after they see it, but there were a few exceptions—was Porter one? No wonder Ed liked her so much.

"Totally." Ed puffed up his chest. "Gene is a rock god if ever there were one."

"You used the Rock God's Reward?" Porter asked, leaning forward in the seat, her bare leg rubbing against mine. "You told me that was only for special occasions. Ed Lovely, so help me, if you did that just to gather up groupie panties I'm going to—"

"Nope. No panties." My roommate held up his empty hand. "But we got some crackers, burned up a ton of Shades, and Gene here worked on his Magick game. All in all I'd say it was a pretty good evening."

"Pretty good?" Porter asked, her elbows on the table. A few stray locks slipped out of her loose bun.

What does she look like with her hair down?

Ed smiled, his dimples on full display. "Yep, but you know what would make it great?"

"What's that?" she said, leaning forward enough for her butt to come off the seat.

Do not look. Do not look.

I looked.

Thankfully Ed didn't notice, he was too busy leaning in himself. "I mean really, really great?"

"What, Eddie?"

"Free beer."

"What?!" Porter dropped back into the seat, her thighs

brushing against mine for a second time. "You came here just to get free beer?"

"And to see you," Ed said, backpedaling at his girlfriend's tone.

"I suppose *you* want free beer too," Porter turned her attention to me.

My stomach clenched up at the sight of those sparkling eyes so close to mine. "Uh..."

"Whatever, two full-priced beers for the rock god and his air-guitar Magician," she said, scooping up the menus and climbing out of the seat.

"Wait, Porter." Ed reached for his girlfriend, but she was already too far away and didn't appear interested in turning around. "Dang it."

"That went well." I unfolded a fresh napkin from the dispenser.

Ed slumped back in his seat. "Nah, she'll be fine. It happens from time to time. Porter's great, but sometimes she doesn't understand the Demon Hunter lifestyle."

"You make it sound like you're not remotely to blame."

My roommate nodded. "I'm not. It comes with the territory, Gene. It's tough work out there night after night dealing with the monstrous evils hellbent on our destruction."

"And it deserves free beer?"

"Well... Yes, dang it. It's not a big thing to ask for. I mean, its *domestic*. It's not like she's going to run us out some expensive imports."

Clunk, clunk!

Porter slammed two tall, golden mugs on the table. That wasn't the cheap local beer this restaurant was known for.

"Excellent! Thank you, sweetheart," Ed said, wrapping his fingers around a sweating glass handle.

"Sure thing, sweetie." Porter dropped the check on the table.

Even from my seat I could tell it was decidedly not free, nor remotely cheap. "Enjoy."

"Uh..." Ed frowned at the bill. "I thought we were going to—"

"Oh, right." The waitress spun around, the pencil in her hair barely holding on, and scooped up the bill.

"Thanks, P." Ed held up his mug. "Cheers, Gene. Here's to Demon Hunting and making the world a better place."

Clink.

Porter returned with a box under her arm. She dropped it on the table with a heavy thump then slapped the bill down on top of it. "There's a fee for having your junk shipped to my place." She scribbled something on the paper in dark marker, then slid it back across the table. "Next time you order something from Peru, try to remember to pay customs."

Ouch.

6

SPECIAL DELIVERY

"*I*t's here!" My roommate practically knocked over his beer pulling the box to his chest.

"What's here?"

Ed ignored me and immediately tore into the packing tape. "I thought for sure he'd never make it, but Mom told me her old boyfriend was good for the cash."

"What is it, Ed?" I asked, pressing my back against the seat. I wasn't entirely comfortable with what might be lurking beneath the foam and packing-peanuts.

My roommate tossed aside a packing slip and dug his hands deep into the contents. "Excellent packing job, Markus."

"Who's Markus?" I dragged the packing slip over and unfolded it.

Dear Edwin, Your mother tells me you're neck deep in the business. That's great. I figure if you've got your 'neck' in it you might want to get a 'head.' The Fun Uncle, Markus.

"Oh, man. Oh, man!" Ed was like a kid at Christmas. He sifted through the box as if he was panning for gold. "Ah, ha!"

Ed's fingers re-emerged with a thick braid of black hair

wound around them. Small loops of leather and bone punctuated the hair like ponytail bands.

"Ed…"

My roommate beamed, his dimples showing off their own dimples. "Gene, I can't believe I got it."

"What, Ed? What did you get?"

A softball-sized, heavily wrinkled head popped out of the packing foam, dangling from what turned out to be a topknot of braided hair. Thick black threads tied the shrunken head's eyes and lips shut.

"Holy crap, Ed!" I said, pushing myself as far back against the seat as I could.

"I know, right? Isn't it awesome?" My roommate set the empty box on the seat and placed the head on the table between the two of us.

"I guess that's one way to look at it," I said, sliding my beer away from the wrinkly thing's lips.

"I've been waiting for one of these to come available since forever."

Ed's face positively shined; his excitement was genuine and all but impossible to hide.

I frowned. "You've been on a wait list for… that?"

"Of course! They are so hard to come by—I mean how often do you think it is that a Magician…" Ed's voice trailed off, as if he remembered something and had decided against mentioning it.

"That a Magician does what, Ed?"

My roommate held up his beer. "It's not important. What *is* important is my Demon Hunting game just leveled up."

"Ed…"

My roommate flagged down a passing waitress. "My partner and I are going to need a plate of nachos to go with these beers. We need to welcome our newest roommate." Ed held up the wrinkly head by its top knot.

"Porter warned me about you."

Ed didn't skip a beat. "Excellent, just put it on my tab. We'd like jalapeños and shredded chicken."

With a curt roll of her eyes the young woman left us to enjoy what remained of our beers.

"Why do you have a shrunken head?"

"Huh," my roommate put down his beer, "I forget sometimes how little Magick you know. I'd swear you had zero parenting. Did you grow up in the woods or something?"

"No."

Ed reached over and scratched behind my ears. "Yeah, no fleas. I guess you're right. Still, you don't even know what a Yaga Doll is? Unbelievable."

"You're going to make me ask, aren't you?"

Ed teased at the thick thread that held the tiny head's lips sealed. "I sure am."

Sigh.

"What is a Yaga Doll?"

Ed deflected my questions and continued to admire his newest toy. In no time, a plate of nachos swung by and Ed redirected yet another server to our table. He asked the confused young man for another round of beers.

"I should get your server…"

"No need. Just get us two more of these." Ed pointed to the almost empty mugs. "And put it on my tab."

"Ed, please. What is a Yaga Doll?"

My roommate set the shrunken head on the napkin dispenser, then slid the nachos between us. "Right, Yaga Doll. Where do I start? Do you know the story of Baba Yaga?"

"No."

Ed shook his head. "Okay, wow. Are you certain you're a Magician? Maybe you're just really great at special effects?"

"Ed!"

My roommate shoved an overloaded chip in his mouth.

"Baba Yaga, the forest witch of Russian fables. We don't know for sure if she was real or not. I mean, there are real witches, similar to Magicians, just different. It's all about the flow of Magick and how—"

I clanged my empty beer against the table. "Lovely! Yaga Doll."

"I'm getting there, but it's a process. You want the story or not?"

"I want to know what that thing is," I said, keeping an eye on the wrinkly head sitting quietly on the napkin dispenser.

"And I'm trying to explain it to you. We've really got to work on your patience."

Two more beers arrived and our empties were carted off.

"Mmm." Ed washed down a few loaded chips with the ice-cold beer. "Wow, that really is the premium stuff. It's amazing how much better they can make beer, isn't it."

"Yaga Doll."

My roommate lifted up the shrunken head's tiny goatee to extract a few napkins. "Right. No more fooling around. This is important. So, the term Yaga Doll comes from the skulls Baba Yaga is said to have kept around her hut. It was a hut that sat on chicken legs, so it moved around. Which is weird when you think about it. I mean, if the hut moved, did the skulls on posts move too? They never covered that in the stories. And, if they didn't move, then why bother having a house that moved at all?"

My knuckles whitened against the mug's handle.

"Anyway. That's not the point. You see, in the stories, this little Russian girl goes to visit Baba Yaga, and somehow she ends up with using one of the skulls like a search lamp."

"Huh?"

My roommate wiped spicy chicken from his chin. "I know right? I mean, why not use a torch or something, but that's not the point. The point is the skull's eyes were like laser beams. When she showed the skull to her evil family—and her family was super evil—it burned them alive." Ed made an exploding gesture with his hands.

"Exploding eye lasers?" I asked, now sliding down the booth to give the wrinkly head an even wider berth.

"I wouldn't so much say exploding, more like green beams of righteous destruction."

"That's so much better."

My roommate nodded and pulled another nacho out of the pile. "I know, right? And I haven't even gotten to the good part."

"There's more?"

"Heck yeah there's more," Ed said, shoving a chip sandwich in his mouth. "Lemme show you." The Demon Hunter pulled at the threads that held the tiny head's mouth shut.

An oddly frustrated Magick bubbled up from the edges of the diminutive head. "Ed, what are you doing?"

"It's cool. I've seen this before."

"Seen?! You mean to tell me you've never owned a Yaga Doll?"

My roommate shook his head. "Nope. Like I said, they're very hard to come by." He pulled out the knot and started unraveling the stitches.

"Please don't tell me it breathes fire."

"No. But wow, now that would be really cool. Okay. So, try not to freak out," he said, undoing the last stitch and setting the wound-up pile of thread on the table.

I put my beer down and waited. "Does something happen?"

Ed hesitated, then banged his hand on the table. "That's right. I forgot. I need to give him a name."

"You've got to be kidding."

My roommate's expression became somber. "I never kid when it comes to Yaga Dolls."

"Right. Sorry, I forgot. Very important death lasers."

"Hmm, Death Lasers isn't bad, but it's too 'on the nose,' if you will. What about Wrinkly?"

I chuckled as the beer buzz worked its way between my ears. "You're gonna give him a complex. You might as well call him Shorty."

Ed drained the last of his mug. "That's it. Perfect. Thanks, Gene." The Demon Hunter looped his hand through the Yaga Doll's topknot and raised him up off the napkin dispenser. "I, Edwin Lovely, do hereby christen you Shorty." The wrinkled, prune-like head twisted gently at the end of its braid. "Well, that was anti-climactic—"

The tiny head's mouth dropped open and let out a wide and impossibly animated yawn, then smacked its leathery lips.

"Ed," I cried, pulling his hand down while checking to see if anyone was watching. "People will see."

The Demon Hunter nodded, as if suddenly aware of his surroundings for the first time. "Oh, right."

"Speaking of seeing, would one of you two knuckle-heads mind removing my eye threads?" Shorty asked, his head now hovering precariously close to what remained of our nachos.

"Ed!"

My roommate tucked the shrunken head into his jacket and pushed the bill over to me. "Right. Let's go. You get the check, and I'll fill you in on the rest on the way back to the dorm."

"Wait. I thought you said the beers would be free—"

The Demon Hunter was already gone, out the front door and as far from the bill as possible.

Sigh.

7

ROAD LESS TRAVELED

I caught up with Ed not far from the restaurant. He'd stuffed the Yaga Doll inside the front of his comically overloaded vest. Shorty's wrinkly forehead and topknot peeked out against the folds of my roommate's unwashed flannel.

"You never finished," I said, jogging up to him. "How does a Yaga Doll help?"

The Demon Hunter directed me off the sidewalk and between some of the larger buildings on campus. Ed liked to take the roads less traveled whenever he could. "Dark powers take the dark paths, Gene," he'd say whenever I asked why we couldn't just cut across the quad.

The University of Florida's soaring brick structures erupted from the lush green grounds like towering stacks of orange-red blocks. Built in one of the historically more swampy areas of the state, the school had been forced to walk a fine line between traditional southern brick buildings and a surrounding wetland that wanted nothing more than to drag them into the inky depths. In a compromise, the founding fathers had elected to create pockets of marsh wherever possible. Ed's chosen path took us alongside one such pocket.

"Huge advantage, Gene," Ed said, high-stepping through some tall grass along the water's edge.

"How?"

"You ever own a dog?" The Demon Hunter extended a hand to catch the tops of the cattail plumes that ran alongside the pond.

"No."

"That's a shame. Dogs are really great."

"You ever own a dog?"

"Nah. Mom never had much time for dogs, but my friends did."

"Ed, we're going off topic here."

My roommate climbed the short bank up to a jagged and broken patch of sidewalk. "Right, sorry. Where was I? Oh, yes, the Yaga Doll has an excellent sense of smell."

I frowned. "Ed, it has no lungs."

"He."

"Huh?"

The Demon Hunter shook his head. "He's not an it. His name is Shorty."

"Oh, right. Well, Shorty has no lungs. How does he smell?"

"You're the Magician. You tell me."

Conversations with my roommate often went this way.

"Fine. So, Shorty has a great sense of smell, which makes no sense given his lack of lungs or any discernible diaphragm, but I'll give you the benefit of the doubt. Moving past that, what is he great at sniffing out? Please don't say Shades. I've had enough negative-energy shadow monsters for one night."

"Monsters, Demons, you name it." My roommate turned at the last second, and instead of guiding us toward the dorms and into the center of campus, selected a more circuitous route outside of the common areas.

"What? Are you serious?"

Ed nodded, his fishing vest of Magickal trinkets jingling

with each step into the dark and overgrown edges of yet another campus pond. "I don't joke about Yaga Dolls, Gene."

"Wait, wait. Are you telling me that this shrunken head is going to help you find, and then potentially destroy—"

"Banish."

"Okay, banish, a Demon?"

"Exactly."

My roommate cut across a wide patch of ferns by the water's edge, then unzipped his vest in the dark of the thick vegetation.

"Where are we going?"

Ed pulled Shorty out. "We're going on patrol."

"Patrol?"

The Demon Hunter nodded and held up the shrunken head in the late-evening air. "Yeah. I want to see just how good his sniffer is."

Splash!

An undersized gator slipped into the dark water not far from where we stood, its bright gold eyes reflecting in the distant lights of the main campus buildings.

"Are you expecting to find anything?" My beer buzz was starting to fade and the thought of another run in with the supernatural so soon was not enticing.

"Hoping, but not expecting."

"Well, that's go—wait, hoping?"

Ed ignored me and held the tiny head in front of his face. "Shorty, time to get to work. I need to know what you smell."

"What's in it for me?" the tiny head asked, his voice surprisingly direct.

"Tell me what you—wait, did you just ask what's in it for you?"

The wrinkly skull nodded at the end of his complex braid. "Yup."

My roommate frowned. "I named you, I am your master, and

I command you to use your nose to tell me if there are any Demons in the vicinity."

"Uh, huh."

Crickets chirped and a distant frog croaked before jumping into the dark water, but Shorty did nothing.

Ed tilted his head. "Shorty?"

"Yup."

"Are there any Demons nearby?"

"Yup."

Ed's face lit up. "That's great!"

"No, it's not!" I said, quite sure I did not agree with my roommate's definition of great. "That's really not great news at all."

The Demon Hunter dismissed me. "Shorty, is there more than one?"

"No."

It was hard for Ed to hide the disappointment in his eyes.

Thank god.

"Shorty, what are we dealing with?"

Please not Shades, please not Shades.

The tiny head wrinkled its nose. "A Reaver."

My roommate froze, his eyes wide. "I'm sorry. You're going to have to say that again. I could have sworn you said a Reaver."

"Yup."

The Demon Hunter frowned.

"Ed?"

"Where is the Reaver, Shorty?"

The tiny head sighed. "I'd love to tell you, but I haven't had anything to eat in a while. I'm afraid I'm just too hungry to focus."

"Gene, give me one of the packages of crackers you shoved in your pocket."

How did he know I shoved crackers in my pocket?

"I don't have any."

Shorty sniffed at the air. "He's lying."

Stupid Yaga Doll.

"Crackers, Gene."

I fished the plastic wrapped sleeve out of my pocket. "I was saving these for later."

Shorty licked his wrinkly lips.

Where does that tongue go?

"Feed him the crackers," my roommate said, pointing Shorty's wrinkly face at mine.

"I am not feeding that thing crackers."

"Gene, you don't know this, but Reavers are insanely dangerous. I don't know how one got here, but I sure as hell am not going to let it stay."

The tiny head snapped his teeth open and shut like a hungry hippo.

"Ed..."

"It's not up for debate. Feed him the crackers before someone gets hurt. Reavers are a product of the Gloom, Gene. The *Gloom.* Don't you want to know why there are Gloom beasts on campus?"

Sigh.

I opened the package and selected a largely whole cracker sandwich. "He better not bite my fingers."

Shorty snapped his teeth again.

"He won't. Will you, Shorty?"

The tiny head twisted at the end of his braid. "Nope. Well, maybe just a little."

"Ed!"

"What if Morgan's in trouble, Gene?"

My roommate knew how to go for the soft spots.

"Why would you say that?" I asked, shoving the cracker sandwich in Shorty's mouth and yanking my fingers back before I lost them.

The doll crunched on the salty cracker while Ed turned his

attention to me. "Because it bears repeating. We have an important job. We are the last line of defense between this world and all the terrible things that exist beyond it." Ed spread his arms wide. "Darkness thrives in the absence of light, Gene. It can't be a coincidence that Shorty smells a Reaver on the same night we face down a horde of Shades. There is something wrong with the Gloom, and that's not good for anyone."

Shorty snapped his teeth. "More!"

I shoved another cracker into his mouth, this time getting the distinct hint of shrunken-head saliva on my fingers. "Ugh."

"That's enough," Ed said, pulling the hungry Yaga Doll up to his face. "Now it's time for you to tell us where the Reaver is."

"One more cracker?"

"Shorty!"

The tiny head sighed. "Fine. Hold me up so I can get a good sniff."

Ed held the shrunken head up as high as he could, twisting slowly so the Yaga Doll got a full rotation.

"Stop," Shorty cried. "There. It's that way."

Like a wrinkly and entitled compass rose, the Yaga Doll's nose pointed away from the center of campus, away from the bright lights and brick buildings, and directly at the shadowy edges of the closest residence halls.

The dorm was old, even by university standards. Air conditioning had been added as an afterthought a few decades ago, and based on the dripping black lines of condensate mold it hadn't been updated since installation. There were a host of issues with that old brick and stone building, and I knew about them all. I knew all about them not because I lived there, at least not officially.

"Ed…"

"Isn't that Morgan's dorm?"

"Yes."

My roommate tucked Shorty inside his vest. "Yeah, well it's

also Porter's dorm. What are we doing standing around talking? Come on!"

Ed grabbed my arm and together we raced up the bank and onto the sidewalk.

Please be okay. Please be okay.

8

THREE'S COMPANY

I shot ahead of my jingling roommate.

"Wait up, Gene," he cried, the fishing vest of arti-facts and Shorty doing their best to weigh him down.

I hopped off the sidewalk and cut through the damp grass. "What is a Reaver, Ed?"

Ed puffed along behind me. "Chaotic rage Demon…"

"Rage Demon?"

"It's not high on the intelligence scale. I'd put them at about a two out of ten for smarts."

"That's a relief."

"Not really. I'd put them at about a nine on the destruction scale."

My stomach curled in on itself.

Morgan!

"Gene." Ed pointed to a gap between a pair of brick build-ings. "Shortcut. Follow me." My roommate slipped into the narrow alley and waved me on. We shimmied around boxes and past a few tightly wedged trash cans only to pop out not far from Morgan and Porter's dorm.

The old brick building was one of the first dorms on

campus, and was always the last to receive any manner of updates. Sweeping concrete and stone arches held up aging brick walls that dripped spanish moss. Grand oaks dotted the lush green grass in front of that ancient building. Their wide canopies stretched to the second floor and beyond, filling the sky above and blotting out much in the way of moonlight. Smooth stone stairs led up to an oversized set of oak doors. Twin gaslit lanterns flickered on either side of those doors, pushing back on the darkness that surrounded them.

Ed popped Shorty out of his vest and held him up. "You got the scent, Shorty?"

The shrunken head sniffed the air.

"Nothing."

"What?" Ed turned the Yaga Doll around to face him. "What do you mean you don't smell anything? You told us to go this way."

"Nothing here right now, boss."

Ed paced between the trees. "Come on, you've got to pick up on something. It's not going to go cold just like that."

The sound of voices coming up the sidewalk got my attention. "Ed, people coming."

My roommate shoved the Yaga Doll back beneath his vest. "Dang it."

"I think you'll like her," a sultry feminine voice said.

I knew that voice.

Morgan.

My girlfriend wandered up the sidewalk, her boot-like heels pounding on the hard pavement. At her side was a slightly older guy; given his beard and button-down shirt, I figured him for a grad student.

"You think?" he asked, adjusting his shirt and clearly debating whether he should roll up his sleeves or leave them buttoned.

Morgan laughed, her voice light and jovial. "You bet. Listen,

I'm not supposed to say anything—" she leaned on his arm —"but I've got a pretty good feeling about you two. It's almost like you were made for each other."

"Really?"

Morgan tugged on his sleeve. "Completely. I never lie about something like this. Marcy should be down any—" My girlfriend stopped, seeing me standing on the sidewalk and Ed still pacing under the trees. "I'm sorry, Kevin," she said, gently tossing her head to get those long green locks out of her eyes. "Gene, what are you doing here, sweetheart? I thought you and the urban fisherman had work to do tonight?"

"We did," I said, gauging Kevin and not exactly sure what to make of him.

For his part, the other guy appeared confused. "Morgan, if you need me to come back another time—"

"Nonsense. Kevin, I want you to meet my boyfriend and single smartest undergraduate on campus, Gene Law." Morgan let go of Kevin's arm and swept up to plant a quick kiss on my cheek. The smell of cloves and incense came with her, and set my heart beating just a bit faster.

"Uh, hey," I said, extending a hand. "I'm Gene."

"Nice to meet you." Kevin ignored me and eyed the dorm steps. "So, uh, is Marcy is coming down soon?"

Morgan glanced at her watch, pushing up the long and flowing sleeves of her silky shirt. My girlfriend rarely dressed below semi-formal, and tonight was no exception. That almost sheer top disappeared below a tight leathery corset, all of which ended at a pair of skin-tight leggings. Morgan knew how to get attention.

Save the hungry eyes for Marcy, Kevin.

"She should be." Morgan frowned and turned her attention back to the dorm. "I told her to meet us out here right about now, but you know how girls are."

"I guess." Kevin fumbled with his sleeves again, apparently

deciding they looked better rolled up—based on his arm hair I wasn't sure that was the best decision.

"Give me a second to talk to Gene and then I'll head up and check on her. Don't you go anywhere."

Kevin nodded, too fixated on his sleeves to do much more.

Morgan pressed her hand against my hip and guided me away from the fidgeting grad student. "Gene, don't get me wrong, it is so nice of you to stop by unannounced," Morgan's fingers found their way across my butt, "but did you have to bring your roommate?"

Ed continued to pace between the oaks, periodically stopping to talk to what looked like his stomach.

I caught Morgan's hand and removed it from my rear end. "He's why I'm here. Ed got a Yaga Doll."

Morgan's eyes flashed and her vibrant liner caught in the flickering gaslights. "How on earth did Edwin Lovely get a Yaga Doll?"

"Wait, you know what that is?"

Morgan frowned slightly. "Of course I know what that is. What I want to know is how he got one, and why you think it's okay that he even has one?"

"I… Uh…" Morgan's questions caught me off guard as they often did. Unlike my almost non-existent Magickal knowledge, Morgan was a walking encyclopedia of Magician lore.

"You don't know where Yaga Dolls come from, do you, Gene?"

"Peru?"

Morgan smiled, her lush lips setting my heart beating ever faster. "That's why I love you. There's so much of this wide world you know nothing about, and I get to be the one that shares it with you."

"Thanks, I guess?"

Those soft lips planted a kiss on mine, and for a moment I couldn't remember what I was worried about.

"Gene," Ed waved from under a nearby tree, "I think he's picked up on something."

The Reaver, crap!

"Morgan, listen, Ed says Shorty has picked up the scent of a Reaver—Chaos Demon—and he thinks it's nearby. We need to get out of here."

"Is there a problem?" Kevin asked, his face sweating in the cool night air. "I mean, if there's a problem you can just tell Marcy that I'd be happy to meet with her on a different evening."

"No," Morgan snapped at the nervous suitor. "Everything is fine." She turned back to me and directed her eyes toward the distant Demon Hunter. "You and crazy boy need to go home. I promised Marcy I'd set her up with Kevin, and I aim to keep my promises."

"Couldn't you just do it some other night?"

Morgan shook her head. "No. This is the only night they both have off. Listen, Gene, not everyone has what we have," Morgan tugged at the front of my shirt, "but that doesn't mean I'm not going to at least try. It's all about making the world a better place."

"Gene!" Ed waved his hand again, this time pointing to the bulge beneath his vest. "We need to clear the deck. Shorty says it's coming."

"Morgan, I really wish you would reconsider. I mean, Ed says—"

She placed a finger on my lips. "It's so sweet of you to worry, but I am more than capable of protecting myself."

"Yeah, but Ed says..."

Morgan's Magick sprung to life around her with the subtle precision of a ticking clock. Like a jeweler's masterwork, Morgan's power was precise as it was effective. "I told you. I can take care of myself."

"But, Morgan—"

Ed raced out from under the oak tree. The shrunken head was out from its hiding place inside his vest and dangling from the braided topknot. "It's coming!"

Kevin's hands twisted nervously. "It looks like you guys have a bunch of other things going on. Please just tell Marcy that I would love to meet her, perhaps at some point in a month or two when we're both free again."

Morgan grabbed his arm. "No, it's fine. Really. My boyfriend and his roommate were just leaving."

Ed shoved the shrunken head into my hand. "Gene, hold Shorty while I look for something."

Clunk!

The heavy oak doors swung open and a petite young blond skipped down the steps. "Morgan, I tried that perfume you told me to use. Damn, girl, that's good stuff!"

Shorty bounced like a yo-yo at the end of his braid. "Reaver!"

9

REAVER FEVER

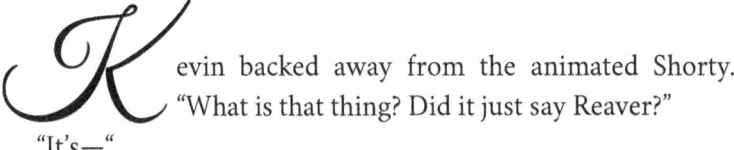evin backed away from the animated Shorty. "What is that thing? Did it just say Reaver?"

"It's—"

"Nothing," Morgan said, stepping in front of the wrinkly ball of excitable flesh. "Kevin, I want to introduce you to Marcy."

"I smell Reaver!" Shorty shouted, alternating between words and equally annoying siren sounds. "Woo! Woo!"

Morgan frowned. "Would you please shut that thing up?"

"Ed, I don't think there's any Reavers here," I said, the shrunken head's lips wet against my palm. "Maybe Shorty got confused by the perfume."

It was a heady scent: musky, with a hint of something else, something I couldn't quite but my finger on.

"I'm telling you, Gene." Ed hunted through his pockets in a frantic search for something. "There's a Reaver here. It's possessing one of them and I'm going to get it out."

Morgan took Marcy's hand and directed her toward the concerned-looking grad student. "Marcy, this is Kevin."

The petite blond waved and used her other hand to brush down the edges of a form-fitting dress. "Hi, Kevin."

Something red appeared briefly on the back of Marcy's hand.

Is that a sigil?

"Hey, Marcy." Kevin nodded, then immediately turned back to Morgan. "He said Reaver."

My girlfriend waved her hand. "It's nothing. They're just a bunch of goof balls. I got this great place picked out for you two. It's very secluded and not far from here. I think it would be a perfect way for you to get to know each other."

Chomp!

"Ouch," I pulled my hand away from the Yaga Doll's biting mouth.

"The Reaver is hiding," Shorty said.

Ed dug through his pockets. "Way ahead of you, Shorty. If I could just find The Skunk Paw of Sellix then we'd be able to—"

Morgan wrinkled her nose at the word skunk. "And that's enough of that. You two are going to have such a great time. Just head down there and take the second left. There's a really nice set of picnic tables."

"Ah ha!" My roommate retrieved a lumpy-looking paw out of his vest. "I knew I had it. Gene, get ready to pull the strings off Shorty's eyes."

"Wait, what?! You said his eye beams are like death lasers."

My roommate held the stinky gray paw up to his face. "I sure hope so, cause we're going to need them once we get everyone into their true form."

Kevin stepped in front of Marcy. "I don't think you want to do that."

"Oh yeah, smart guy, what else don't you think?" Ed licked the paw.

The skunk's tiny digits wiggled, their motion filling the air with a vile and revolting Magick. Like standing next to a trash heap or day-old-roadkill, the scent burned my nose and stung my eyes. "Ugh, Ed, that smells terrible."

"Exactly."

Kevin pushed Morgan aside to face the Demon Hunter. "You don't want to do that, child." His voice shifted and grew deeper, while at the same time rumbling against a widening chest.

Ed backed up from the angry grad student. "Death Lasers, Gene."

"I'm trying!" I said, tugging at the black threads that bound Shorty's eyes.

Kevin's face twisted, pulling and stretching like something underneath was trying to break free. His skin curled like cheap carpet, while those rolled-up sleeves expanded to almost cartoonish proportions.

"Any time now, Gene!"

Marcy screamed and the air filled with the first inklings of Morgan's Magick.

Shorty's face bounced at the end of the topknot, making it next to impossible to get the threads undone. "Almost there."

Rip!

Like an insect shedding its skin, Kevin's grad-student body sloughed off like a discarded cracker wrapper, exposing the glistening exoskeleton of a massive mantis. Long whiskers waved gracefully in the evening air from an angular and chitinous head. Two large and multi-faceted eyes glittered in the glow of the nearby gaslights.

I frantically yanked at the threads. "Almost there."

"That's not a Reaver," Ed said, dropping the Skunk Paw of Sellix.

"Huh?"

The monstrous mantis unfolded his hook-like claws, those razor-sharp appendages slicing the air like premium cutlery.

"Illickthid," Morgan breathed. Her Magick ramped up behind me.

The monstrous insect's long antenna-like whiskers twisted in the air. "There is a Reaver here!"

"I told you," Shorty cried, twisting at the end of his topknot.

Marcy...

The young girl took a few steps back, her clutch clattering to the ground. "Morgan, what's happening to me?"

Red splotches appeared on the blond's formerly perfect skin. They spread like spilt paint, consuming her arms and covering her bare shoulders. The young woman doubled-over and a fit of coughing sent her to the ground.

I dropped Shorty's thread. "What's happening?"

Morgan pulled me back. "Be careful, Gene."

"What is it?"

Hook-like claws shot past my head, knocking the Yaga Doll out of my hand and sending it tumbling beneath the oaks.

Long insect legs pushed their way between us and put the mantis in front of the fallen Marcy.

Insect claws sliced at the air.

"Ed, what do we do?"

"Grab a crab-leg, buddy." My roommate wrapped his hands around one of the Illickthid's many appendages and pulled.

I followed his lead and grabbed my own mantis leg. "What about the Reaver?"

"It's a possession." Ed said, his vest jingling against the Illickthid's monstrous strength. "If he kills the Demon, he's going to take the girl with it."

"Why would he do that?"

"Illickthid's are sworn enemies of Chaos Demons—goes back thousands of years, but I don't have all the details. I'm still trying to figure out what the odds are that we'd have two of them together in the same space at the same time."

"And that you'd skunk them."

The mantis's many feet dug into the hard concrete and yanked us forward like clingy toddlers.

My roommate adjusted his grip to keep his face from

scraping on the ground. "Crap. Morgan, can you do something?"

My girlfriend was somewhere beyond the oversized bug carapace, but I knew she was there. The tell-tale ticking of her complex Magick was a dead giveaway.

"Morgan's doing something."

"That's great," Ed said, clearly straining against the Illick-thid's considerable strength. "Where's Shorty?"

"I lost him in the bushes."

"What?!"

Crunch!

An explosive force knocked the Illickthid backward and took Ed and I with it. The three of us skidded across the side-walk, myself narrowly avoiding the monster's claws. "What the—"

A misshapen form rose out of the tattered remnants of Marcy's dress. The beast resembled the lumped together remains of melted rubber action figures. Twisted limbs and bulbous flesh stood mashed together in grotesque detail. Mouths cried and eyes glared from almost random positions. Deformed muscles swung thick and wild arms. To call the Reaver a Demon of chaos was almost kind. The Reaver was chaos, in all of its confusing form.

"Morgan!"

My girlfriend lay with her face turned away from me not far from what had been Marcy.

"Ed, Morgan's in trouble."

"Go!" My roommate pulled a gumball out of his vest pocket and popped it in his mouth. "I'll slow him down."

Ed bit down on the gum while I hobbled past the recovering Illickthid.

"Morgan." I slipped under a wild swing from that crazed mound of disfigured flesh. "Wake up, Morgan!"

My clove-scented sweetheart didn't move.

Damn it.

Mantis claws sliced the air, the Illickthid lunging forward only to be caught by something. Ed's gumball, now fully chewed and rapidly approaching the size of a basketball, held one of the creature's many legs tight.

Nice one, Lovely.

The Reaver pressed its advantage, massive and muscular arms swinging with reckless abandon against the trapped Illickthid. I took this opportunity to slip past the Chaos Demon and make a break for Morgan.

"Are you okay?" I asked, gently turning her to the side, only to find blood trickling from a small scrape above her ear.

Crap.

The Illickthid tore free from the chewy wad and turned its attention to what had been Marcy.

My roommate backed away from the heavyweight fighters. "A little help here, Gene."

"Morgan, you've got to get up!"

My girlfriend remained still, her chest softly rising and falling beneath the flickering lights of the dorm doors.

"A little Magick would be good now." Ed's face popped up beneath the Illickthid's many legs. "Like now. Right now."

Razor sharp claws cut into the Reaver's mutilated flesh.

Stop wasting time, Gene.

I closed my eyes and reached into the well of cosmic power that churned inside my chest.

The Yaga Doll... But would that hurt Marcy?

Illickthid claws slashed and chaotic fists swung wildly. One of these two would win, and I had very little interest in seeing what would happen to us in the aftermath. There was only one logical choice.

Get Shorty.

I took a deep breath and coaxed the Magick into my hands, then reached out into the night air. "Venit!" I cried, willing the rubbery little head to me while hoping to hell I knew what I'd do if it actually made it here.

LETTING GO

*L*ike a wrinkly fastball off the mound, Shorty's head erupted out of the distant bushes.

Whump!

The Yaga Doll hit me in the gut and ejected the air from my lungs while the rest of me scrambled to hold on to the oversized raisin.

My roommate backed away from the supernatural death match in front of him. I tore at the threads and peeled apart the thin black cord that kept Shorty blind.

"Don't look at it!"

Too late.

The tiny head's eyelids fluttered open, revealing glowing green eyes that shone like halogen bulbs. I tried to look away, but the monster's pupil-less gaze held me tight.

"How are you not burning?" Shorty asked. It's glowing eyes enveloped me.

"Damned if I know," I said, mesmerized by the brilliant green. "What do I do?"

The oversized raisin smiled.

"Point him at the Reaver, Gene," Ed said from somewhere beyond the melee.

"Best do it before you burn up, Magician."

I fought to close my eyes, to find the strength to look away from the unholy power of the Yaga Doll's gaze, but I couldn't move. Shorty's green glow consumed my arms, and then my chest. In seconds, it was hard to see where the shrunken head stopped and I began.

Ed shouted something, but his voice faded in the roar of the Yaga Doll's Magick. There was power trapped inside that wrinkly skull, a force of destruction that was both familiar and alien.

"Whatever is keeping you safe from me will not last forever," Shorty said, his voice booming between my ears. "We've got a Reaver to destroy."

Yes, yes we do.

Renewed by the Yaga Doll's encouragement, I pulled my eyes away. The intensity of Shorty's gaze left me partially blinded. It was like staring at the sun. I was lost in a sea of hazy shadows and misshapen figures.

"There!" Shorty's head no longer bobbed at the end of the topknot, but now focused on a distant shape. Blurry figures and unfocused afterimages played out across my eyes, but I didn't care.

So much power...

The Yaga Doll's Magick roared in my hand. It was like holding up a firehose of pure cosmic energy, yet the power I held wanted nothing else but to destroy. Thanks to the doll, we were unstoppable. There was nothing that could withstand our cleansing fire.

Laser-like light erupted from the shrunken head's eyes. Twin rays of intensity cut the air like searchlights at a movie premiere and bored down on the hazy shapes. My roommate shouted something, but again his words were lost in the Yaga Doll's fury.

"More power!" Shorty cried, his fiery voice echoing in my head.

There was more, a lot more. I'd spent years building up tiny fortifications around my Magick. I didn't realize it at the time, but I'd built reasons to hold back—some good and others not so much—but now, in the heart of Shorty's unholy fire, I let them burn away one by one. There would be no more self-imposed constraints around, no more questions, and no more fears. I would unleash the gates of hell itself if it meant reveling in the Yaga Doll's swelling destruction.

"Gene!" Ed's voice cut through the roaring Magick, the dim blur of my roommate appearing next to me, his hands waving frantically. "Stop, it's going to consume you!"

"More," the tiny head shouted, its demands bouncing around in my head like a hungry dog.

Ed...

The Yaga Doll demanded power, and power was what it got. Magick poured out of me like a crashing wave. Cosmic energy pushed down for far too long surged into the Yaga Doll. Its wrinkly flesh glowed with the light of a dozen suns.

Ed's hands reached for me. "Drop it before you destroy them and yourself."

Eye beams like high-powered lasers filled the air with an acrid smoke and the sound of sizzling flesh.

What have I done?

I tried to pull back, but I couldn't. Instead the power surged.

"More!" Shorty screamed, but his demands were no longer enticing. I had become a slave to the Yaga Doll and its fury. I wasn't a force of unstoppable nature. I was simply a reservoir of power for the hungry head's anger.

The Yaga Doll's pull was too strong, too powerful. I couldn't stop, and I couldn't let go—Shorty had become an extension of me. The shrunken head was fused to my fingers like a live wire: even if I'd wanted to let it go, I couldn't.

Shorty laughed manically in my hand—his burning eyes were a lighthouse in the maelstrom of raging Magick.

Ed grabbed my shoulder. "Gene, I've got to cut you off. This is going to hurt, but there's no other way. If you don't stop soon you'll destroy the Illickthid, the girl, and then yourself."

The watercolor image of my roommate swirled against the backdrop of Shorty's unquenchable fire. He pulled something from his vest, then froze, his fingers unmoving in the fiery Magick's light. "Gene—"

Pling.

Whatever it was he'd been holding hit the ground, and Ed's voice faded away, only to be replaced by a different one, one I knew from many a sultry evening beneath the sheets.

Morgan!

They were still my roommate's lips moving, but they weren't his words. Morgan had taken control of Ed's body. The ticking precision of her Magick slid into position like gears in a great engine. "Gene, ignore him. He's not a Magician, he doesn't understand us. How could he? He wants to keep you from becoming all you can be. He wants to keep you down, to suppress the power that roars inside you. Do you want that? Do you want to be like him? Gene, you can do this, I believe in you. Let it free and be who you were made to be!"

Magick raced down my arm and into the Yaga Doll. Somewhere at the end of those fiery beams flesh popped and burned.

"Morgan... I have to... stop."

"No, Gene," my girlfriend's words played out across Ed's lips. "You need to dig deeper. The Illickthid won't stop with a Reaver. It'll tear its way through the rest of us. You have to destroy them, you have to break them both. You are the only one who can do it. You are the only one that can save us."

"But Marcy—"

"Show me the Magician I knew was hiding beneath the

surface. Show me that power. Show me the real Eugene Law.
Show me who you are!"

Morgan's Magick clicked into place, like the turning of the
world on its axis, and her power dug into the edges of the
barriers in my mind. With a gentle touch, my girlfriend untied
many of the protections that stood between my soul and the
cosmic power fighting for control of it. Magick surged, and I
screamed. The Yaga Doll cackled, and cosmic energy roared
through it like the heat of the sun focused through a magnifying
glass—everything burned.

"Yes, Gene! You've done it," Morgan said from inside my
roommate. "I always thought you had power, but this much? I
am in awe. Never did I imagine you hid this much. You could
rival the Magicians of old. You could take your place in the
history books as one of the greatest to have ever lived. Together,
you and I will change the world. We will be unstoppable, a force
of nature—"

My roommate stuttered, Morgan's voice breaking up against
the hazy face of a very angry Ed Lovely. "Get the hell out of my
head." Ed balled up his fists.

"Gene," it was Morgan again, "don't let him drag you down.
A power like yours comes along only once in a generation, if
that. There is so much more you could be—so much more—and
with my help you will get there. I will help you blossom."

"I… can't…"

"Oh, but you can, and you did! You already did it, Gene. The
Illickthid is a melted husk, and the Reaver is gone. Neither of
them could withstand the power of Eugene Law.

"Ed!" Porter's voice cut through the swirling confusion.
Porter! Oh no, is she hurt?

Morgan's Magick shuddered, and like grinding gears, it
faded beneath the anger in Ed's eyes.

"Enough!" my roommate shouted, shaking his head and
forcing Morgan from his voice. "You've got to stop, Gene. I can't

let you end up like Shorty. I'm sorry, but you left me no choice, buddy."

I'm sorry, Ed, I didn't mean to.

The last thing I remembered was the Demon Hunter's fist and a brilliant explosion of stars before my world went white. Shorty's terrifying laughter chased me into oblivion.

RAZOR SHARP

"Gene, wake up."

Shorty's roaring Magick was gone, but it had left me with a nice ringing in my ears as a stark reminder of the Yaga Doll's anger.

Or was that my anger?

"Ed, are you okay?" Porter asked, her voice concerned yet distant.

"I'll be fine."

The Demon Hunter didn't sound fine.

Soft hands caressed my face and brought with them the soothing smell of mint and cloves. "Come on, Gene. Crawl your way out of it. I know you can. You've been hiding some tremendous power from me."

"Morgan?" I asked, opening my eyes to the flickering gaslights and something else.

Oh my God.

The charred remains of the monstrous Illickthid and distorted Reaver flesh lay in a hopeless lump of still-smoking ash.

"I did that?"

Morgan helped me up, her bright eyes twinkling in the broken light. "You did. Oh, Gene. You saved me, you saved all of us."

"I did that…"

The memory was still hazy. I had flashes of Kevin, the grad-student-turned-monster, and then there was Marcy.

Oh my God Marcy…

My stomach churned at the thought. It was all I could do to fight back the beer and nachos threatening to come back up all over the sidewalk and my girlfriend.

Ed stood not far from the smoldering remains, the tattered and scorched fragments of a broken Yaga Doll in his fingers. Clearly concerned, and not entirely sure what to make of what just happened, Porter placed a gentle hand on his arm. "Are you okay?"

My roommate shoved a broken sack of wrinkly flesh into her hands, then unloaded on my kneeling girlfriend. "What the hell did you think you were doing?"

Morgan took her hands off my face and shrugged. "What was I doing? What were you doing? You were the one that brought a Yaga Doll to my dorm. You're the one who told Gene to use it. I'm just glad I was here to keep him from making a mistake that could have hurt you, Porter, or others."

Ed's face was beet-red and his hands were waving faster than my still blurry eyes could follow. "You know the rules. You of all people should know the rules, Morgan Crowley. That was Ten Spins' Soul Push, wasn't it?"

My girlfriend wrapped a hand around my shoulder and pulled me gently toward her like a mama bear protecting its cub. "Maybe it was, maybe it wasn't. It doesn't matter. What matters is I made sure you survived. We made sure all of you survived."

Ed swung a wild finger around to point at the smoking remains. "What about them? Did they survive?"

A faint breeze kicked up and brought with it the gut-churning smell of burnt hair and wet dog. I swallowed back at the bile rising in my throat.

"What are you talking about, Ed?" Porter waded gently into the conversation, zipping a thin jacket tight to her chest. "What's a Soul Push?"

"Gene's girlfriend thought it would be fun to push my soul out of the way and take over my body."

All the color drained out of Porter's face. "She can do that?"

Morgan didn't skip a beat. "She sure can. But just because she can doesn't mean she would unless it were dire circumstances. Your boyfriend put us all at risk bringing that Yaga Doll here, but once he did, there was only one solution. Gene had to see us through to safety—no matter what the consequences."

Porter grabbed my roommate's hand, concern evident on her face. "Eddie, are you okay?"

"Yeah. I'll be fine." Ed scooped up a small metal toy jack, its diminutive spokes shining in the flickering light. "You weren't expecting me to have Sanity's Jack, were you, Morgan?"

Morgan shook her head. "Of course I expected you to have it. In fact, I wouldn't have pushed you to the background had I thought you didn't have a way to hold on."

"You're lying." Ed shoved the tiny metal toy into one of the pockets of his jingling vest.

Porter tucked what remained of the melted and broken Yaga Doll under her arm. "What do you mean 'pushed you into the background'?"

Ed fumed. "Should I tell her, or would you like to?"

Morgan didn't respond. Her hands caressed my tired chest.

"Fine, I'll tell her." Ed turned to the petite waitress. "The sea of consciousness. It's a mental manifestation that comes with the Soul Push. You have to scramble to stay above the waves. If you aren't careful…"

"What? If you aren't careful what, Eddie?"

"You drown," Morgan said, without a hint of concern in her voice.

Porter almost dropped the shrunken head. "Drown?!"

Ed threw his arms in the air. "You risked my life, Morgan. You used some of the most dangerous Magick ever created without a care in the world. You could have killed me—or worse."

"Would you have preferred to end up at the receiving end of the Reaver's fists? Or what about the claws of its mortal enemy? You're alive, Edwin Lovely—you should be thanking me. You should be thanking Gene. Without his Magick we all might not have survived."

"Yeah, well tell that to the two of them." Ed pointed at the charred and smoking remains. "How did they fare?"

"Ed..." Porter took a step back from the smoldering pile. "It moved."

"What?" The Demon Hunter turned his attention to the ash and melted flesh.

The pile shifted, and a small voice escaped the burnt remains. "Help..."

"Marcy?" Morgan left me back on the sidewalk and raced back to the smoking heap. "Marcy, can you hear me?" Morgan pulled at edges of melted exoskeleton, tearing it off in great chunks and tossing it aside. "Marcy?"

Pinky and healthy fingers appeared from the dark char and coal. "Morgan? Is that you?"

"Don't just stand there." My girlfriend yanked at a large piece of still-smoldering exoskeleton. "Help me! We're coming, Marcy."

Ed and Porter joined her, and in a few seconds they had the young girl's arm free.

"We're coming, Marcy," Morgan said, directing Ed and Porter to grab the opposite edge of a large piece.

"Morgan," Marcy's voice was thin and shaken. "Morgan, I

remember. I remember all of it."

"Pull." Porter pried back the side of burnt exoskeleton, while Ed snapped off the pieces surrounding Marcy's head.

The young woman's unfocused eyes appeared beneath the ash and soot. Confused and full of pain, Marcy searched frantically. "No, no I can't do this," she cried, her tear-filled eyes lost in a memory only she could see. "Please no, please don't. Morgan I—"

My girlfriend didn't hesitate. She placed her hands on Marcy's face and spun up her Magick. "Ssh," Morgan said, using her fingers to brush the matted hair out of Marcy's eyes. "It'll be fine. I promise you, it'll be fine. You hear me?"

Marcy's eyes continued to search frantically. "Morgan, don't let it—"

"I won't. I promise you, I won't."

My girlfriend gently placed her thumbs beneath Marcy's cheeks, tracing a tiny pattern in the ash with her fingers. Even from my spot on the sidewalk, the symbol brought back memories of its own: the dark and mysterious pattern that had fallen from Morgan's books.

"What is she doing, Ed?" Porter asked, stepping back from the frantic young woman.

Marcy's eyes went wide and a startled cry escaped her lips. "Argh, that hurts. Stop, please stop!"

Ed reached for Morgan, but she snapped at him, "You want to leave her brain dead, then go ahead and touch me."

"Memory Scalpel..." Ed breathed, clearly not sure how to proceed.

"Right. No one wants to remember a possession—no one. You want to remember what it was like having me in your head?"

Ed opened his mouth and then closed it again.

"Exactly," Morgan said, her Magick ramping up dramatically. "Do not interrupt me."

Memories flashed through the churning power. It was hard to follow—there were tears, anger, shame, and disappointment. A cornucopia of emotions blurred into a hazy and painful watercolor. Details were lost in a wash of mental fragments too hard to piece back together.

"Wait," Porter said, coming to her boyfriend's side. "Don't we want to know how it happened?"

Ed shook from his trance. "She's right, Morgan. If we've had run-ins with both Shades and a Reaver in the last twenty-four hours, that means something isn't right. We need to see what she knows."

But Morgan didn't stop. She poured it on. Even in my haze I could feel it—the power my girlfriend wielded was precise, almost surgical. Morgan dug through the girl's memories one by one, slicing them out with expert precision and removing any chance we'd figure out how it happened.

They're right.

I tried to get to my feet. "Morgan, stop, wait!"

The sigils scrawled against the girl's cheeks flashed with an angry red glow, and then faded—the Memory Scalpel had done its job and left its patient on the cutting-room floor.

"It's done," Morgan said, taking her hands off Marcy's face.

With a faint smile, the young girl collapsed against the sidewalk.

The distant sound of sirens echoed beneath the trees, while bright red-and-blue lights flashed between the dark branches.

Porter turned her attention to the fallen Marcy. "Why did you do that?"

Morgan stood, only to sway gently, her feet unstable. "I did what I had to do. There was too much pain. I couldn't let her live that way. I hope you never have to know what that's like, Porter, I truly do, but if some monster should crawl inside your skin, I bet you'll beg me to make you forget the whole thing."

Morgan clutched at my arm. "Gene, help me get home."

"What about the—"

Her fingers tightened against my arm, and the nails bit into my flesh with a surprising amount of strength. "Please, Gene. Let's go home."

The siren roared again, and Ed helped Porter remove Marcy from the disintegrating mess of burnt flesh and exoskeleton. "This isn't over, Morgan."

"You're wrong, Ed. Thanks to Gene, it is."

PART II
FRUIT OF THE TREE

SCENT OF A WOMAN

*W*e hadn't made it much past the heavy oak doors to Morgan's dorm before the police and fire department showed up. I hesitated on the other side, wondering if I should be out there with Ed and Porter.

"They'll be fine," Morgan said, letting go of my hand and pointing to the concrete steps just inside the entrance. "I'm still a little woozy."

"What about Marcy?"

My girlfriend smiled and tucked an arm under mine. "See, that's what I like about you, Gene—always worried about others. She'll be fine. As far as she's concerned she'll wake up and remember it as a fun date, and that maybe she had a bit too much to drink."

Date? Kevin.

"Wait, what about that Kevin guy? What was he? What did you call him?"

Morgan gently dragged me toward the steps. "Illickthid—old-time mantis creatures from before there were people in Florida. I honestly thought they were extinct."

"But he looked just like—"

"A person?" Morgan nodded, taking the first step. "That's what they do. Listen, Illickthids are scary tough and not something to mess around with. Those hooked claws can cut you to ribbons, and they're not afraid to use them. I can get angry at Ed all I want, but the Yaga Doll was instrumental in saving all of our butts this evening."

We hit the first landing and I blinked a few times, trying to push Shorty's afterimages from my eyes. "I guess—"

"Look at me," Morgan said, pausing briefly to check my eyes. "Can you see?"

I blinked a few more items, letting the sparkles fade around the edges. "Yeah, sort of. Still having a few afterimages."

Morgan pressed down on my cheeks and peered into my sore eyes. "I should say so. I'm still trying to understand how you took a Yaga Doll at point-blank range and are standing here to talk about it."

My mind drifted back to the burnt pile of ash no doubt slowly disintegrating on the sidewalk out front—could that have been me?

"I have no idea."

"Yaga Dolls have a history, Gene," Morgan said, taking her fingers off my cheeks and dragging my attention back onto the stairs.

"Where do they come from?"

Morgan took a few steps, then paused. "I don't want to go into it right now. I'll explain it to you later."

"But—"

"Later, Gene. Later."

We took the next set of stairs in silence, neither of us doing much more than focusing on our feet. It wasn't until we reached her floor and pushed open the door that I decided to press a different question that had been bothering me. "What's a Reaver?"

"Distilled chaos, Gene."

"Huh?"

"Chaotic monsters from the edges of the Gloom. Think of them like a manifestation of irrational fears, fused together in a wet mess of anger and frustration."

"That sounds lovely. Speaking of Lovely, Ed says they're rare."

Morgan leaned her back against the dorm door, letting it close slowly behind her. "He's right, they are. However, what Ed doesn't know is that the university has a history which makes Reavers a distinct possibility."

Wait, did she say Reavers? As in more than one?

Morgan took my hand and led me down the hall toward her room. Posters of male actors and musicians hung from the walls every few feet, taped over with white stickers and inked in vibrant marker with the names of the girls living in the closest room.

We hadn't made it halfway down the hall before one of the doors swung open and a curly redhead stepped out to block our path.

"Morgan, I'm out of the good stuff," she said, adjusting a tube top that barely contained her ample chest. "I need more."

"You couldn't have used all of it, Jess," Morgan said, clearly tired and trying to navigate past her curvy floor-mate.

"That stuff is amazing—of course I've used all of it. Holy crap, girlfriend. The guys are just eating out of my hand," Jess said, setting up in front of us. "Besides, you got Gene here, it's not like you need it."

Morgan sighed and fished a small glass vial of pink liquid out of one of the many hidden pockets of her corset. "Here, but this is it for a while, Jess. You gotta go easy on this stuff; it can have repercussions."

Jess snatched the glass from Morgan's hand like a parched castaway would sieze a bottle of water. She popped the top off and pressed the vial up to her nose. "Oh yeah, mango and lilacs.

I don't know how the heck you do it, Morgan, but I love it just the same." She swung around and kicked open the door to her room. "Hey, bitches! We gonna get our freak on tonight!"

"Since when are you in the drug business?" I asked once we'd made it safely past the party room.

"I'm not in the drug business," Morgan said, more than a hint of frustration in her voice.

I hadn't detected any Magick in the pastel-colored perfume. "Then what is it?"

"It's perfume, Gene."

"You're making perfume?"

Morgan sighed. "If you must know, yes. I need the cash. Not all of us fall into scholarships and grants—some of us have to work for our money."

"Sorry, I didn't mean..." She was right. I had been tremendously lucky, not only getting into Florida, but in somehow landing scholarships and grants that covered just about everything. I'd been taking that for granted, and Morgan had just called me out on it.

"Whatever, it is what it is. Making that stuff is something my Dad's second girlfriend taught me how to do. Lately I took it back up to cover some unforeseen expenses."

"Hey, if you needed money—"

"Stop, Gene. I'm fine." Morgan's clipped tone told me it was best not to press further.

We reached the end of the dorm hall and her single room in silence. My girlfriend had long since removed her pop-star poster name plate, preferring to keep her door simple and nondescript, but that had been before. Something new lay lightly inked on the cheap wood.

A sigil?

"That's new," I said, leaning in to inspect the complex design. "What does that do?"

Morgan snapped my fingers away before I could touch it.

"Enough questions, Gene. What is this, the Spanish Inquisition?" My girlfriend didn't wait for a response before she brushed a hand across the symbol and let a tiny hint of her precise Magick slip from her fingers.

Click.

My girlfriend's undersized single was nothing if not organized. An expertly made bed lay pressed up against the far wall, while next to it a tiny nightstand held an old-time alarm clock, along with a small leather-bound notebook. A wide area rug covered the floor, leaving only a tiny sliver of polished concrete visible along the edges.

Morgan pushed me onto the bed. "You've been holding out on me."

I blushed. "Actually, I think we've been plenty—"

"Magick, Gene. You've been playing me. Since when do you swing that kind of power around?"

My mind drifted back to the early evening, the Shades, and pumping Magick into Ed's Rock God's Reward. "I don't know. Tonight with Ed I sort of let go. There were these Shades and—"

"Shades?" Morgan sat down next to me, her wide eyes full of concern. "You and Ed ran into Shades? I thought you guys were off doing some sort of exorcism or something."

"That's how it started, but things got out of hand rather quickly. You know Ed."

"Sadly, I do."

I laid back on Morgan's soft bedspread, placing my head on her oversized pillow and stretching my feet out. "Well, it started as a Poltergeist that Ed said always showed up at ten-thirty."

Morgan helped me pull off my shoes. "Ten-thirty, huh—a punctual spirit?"

"That's just it," I said, putting my hands behind my head. "It wasn't a spirit, it was chaotic Magick—some seriously unpredictable stuff. I don't know where it came from."

Morgan kicked off her heels and carried both our shoes

toward the door. "Unconstrained Magick? That is very interesting. What about the Shades?"

"Gone," I said, letting out a long sigh.

Morgan hesitated, her back to me. "Gone?"

"Completely. I don't want you to get too excited, but you are in the presence of a Magickal rockstar at his finest. All we were missing was the groupies. Maybe you could help me with that?"

Clunk.

Morgan dropped our shoes. "The Rock God's Reward isn't strong enough to take out a horde of Shades."

"Funny, that's what Ed said."

Click.

Morgan turned the light off and left me with just the pale outline of her body against the moonlight that slipped through the closed blinds. "You never cease to amaze me, Eugene Law."

"You're telling me. Sometimes I amaze myself."

13

A LOVELY INQUISITON

*D*appled light from the morning sun trickled through Morgan's half-shut blinds. They warmed the bedspread, before finding their way to my face. I promptly rolled over and pulled on the thin sheets, but found them unwilling to budge. Morgan had tucked them too tightly into the end of the bed.

"Ugh, close the blinds," I said, burying myself beneath the pillow.

No response.

I slipped a hand out to the side my girlfriend should have been on—no Morgan.

"Morgan?"

Nothing.

I pushed myself up and confirmed I was both alone in the bed and the tiny room.

Where is she?

I kicked off the clingy sheets and knocked a small piece of paper to the ground in the process.

Gene, had a few quick things to take care of this morning. Want to meet for breakfast?

The note went on to detail the exact location and time—Morgan was nothing if not precise.

I chuckled and went to shove the note in my pocket, only to realize I wasn't wearing pants. They hung from one of the bed posts like an animal pelt. Next to them, at the end of the bed, my shirt and wadded-up socks were nestled together like a mother hen and her chicks. The three amigos of Gene Law fashion were wrinkled almost beyond recognition, but I wasn't out to impress anyone today.

Saturday...

I yanked my jeans off the post and pulled them on, stumbling my way out of Morgan's bed in the process. I contemplated leaving her sheets unmade, then quickly thought better of it. That was an argument I wasn't keen on having again. A complex series of tucks and pulls, followed by a re-alignment of the bedspread and proper fold-over of the pillow area, and I was done. I took a moment to step back and admire my work. It wasn't Morgan-grade, but it was infinitely better than anything that passed for clean on my roommate's side of our room.

Ed... Was he right to be angry? Would I have been angry too?

I contemplated all of this as I pulled my shirt over my head.

But wasn't it really his fault all along? Had Morgan not pushed him aside, could things have gone worse for all of us?

I tabled that thought and scooped my wallet off the nightstand, checking it for cash.

Enough for coffee.

Morgan's antique alarm clock slowly ticked away in front of me, its tiny hands sweeping in time with the headache bubbling up in the base of my skull. The old clock's face and I were in agreement—it was way past caffination hour.

Where are my keys?

I checked the nightstand again, but they weren't there. A quick pass under the bed didn't reveal anything either, just a remarkably dust-free patch of polished concrete.

I turned my attention to Morgan's desk, but just like her bed, the standard-issue oak-topped desk was a temple to organization. Pencils and pens stood in tightly packed holders, while next to them a stack of blank pages waited patiently to be used. I pulled on a couple of the drawers, but Morgan must have locked them, because not a single one budged.

I signed and tried to replay my actions from the night before.

Morgan turned off the light and I tossed my—that's it.

I spun around to find my keys laying on one of the lower levels of her bookshelf. A single dorm room wasn't large, but my girlfriend had still found a way to get a set of shelves big enough to hold all her various texts into the room. I picked up my keys and hesitated, taking a minute to run my hand over the covers: The Jacobean Prefect, The Gorbel Conjecture, Mejinks and The One Thousand Tongues. I didn't know what any of these were, and to be honest the few times I'd tried to follow them I quickly became bored to the point of tears.

I pulled one of the books off the shelf, checking for that paper I'd seen the other night, but found nothing. A few more volumes proved to be the same. Each one was full to the brim with complex Magickal theories and concepts, but not one of them providing anything remotely similar to odd-looking sigil that had graced the scrap of paper I'd found the other day.

I pushed the books back on the shelf, pausing to confirm each one was in the same place I'd found it, then grabbed my shoes by the door. After lacing them up I checked one last time to make sure everything was in order, then slipped out the door and down the quiet dorm hall.

I left the dorm and stepped into the cool morning air. Fall was coming to Gainesville, and that meant a welcome respite from the summer heat. The street outside Morgan's dorm was largely devoid of life. A few birds chirped in the wide oak canopy above my head, clearly more interested in catching their morning worm than paying any attention to me, while a wide array of cars sat parked in sequence against the street's edge. Having a car would have been pretty helpful, but that was not in the cards for me. Scholarships paid for tuition, not wheels. I skipped down the steps and paused, the blackened and burnt sidewalk spot a stark reminder of last night. The details were a hazy memory, everything except for Shorty's eyes. The Yaga Doll's green gaze felt like it would be forever burned into my mind.

"Stayed with Morgan last night, eh, Gene?"

I practically jumped up at the sound of my roommate's voice. Ed popped out from behind one of the trees. He wasn't wearing his vest—even Demon Hunter Edwin Lovely took the weekends off.

"Yeah, I stayed here." There was a curt tone to my voice I hadn't been expecting. Ed noticed it, and didn't appear impressed.

"Where's Morgan?"

"Out running errands," I said, leaving the burned-out sidewalk and joining my roommate under the ancient trees. "Listen, whatever it is you have to say to her, you can say it to me."

Ed shook his head, those long blond bangs swinging from side to side like a pair of windshield wipers. "I don't think so, Gene. We have an issue, her and I."

"Is this because of the Ten Souls thing?"

Ed frowned. "It's Ten Spins' Soul Push, and you should be very concerned your girlfriend was willing to use any of that foul Magician's designs. He was quite a piece of work, and that's just the sigils we know about. I expect there's a lot more we aren't aware of."

"Ed, you're alive, as am I, and Porter. We all survived, and honestly when all that went down last night I wasn't sure that was a given. Don't push the issue."

Ed's hands opened and closed a few times. Having lived with him the last few months, I had a handle on when he was angry. While it was certainly rare, when Ed had a bee in his bonnet it wasn't readily forgotten.

"This from the guy you could barely call a Magician on his best day."

"Ed, don't do—"

My roommate shook his head and pushed off the large oak. "If you were one, you'd know just how dangerous what your girlfriend did was, and exactly why I'm here right now."

"Oh, really? Then tell me, why are you here, Ed? Did you come over here to hurt Morgan? Is that why you're here? Because if that's the case you're going to have to go through me to do it." Blood rushed to my face, and brought with it a chilling surge of Magick. The cosmic energy seethed beneath my chest, startling me, and Ed as well.

"So that's how it's going to be? You're willing to throw our friendship away over her?"

"You're the one that came to the dorm on a Saturday morning, and you're the one skulking under the trees, ready to pounce on Morgan as soon as she walked outside."

I pushed the Magick back down, fighting that jack back into its box while hoping I could keep the lid clamped down before something I regretted popped out.

"What happened to the Gene Law I knew? He was cool. This guy has lost his way hanging around with a—"

"Don't say it, Edwin Lovely," Porter shouted, coming around the corner, her hair up in a pony-tail and dangling above the restaurant visor's back strap. "I know you're pissed, but don't take it out on Gene. I promise you'll regret it if you do."

Ed threw his hands up and stormed off, huffing his way between the oak trunks before disappearing behind the building.

"Thanks," I said, letting the Magick sink back into my churning gut.

Porter gave me a curt nod and zipped up her thin jacket. "Walk with me, Gene."

"I was going to get—"

"Coffee? Yeah, so was I. We need to talk."

14

PERKS

*P*orter tucked her hands in the pockets of her jacket and hunched her shoulders. A cool morning breeze kicked up and ruffled at the ends of her undersized uniform shorts. "Come on, Gene. It's cold as hell out here." Ed's girlfriend stepped off the sidewalk and cut across the narrow street away from the dorm. "Perks?"

"Works for me."

Perks was a relatively new coffee place off University Avenue. Capitalizing on the custom coffee craze, the hole-in-the-wall cafe was almost always crowded, and today was no exception. A small line of patrons had queued up out front, their bleary eyes and sagging cheeks carrying them in one by one on shuffling feet. The entire display had all the colorful excitement of a funeral procession. We took up a spot at the end of the line, Porter bouncing softly to keep the blood flowing to her chilly legs.

"What do you get?" she asked, retrieving a hand from its pocket long enough to zip her jacket up to the top.

"Coffee, black."

"Gene." Porter shook her head. "That's so boring."

I shrugged. "I'm not an exciting guy."

Ed's girlfriend paused long enough to give me one eyebrow gesture that said otherwise. "Right…"

"What are you getting?" I took the next spot as the line moved.

"Same."

"Porter, you're so boring."

The petite girl shrugged her already hunched shoulders. "I'm from Missouri."

The line snaked forward another spot and we moved ever closer to the front door.

"You didn't ask me over here to talk about coffee." I moved to block the breeze from cutting through her.

"No, I didn't." Porter paused as if searching for the right words. "I've got a bunch of brothers, Gene."

"Uh, okay, that's really great for you."

Porter shook her ponytail. "No, damn it. What I mean is, I've seen how brothers are, and you two are about as close to brothers as you can be—without sharing the same blood, that is."

My mind drifted to our dorm room, and the stark contrast between Ed's side of the room and mine. Whereas the Eugene Law side was a precise array of orderly lines—maybe not quite as straight as Morgan would have preferred— it was still far and away better than the unruly pile of disorder that was my roommate. Ed preferred to keep his clothing in descriptive lumps on the floor: the clean pile, the maybe clean pile, and the 'it really should be cleaned' pile.

He frequently got them mixed up.

"I'm not sure about that…"

Porter laughed, and the genuineness of that sound caught me off guard. There was no hidden agenda in her tone. She didn't appear to be carefully measuring her responses or gauging my reaction. It was oddly refreshing to talk to someone and not have to stay ten mental moves ahead.

I see why Ed likes you...

"I've seen your room," she said, following the line forward another space. "But listen, you guys have something special. You really shouldn't take that for granted. Life's too short."

Porter's words touched a nerve. I wasn't the one taking our friendship for granted—that was Ed, the guy who'd hid under the trees to pounce on Morgan as soon as she'd come out of the dorm.

"Tell that to your boyfriend," I said, perhaps with a little more venom in my voice than I'd anticipated. "He's the one that showed up at the dorm this morning."

Porter frowned. "I told him not to do that."

"I see that he's just as good at listening to you as he is at listening to me."

"Pretty much."

Coffee patrons inside the door shuffled forward and we took our place inside. The warmth of the buzzing crowd and percolating machines washed over us like a soft blanket. Porter immediately unzipped her jacket and let those overly tight shoulders drop. There was an athletic grace to how she moved, and I couldn't help but admire it. My frustrating lack of coordination made the petite brunette's actions seem downright impressive, and she hadn't done much more than bob and weave since we'd shown up.

"Think he'll get over it?" I followed her to a small display of collegiate-licensed coffee cups and travel mugs.

Porter picked up one of the gaudy mugs and turned it over in her hand, checking the price before immediately setting it back down. "Wow. Sorry, as much as I would love to have a mug shaped like a human-sized alligator crushing a—what is that?"

"A spear."

"Right, a spear—because why not, right? Anyway, as cool as

it would be, I'm gonna have to pass." She set the mug back down. The alligator man's flexing muscles put me to shame.

Porter shook her head. "Can you imagine seeing something like that in real life? I mean, that's just creepy. Then again, I'm talking to Ed's best friend. You guys corner the market on creepy." The petite brunette moved another spot forward in the line. I followed her, but stopped briefly to line the Alligator Man mug up with its brothers.

If only she knew they actually exist... Easy there, Gene, save that for another day.

"What has Ed told you about us?" I asked, letting my voice drop in volume.

Porter and I reached the counter. "Hold that thought, Gene," she said, turning her attention to the cashier. "Morning, Melissa! How's Timmy?"

The thirty-something clerk beamed. "Growing like a weed, P. Hold on, I have a new picture." She tucked a hand in the pocket of her apron and fished out a polaroid, and handled it to Porter.

"He has gotten big, wow! What are you feeding him?"

A cherubic youth smiled in the hazy photo, his diaper-only dance apparently caught mid-thrust.

"Anything that isn't tied down," the cashier said, accepting the photo back with a broad smile of her own. "He's a Cheerios eating machine."

"That's great, Mel. He's got his mom's smile."

"You're a sweetie. What can I get you? The usual?" Melissa looked at me and paused. "P, is this Ed? He's even more handsome than you told me."

I couldn't tell for sure, but I was reasonably confident Porter turned a few shades of red at that comment. "No, no. This is Gene. He's Ed's friend."

Melissa frowned. "I'm sorry."

"It's fine. I promise I'll bring Ed by one of these mornings. He's typically not one for waking up early."

"Very few of them are."

"Mel, I need two blacks and a breakfast care package."

The cashier nodded. "You got it, P."

I pulled out my wallet, but Porter put a hand on mine. Her soft skin was warm even in the stuffy confines of the cafe. "I got it. Accept this as a peace offering from Ed and I. He'll cool down —not as fast as this coffee, but he will. I promise."

"Uh, thanks."

Porter pointed to the coffees. "You carry those. I'll get the bag."

Melissa returned with a small paper bag and shoved what appeared to be some sort of breakfast sandwich inside, while Porter grabbed an orange and banana off the counter and placed them in the bag as well.

Ed's girlfriend paid for everything, fishing out crumpled bills from the tiny pockets of her uniform shorts and handing them over. "See you later, Mel."

"You got it."

We navigated our way back through the crowded cafe, careful to not spill coffee or stumble over anyone.

"Got yourself some breakfast, eh?" I asked when we were back outside in the cool morning air.

Porter set the bag down and zipped up her jacket, those shoulders again pinching up against the chilly breeze. "Nope."

"Breakfast for Ed?"

Porter shook her head and picked up the bag. "Nope. You mind holding that coffee for me for just a minute?"

"Sure."

Ed's girlfriend turned her attention to the street. Then confirming no cars were barreling down it, shot across, the bag tucked up her arm.

Don't look at her butt.

This time I didn't, but only because I was too busy trying to figure out where she was going. Porter hopped up on the opposite curb and approached a huddled man pressed up against an empty building.

I couldn't tell what the two of them were saying, but I didn't need to—the body language told me everything I needed to know.

Porter crouched down and put a hand on the man's shoulder, passing him the bag and eliciting a wide grin in the process. He dug out the orange and they shared a laugh. A few more words and a high-five later, and Porter was back dashing across the street to me, her ponytail bobbing with each graceful step.

I was lost in that visual when Morgan's jarring tone knocked me right back to the present. "Good morning, Gene. Oh look, it's Porter."

15

IT'S JUST COFFEE

*P*orter hopped up on the curb and slipped the coffee out of my suddenly cold fingers. "Thanks, Gene. I had fun catching up. See you later."

"Uh, sure," I said, giving Porter a half-hearted wave, then directing all my attention to the unhappy Magician standing next to me with a modest bag of sweet-smelling food in her hand.

"Spending time with Ed's girlfriend?"

"No, she happened to be outside the dorm and wanted to talk. So we just walked over to Perks and she bought me coffee."

"Just talk, eh?" Morgan asked, raising an eyebrow.

"Yeah, she was concerned about Ed coming to the dorm earlier in the morning looking for you."

Morgan's eyes flashed ever so slightly. "What did he want?"

"He's still angry about last night. I told him what you said. We had a few words."

"Then what happened?"

"Porter showed up and he left."

The way I'd laid it out made everything seem very upfront

and above-board, but I couldn't shake the sense I was playing footsie with a loaded bear trap.

"I see." Morgan let her words hang uncomfortably in the air. "And that's when she invited you on a date? Did you two have a nice time?"

"Yes—wait, no. I mean, it wasn't a date. She just wanted to talk to me about Ed. She was sorry he got so mad, and said we were like brothers, and that I should really put it behind me. Other than that it was just coffee, see?" I held up the paper cup. "Just coffee."

Morgan brushed her long green hair back, then stuffed the bag into my hand. "Well, I got us beignets, but we can always call Porter back and see if she'd rather have breakfast with you instead?"

"No, that's fine. I mean, we can just—" I opened the bag and shoved my face in, taking a deep whiff of the powdered fritters and hoping my over-the-top actions could get the topic changed quickly. "Wow, these smell amazing. Did you get them at that New Orleans cafe up the street?"

"Yes."

"Thanks! Where do you want to go to eat?"

Morgan slipped the coffee out of my hand. "Walk with me, Gene."

I followed Morgan down the block, passing in front of stores just opening for the day. "Is everything okay?" I asked after we'd gone another hundred yards without speaking.

"Fine, why wouldn't it be?"

I might not have been the smartest man on the block, but I knew when 'fine' didn't mean fine.

"Well, you've been quiet."

"I'm just enjoying this beautiful morning." Morgan shook out her hair and took a deep breath. "It's lovely, isn't it? Crisp, cool, and perfect for breakfast with someone special. Don't you think?"

"Completely."

Where is she going with this?

Morgan paused in front of a flower shop. The store hadn't opened yet. A single broken pink carnation lay on the sidewalk outside. She picked it up and brushed dirt off the petals.

"Where are we going, Gene?"

"Excuse me?" I asked, checking the upcoming corner. "Uh, looks like that's Thirteenth Street coming up."

Morgan tucked what remained of the flower's stunted stem in the pocket of her dark jeans. "You know what I meant, Gene."

"I do?"

Morgan sighed. "Where are we going with all this?"

"You mean us?" I asked.

"Yes, I mean us."

"Well, I thought things were going pretty good. I mean, last night was a lot of fun and—"

"Gene, I'm not talking about that."

"What are you talking about?" I asked, wondering what cold beignets would taste like, and whether my stomach would be up for them regardless.

Morgan took a sip of my coffee. The breeze caught her hair and twisted it gently. "I'm talking about your Magick. All that power you have squirreled away inside, and how you have been hiding it from me. Why would you do that? Are you afraid of me?"

"I wasn't hiding it from you."

Morgan turned to face the rising sun, its soft rays playing across her pale skin. "I'm having a hard time believing you."

"It's true," I said, tucking the bag under my arm. "I just sort of pushed it last night. I don't know, it just happened."

"Were you afraid?"

"Of course I was afraid," I said, putting a hand on hers.

"You were afraid of the Magick?"

"Who wouldn't be?" I set the bag on the ground. "When a

glowing, green-eyed shrunken head hits someone with his death beams it has a tendency to put a healthy dose of fear in a person. It's one of those 'what am I doing with my life?' sort of moments. Well, that and being attacked by Shades."

It was subtle, but I could have sworn Morgan's fingers squeezed my coffee cup just a little bit tighter at the mention of those shadowy negative-energy beasts.

"Not all Magick is scary, Gene."

"I know, I know, but lately I haven't seen much to prove otherwise."

"And you are worried that since you are a Magician some of those terrible and scary things are going to come after you?"

I took back the cup. "Well, I hadn't been before now, but thanks to you I'm sure I'll start worrying about it tonight."

Morgan slipped the pink carnation out of her pocket. The young woman's precise Magick spun in tight rotations around the tiny flower. Her nails left delicate lines in the fleshy pink petals.

"What are you doing?"

Morgan didn't look up—she was too focused on the tiny blossom. "Petals of Belladonna," she said, with the same casual delivery a normal person would have used for 'ordering pizza.'

"And that means?"

Morgan looked up with a sparkle in her eye. "Let me show you why Magick is so important."

She tugged at my sleeve and I followed her across the street and to the corner. We hadn't made it much past that blind turn before I stopped cold.

Street preacher...

Most of them were harmless, but not this guy. The gentleman swinging his arms in wild abandon at the end of the street was a well-known fixture around campus. To say he cared for your immortal soul was a stretch; every time I'd seen him he'd appeared far more interested in hurling insults than anything remotely constructive. "Morgan, come on, let's go back."

My girlfriend smiled, her eyes wide with excitement. "No, Gene. You've only seen the scary side of Magick. I need to show you there is more—much more."

The street preacher tugged at the collar of his starched white shirt, loosening his tie then adjusting thick plastic glasses.

I dropped the beignets and grabbed Morgan's arm. "Wait, stop. Don't do something to him."

My girlfriend's smile vanished. "Is that what you think of me? Are you afraid of me, Gene?"

"No, that's not what I meant. I just—"

The preacher retrieved a bullhorn from next to his feet and fiddled with the controls.

"You are. You're afraid of me. You think I'm some monster that would use her Magick to injure people, don't you?"

The preacher pulled a set of notecards from his breast pocket and leafed through them.

"No, Morgan. I'm not afraid of you, I just don't want—"

"You don't want me to hurt him? Is that right?"

"No. It's not that. Damn it, just let me finish. I don't want to have to listen to him say terrible things about you, okay? I don't need that in my life, and neither do you." I pointed to the mostly warm bag. "You know that guy's trouble. We don't need any of what he's peddling. We've got beignets, let's get you a coffee and we'll go enjoy them together, okay?"

Morgan hesitated, the small flower twisting between her fingers.

"Come on." I scooped up the bag. "It'll be fun. I know, we'll do a picnic under the trees over by your dorm. Sun should get through those clouds any minute. It'll be a fun way to start the day, and I'll even let you school me up in a little Magick. God knows I could use the practice. Wouldn't that be nice?"

Morgan took a step back toward me. "It would—"

Snap!

The bullhorn sprang to life, filling the sidewalk with pops and crackles before a familiar and belligerent voice boomed through it.

"Well, if isn't the harlot of University Avenue come to pay me a visit," the preacher yelled, jumping up to stand on a nearby bus bench and pointing at Morgan's back. "I'd know those devilish locks anywhere. Have you come to work my street?"

Morgan's eyes sparkled and her lips formed a crooked smile.

"Don't do it," I whispered. "Please don't."

"Gene, you worry too much." She blew me a kiss then turned to face the older gentleman. The pink carnation twisted in her fingers. "It's so good to see you, David."

16

GIFT OF THE MAGI

*T*he preacher crooned triumphantly from his perch, the bullhorn spreading his vitriol like a butterknife across the wide sidewalk. He hadn't gathered much in the way of onlookers yet, but I found a few heads popping up to take in the scene.

Morgan!

"Have you come to seek the savior's forgiveness?"

My girlfriend shook her head gently, those long tresses falling around her face. "No, not today. I came to bury the hatchet with you, David."

This caught the older man off guard, but only briefly—he wasted little in the way of time turning Morgan's words against her.

"Now the serpent was more subtle than any beast of the field which the Lord God had made…"

At this moment, Morgan's Magick was anything but subtle. It spun and clicked like the inner workings of a Swiss watch. David might not know it was there, but I sure did, and it scared me.

Is she right? Am I scared of her?

"But didn't Moses fashion a staff out of the fiery serpent?" Morgan asked, the flower twisting in her fingers.

"Yes, but it was only to—"

"And," Morgan continued. "Does the Bible itself not say that you could take up the serpent and not be harmed."

Dark sweat spots appeared on the edges of David's formerly crisp blue shirt.

What is she doing to him?

"Morgan." I shook the bag of beignets. "Come on, our breakfast is getting cold."

My girlfriend ignored me, her body language mesmerizing. Each step was perfectly aligned to give her the appearance of a model on the catwalk. Whatever she was doing, she wasn't going to stop until it was over.

My outburst gave the preacher a new and welcome target. "Now's your chance, young man, leave while you still can. Do not let the devil drag you further into the abyss. Go and sin no more."

The Magick in my chest churned, and before I knew it a surge of cosmic power roared into my arms and went straight down to my tensing fingers. The white bag crumpled beneath my grip.

Morgan looked back just once, clearly picking up on the surge of barely controlled Magick, and shook her head slightly. "No, Gene. It's not the time for that."

I took a deep breath and fought back against my frothing power. The emotional outburst made it difficult to control. My Magick wanted out, and I was forced to push it down like I was fighting to get an oversized blanket into the washing machine.

Morgan twisted the broken carnation in her fingers. The Magick building around that tiny flower was immense, but subtle. My girlfriend was the master at things like this, her power so precise, and yet so effective.

What is she doing?

"David," Morgan said, closing the last few feet with an elegance of motion that almost resembled diplomacy. "I have a gift for you." She held up the tiny pink carnation, its petals glistening in the early-morning light.

"A flower?"

Morgan let the flower twist in her fingers again. "Not just any flower. This is a carnation. A pink carnation."

"Beware of false prophets..." The preacher's face was a mixture of frustration and confusion. He clearly had not planned on Morgan's arrival, or her gift.

"Oh, David," she said, holding the flower up. "A stalwart man of God like yourself should know the history of the pink carnation."

There it was again, the subtle twist of Morgan's Magick. It permeated everything. Like a thick fog it drifted through the morning air. Gentle as a mother's lips, it tickled at my face and tugged at my shirt collar.

What is she doing?

David brought the bullhorn down and rubbed a hand across his smooth chin. It was clear he was searching his mental archives for pink carnations but not finding much. "Of course I know, but I'd like to see what you think. Tell me what pink carnations have to do with the Lord?"

"Certainly, David," Morgan said, her voice mesmerizing. "It is said that the first pink carnation bloomed from the tears of the Blessed Virgin as she wept at the feet of the cross."

What is she talking about?

"Yes. That's true. Very good. It would appear there is hope for you after all," the preacher said, clearly feigning knowledge of something he'd never heard before.

"The Lord works in mysterious ways," Morgan said, pointing to his breast pocket. "Will you wear it?"

"I..." The hellfire-and-brimstone man hesitated, not sure how to react.

"There are many gifts but the same Spirit, David. Perhaps the Holy Spirit is guiding me now, to give this to you. Would you not accept a gift of the Holy Spirit?"

A small crowd had begun to gather at the periphery and it was clear David knew it. He had an audience and was clearly not the kind to pass up an opportunity.

"I will accept your gift, young lady."

Morgan smiled wide and placed the pink flower in his hand. Magick spun like a wound clock, but still I couldn't understand what it was doing.

David tucked the carnation into his breast pocket. The petals sprouted from the seam like a gently blooming bud.

Morgan stepped back and finally returned her attention to me. That crooked smile was back, along with eyes that sparkled in the dawn. "It looks beautiful. What do you think, Gene?"

"Uh, yeah, it looks fine…"

Magick oozed from the flower like spilled milk. It tumbled down his shirt and across his chest, soaking into the white fabric. I tried to pick at the edges of that subtle power with my mind, but Morgan's Magick was so unlike my own. Her Magick was too obtuse to crack on a good day, let alone a hazy Saturday morning.

"So." Morgan took a few steps back and pointed to the blooming petals. "I think we are good now, don't you?"

The preacher hesitated, his hand across his chest, and his fingers playing with the soft petals. "Yes…"

The carnation's Magick spread further, twisting like a snake around his neck before finding its way to his head. Murmurs bubbled up in the small crowd that had gathered just beyond the two of them. I couldn't make out any of the words, but the general feeling was one of surprise. I had no interest in hanging around should that surprise turn to something worse.

"Wonderful!" Morgan said, her voice airy. "Well, Gene. I

think this is a perfect time to enjoy that breakfast. How are those beignets holding up?"

"Huh?"

Morgan turned to face me, the sparkle in her eyes practically predatory. "Are you ready to go?"

"Yes," I said, still trying to piece together what my girlfriend's Magick was doing. "That would be great."

Morgan left the preacher and joined me on the sidewalk. She took my hand, her fingers warm against the cool of the morning. "Oh, one more thing." She turned her attention to David, who continued to twist at the pink flower in his breast pocket. "You won't be calling women harlots anymore will you, David?"

David's eyes softened. "No ma'am."

"What about prostitutes?"

"Morgan," I hissed, quiet enough for only her to hear. "Come on, let's go. Don't push your luck."

"This has nothing to do with luck, Gene. This is all about what we were made to do. This is who you are, and who I am. We are here to make this world a better place, and that is what I plan to do."

Morgan directed her attention back to the preacher, who had now stepped down from the bus bench. "Well, David? Will you be calling woman prostitutes any more?"

Magick continued to twist and turned in the air around him. Like a complex game of stacking tiles, Morgan's power shifted in and out of positions faster than I could follow it.

The preacher stared off into the distance, his face lost in thought and his fingers continuing to twist at the tiny flower. "No, I don't believe I will."

More murmurs drifted through the assembled crowd. Those that had come for the morning hate were clearly disappointed, and I wasn't interested in hanging around for what they might do to get their fix.

"Morgan, come on."

My girlfriend winked. "This is wonderful news. Don't you think so, Gene?"

"Yeah. Great news. Very happy. Now, let's enjoy these before they become brunch."

What did she do to him?

"Have a blessed day, David," Morgan said, turning away from the preacher and guiding me back in the general direction of her dorm.

"You as well. May the good Lord bless and keep you," he called out behind us.

"What did you do?" I asked as soon as we were out of earshot.

Morgan squeezed my hand and smiled her crooked grin. "I made the world a better place."

17

OH, KNOTS

*W*e hadn't made it more than a block before I pulled back on Morgan's hand. "Stop. I need to know what you just did."

"I made the world a better place," she repeated, that crooked smile still plastered on her face. "Is that a crime?"

"No. At least I don't think it is, but you did something. I felt the Magick."

Morgan swung her hair over her shoulders. "I should have hoped you did. Last I checked you were still a Magician."

"But I don't know—"

"You don't know what I did because you haven't spent much more than a few fleeting moments studying anything I've put in front of you."

"That's not entirely true."

"Really?" Morgan snatched the bag out of my hand and started across the street. "So you can walk me through Eldero's Seventeen Seals?"

I hesitated. "I, uh…"

"That's what I thought. What about The Jacobean Prefect, or The Velcurses Conundrum?"

I raced off behind her, doing my best to keep what remained of my coffee from spilling. "Wait, now that one I have a little experience with—I used that one on the Shades."

Morgan hopped up on the curb and turned around. "You used The Velcurses Conundrum on Shades? First, where did you find negative-energy beasts?"

"Accounting building," I said, surprisingly out of breath from the short jog across the street.

I have to start exercising.

Morgan frowned and crumpled up the top of the bag in her hand. "Walk with me, Gene."

I'd done a lot of walking with women that morning, and very little of it had solved anything—I was still hungry, and my coffee was lukewarm at this point.

"Where are we going?"

Morgan turned the corner next to Perks and took a back alley off University Avenue back to the main campus. "Where is the accounting building?" she asked, cutting across a narrow stretch of sod that separated the city of Gainesville from the university itself.

"It's over there," I said, pointing past Century Tower, the largest landmark on campus. It was a soaring spire, smothered in brick, and sporting a series of booming bells in its topmost alcove.

Morgan stopped. "Is it next to the library?"

The University of Florida was home to a number of libraries, but since Morgan hadn't been more specific, I guessed she meant the oldest and largest of them—the main campus library.

"Yeah, it's not far from there. I can show you if you want."

Morgan shook her head. "No. I'm hungry. Let's have these Cajun donuts before they go completely cold."

Finally, a plan I can get behind...

I cut in front of Morgan and into the Plaza of the Americas, a wide field dotted with grand oaks that spread out like a natural welcome mat in front of the large, rectangular library. Tiny windows punctuated the red-brown bricks like portholes in a land-bound submarine. Inside those squares of blurry glass, students passed back and forth, books in hand and exhaustion on their faces.

I hadn't gone more than twenty feet or so before I realized Morgan wasn't next to me. I found her still standing on that narrow stretch of sod near the edge of campus, her eyes trained on the library's brick walls.

"Morgan?"

"Let's go back to the dorm," she said, turning away.

"Wait, there are plenty of trees here," I said, pointing to the thick oaks that filled the plaza. "We could just picnic here."

It was too late. Morgan already had me in the rear-view mirror, and since she had the beignets wherever she went breakfast would follow.

"Wait for me," I cried, jogging to catch up with her. "What's wrong with the plaza?"

"Nothing." The clipped tone of her voice surprised me. "We need to work on your Magick, Gene, and I don't want any distractions."

"You're kidding, right?" I said, joining her on the narrow sidewalk. "It's not even ten. I expect we would have been the only people on the plaza."

Morgan shook her head. "I don't like that place."

"Huh? What's not to like? Trees, squirrels, grass? Sure, maybe it has a few ants, but we could have avoided them."

Morgan took an abrupt turn off the sidewalk and followed a shortcut similar to the one that Ed had taken the other day.

"Wait, was it something I said?" I followed her into the shadows between the buildings.

Morgan brushed aside weeds in alley before stepping out the far end. "I don't want to talk about it, Gene."

"That's fine, we don't have to if you don't want to," I said, stumbling out behind her and into a small clearing. Brick buildings loomed around us like giant dominos. They blocked all but the noonday sun and formed a wall of red brick around a massive and ancient live oak. The tree had to have been at least five feet wide, with large knots and low-hanging mossy branches. Mold speckled the dense bark, marring the otherwise grandiose tree in splatter patterns of light green. Roots sprouted in thick knots around the grand oak's wide base. Knobby and twisted, they swelled in bulbous patches of noodle-like confusion.

"This is where I want to eat." Morgan pointed to a wide tangle of dense roots.

"Here?"

A cool breeze slipped between the buildings, rustling the branches and wagging the Spanish moss like a kite's tail.

Morgan took a seat beneath the dark tree. She opened the partially crumpled bag and filled the clearing with the smell of powdered sugar. "Yes, here."

I hesitated, the gently swaying of the oak's branches unsettling in the shadowy light. "You sure you don't want to go—"

"No."

I took an uncomfortable seat beneath the wide tree and fished a pastry out of the bag. It wasn't cold, but it wasn't exactly warm either.

"I've never taken you here, have I?" Morgan asked, plucking the half-empty coffee cup from my hand.

"No..."

"That's a shame. I should have, but maybe I didn't because you weren't ready."

I polished off that fritter and pulled another one out of the bag, happy to find this one warmer than the last. "Ready for what?"

Morgan sighed and crumpled the top of the bag. "For real

power, Gene. For the Deep Magick." She let those last words linger uncomfortably in the air.

"Deep Magick?"

Morgan set my coffee down and stood, directing her attention to the dark trunk. "Deep Magick, the really complicated stuff. The things that up until last night I didn't think you'd ever be able to handle."

"The Yaga Doll…"

Morgan ran a hand along the thick bark. She caressed it with the tips of her fingers, not unlike she'd caressed my own chest the night before.

"The Yaga Doll was Deep Magick, yes, but it was only scratching the surface. There is so much more."

I reached for the bag, then thought better of it.

"Come here, Gene," Morgan held a hand out to me. "I want you to feel something."

I brushed the powdered sugar from my hands. "Uh, sure."

"Put your hands on the tree."

I ducked the spanish moss that tickled at my shoulders. The oak's low branches made for a shadow-filled space around the knotted trunk.

I extended my hands, but hesitated, unsure of the tree's grotesque knots. "Why?"

"Gene, stop asking questions, and start getting answers. Put your hands on the tree."

I pressed my palms against the wide trunk, the mildewy bark cold on my skin.

"What do you feel?" Morgan's cheek grazed mine, and her sultry voice warmed my neck.

"Bark?"

"Deeper, Gene." Morgan's hands pressed against my shoulders. "Go deeper. Use your Magick, let it go."

I closed my eyes and reached out for the Magick. Its cosmic power swirled in my chest, excited at the prospect of release, yet confused as to what I wanted it to do. "How do I—"

"Ssh," Morgan said, her nails digging in and pushing me toward the thick trunk. "Let it go, Gene. Let your Magick free."

I did as she asked. I let my Magick go, willing the power down my arms and into the rough bark.

"Yes, that's it, Gene—more."

I pushed harder, digging into the power and willing it into the dense tree.

"Excellent, that's a good start, but you need more. You need to let go of those barriers. You need to believe."

I poured it on, letting the Magick prickle my skin and raise the hairs on my arms.

"Wonderful," Morgan purred, her nails pressing harder against my back. "You've woken her up."

"Huh?" I opened my eyes to find my hands wrapped by withered and rotting hands of oak.

"Now we'll see just how hard you can hit," Morgan whispered, pushing me into the ancient tree.

18

WITHERING

Gnarled and bark-covered hands clutched at mine and pulled me into the wizened oak. "Morgan!"

"Come on, Gene. With all that power, you can handle a single Withering."

Speckled and moss-splattered fingers twisted around my own. A damp and chilling cold raced up my arms.

"Morgan, help me," I cried, pulling back against the tree's grasping and claw-like hands.

"I am helping you. You've got so much Magickal potential, Gene. So. Damn. Much. But you spend every day in frivolous pursuits. You've got real power tucked up in here," Morgan patted my back, "and I'm going to help you get it out."

Panic churned my stomach and the powdery fritters sloshing around inside it. I kicked out and put a foot against the trunk, trying to pry myself from the ancient oak's grasp.

"That's not going to help you," Morgan said, casually stepping around the bulbous roots.

Another hand erupted from the blackened bark. Long finger-like branches clamped down on my shoe and pulled it into the suddenly softening tree.

"Morgan!"

My girlfriend folded her arms. "You've got it in there, Gene, I know you do. Sometimes it just takes motivation. This time motivation takes the form of a Withering."

"Withering?"

"Angry tree spirits. They exist all over campus. I've discovered so many of them. If you don't like this one, perhaps I can find you another?"

"I..."

"This one is here to provide the motivation you lack. I promise you she's quite good at it. Do you know how many young lovers have disappeared beneath this tree?"

The tip of my shoe vanished inside the blackened bark. "What—"

"Exactly." Morgan smiled, her eyes practically giddy beneath the swaying spanish moss. "She's hungry—very hungry. How many years has it been, Selavim? How many?"

Black mildew and patchy moss shifted across the trunk, forming an ancient and angry face. "Many winters..." a halting and raspy voice said.

"See, Gene? It's been many winters, so I'm guessing she's is parched for blood. Is that right, sweetheart?"

Sap-like saliva rolled down the Withering's crooked jaws.

"Damn it, Morgan." My foot continued to vanish into the evil tree. "This isn't funny. Help me!"

"I never said it was funny, Gene, but it is necessary. You're like me when I was younger. I had my father to guide me. You have me."

Strong tree-claws pulled my left hand into the trunk. It sank between the creases of bark, vanishing inside the cold sap until only my wrist remained. "Help me!"

Morgan's sparkling eyes glared at me. "I am helping you. Why can't you see that? How many books have I given you to read? How many, Gene?"

"I don't—"

Morgan clapped her hands in frustration. "You don't know because you've never paid attention. I know you don't read them."

"I'll read them now. I promise! Please just help me." The tree spirit's hand pulled my right beneath the sap-laden bark.

"I bet you will, and when you escape there will be plenty of time for that. But now I have to show you."

"Show me what? Please, I've learned my lesson."

Morgan shook her head, those green tresses blending with the pale spanish moss. "No, you haven't. Even now you are pleading with me when you should be reaching for your Magick. Where is that cosmic power that you seem to have so much of? Huh, Gene? I know its in there, so perhaps now would be the right time to put it to good use. I mean, at least before she reaches your elbows."

The Withering's face sneered. Jagged teeth like the shattered ends of downed branches poked out beneath fungus-covered lips.

Morgan was right—I was losing the fight. The more time I spent pleading with her, the more of me was lost to the ancient oak.

I closed my eyes and tried to push away the visual of that hungry tree.

"That's it, Gene. Now reach for it, reach for your Magick. I know it's there—use it!"

Bark brushed my knee and I gasped. The tree had my leg and clamored for more. My eyes snapped open at the shocking cold and I lost my concentration.

"You're going to have to do better than that," Morgan said, shaking her head. "There is a lot more cold places in this world and the next. You can't let a little Withering sap get to you. Go deeper, Gene. Find that fifth gear I saw you use with the Yaga Doll. Find it before it's too late."

The hungry oak pulled me closer. Both of my hands vanished beneath the darkened bark. My heart thumped in my chest and my breath came in uneven gasps. Morgan simply stood off to the side, her arms folded, and her face a mask of disappointment. "At some point you have to push them out of the nest. They either fly, or they die. I don't want you to die, Gene. I really don't. We have something special, something that doesn't come around very often. What's worse is I can see you know that too. You know just how special we are, and how great we could be together. Gene, there isn't a force of nature powerful enough to stop us if we work together."

The rest of my arms and most of my legs succumbed to the tree spirit's hunger. "Yes. I see that. I see all of that. But I can't do anything if I'm dead."

"Selavim won't kill you immediately, Gene. You'll dissolve slowly inside her sap-riddled trunk. It shouldn't take more than a few years. That's plenty of time to think about what you could have been—what we could have been."

"No!" I reached for my Magick, pushing past the fear and frustration, digging deep for that well of cosmic power that churned in my chest.

"Yes," Morgan cried, her eyes sparkling in the dappled light. "There it is. There is the power I knew you had. That's the man that can face a Yaga Doll and live. Now, channel it. Direct it where you want it to go. There are no sigils to save you, Gene. You need to focus on the words."

Power words...

Visions of uncontrollable Wild Magick played out in my head and I almost lost the tenuous grasp on my own power.

The Withering pulled me closer. Her jagged jaws opened to consume me whole. "What are the words?"

"You mean to tell me you've read through all my books, yet cannot remember the words?" Morgan asked, a hint of concern in her voice.

"No, I can't."

"Try harder, Gene." Morgan took a tentative step toward me and carefully avoided the bulbous roots in the process. "I know you can do it. Try harder, now!"

My cheek pressed against the rough edges of the tree's macabre jaws. Splintered fragments dug into my skin, while what remained of my arms disappeared into the bone-chilling husk. The Magick flickered, confused, unsure, and faced with a situation it didn't understand. I tried to pull it back, to grab at the power, but like a frightened animal it slipped out of my mental grasp.

Panic flashed in Morgan's eyes. Maybe she hadn't planned for it to go this far, but the concern on her face told me perhaps it had.

"Gene," she cried, scrambling over the trunk to place her face as close to mine as she could. "The words are..."

Whatever she said, I lost it in the cold of the Withering's sap. Morgan's sparkling eyes pleaded with me even as her words faded.

I drifted, my heart no longer racing. The evil tree's chilling sap quieted my panic. I had only to let go and I would float away on a dark and tideless sea.

Somewhere nearby Magick surged, carried on the powerful words of a much smarter Magician than me. The heart-stopping cold of the Withering pulled away from that fiery Magick, while sap-laden claws released their grasp.

Thump.

I hit the ground hard and opened my eyes to Morgan's tear-streaked face. My back pressed up against the cool earth.

"You scared me half to death, Gene. Don't ever take me to the edge again, damn it!"

"I—"

Morgan pulled me close and buried her face in my neck. "Never again, Gene. Never..."

19

SWAN SONG

I flexed my fingers again, happy to find them attached.

It had been a few hours since I'd almost lost myself to the rotting heartwood of that hungry tree, but still my hands tingled. Morgan had insisted it was for the best, and that my Magick would continue to get better, but I had a hard time believing her. There was something about being shoved into the waiting arms of a malevolent live oak that made me second guess her intentions.

The entire walk back to the dorm had done little to improve my demeanor. We'd argued, and she'd cried. Effectively zero progress had been made by the time we'd reached her room. Morgan insisted the entire ordeal was necessary, that all Magicians go through something similar and that it was my lack of experience that had kept me from understanding that simple fact. I hadn't bought it, but I also hadn't rejected the book she'd shoved in my hand before I'd left.

A couple hours spent wandering the campus deep in thought had only resulted in more questions and a surprisingly healthy appetite.

The dining hall was open, so I'd slipped in for an early dinner.

That's where I was now, listlessly turning the pages of The Jacobean Prefect, my eyes glazing over at the complex designs and confusing symbols. I picked at a small pile of French fries and sat back in my chair. Salt stung at the tiny cuts on my fingers. I may have gotten my digits back, but the Withering appeared to have left me a memento of our time together. I shuddered at the thought of that vile creature and tried to take my mind off the entire experience. A handful of students moved about the cafeteria around me, carrying trays and gathering up the early dinner fare.

A tall couple worked their way through the line. She handed her long-armed boyfriend a plate of something. He didn't appear overly keen on it, but accepted the offering just the same. There were a few exchanged words, which resulted in a pair of smiles and a laugh. I stuffed a few more fries in my mouth and chewed them with a little more vigor that I expected.

Must be nice...

My eyes drifted around the cafeteria, settling on one couple after another: tall, short, beautiful, and otherwise, the entire room appeared to have become some great convention hall celebrating the wondrous joy of a proper pairing.

I slammed the book shut, all set to storm off and find a dark place to ruminate on the ills of my life, when a familiar face pulled out the chair across from me.

"Hey, Gene, mind if I join you?"

Ed.

"Uh, yeah, I guess."

My roommate flicked his long blond hair out of his eyes, then picked up the ketchup. "How's the burger?"

I pointed to the crusty remains on the edge of my plate. "Passable."

Ed nodded, dumping a wet glob of ruddy ketchup on his bare paddy. "Figured."

"Where's Porter?"

Ed sighed. "Yeah…"

"What happened?"

Ed stacked a few fries on top of the smothered hamburger. "Lord if I know."

"What do you mean?"

My roommate shook his head. "Women…"

"Tell me about it," I said, taking my hand off The Jacobean Prefect long enough to sift through what remained of my fries.

Ed spun the book around to face him. "The Jacobean Prefect —that's some serious stuff. Are you able to figure it out?"

"I'm trying. I should work on my focus, or at least that's what Morgan told me…"

Among other things…

I tried to gauge Ed's reaction to my girlfriend's name—after this morning I wasn't sure where his head was at when it came to Morgan Crowley.

"It's a smart plan." Ed took a bite out of his burger.

"What?"

My roommate nodded. "Yeah, I mean, just the other night your Magick was all over the map. The Jacobean Prefect is gonna work you over something fierce, but she's right when she says you could stand to focus more."

"Wait, you're siding with Morgan?"

Ed shook his head. "No, I'm on Team Gene."

"I don't understand."

Ed sifted through the salty remains of my French fries to locate a particularly crispy one. "What's to understand? You're a Magician, Gene. Somehow, you ended up with all this power and no real understanding of what to do with it. That's a damn shame if you ask me. So, while there are a lot of things Morgan does that I do not agree with, I do agree with her when she pushes you to get better. You are a rare talent, roomie. I want to be able to say I knew you when."

I opened my mouth, then closed it again. I had no idea how to respond to that.

My roommate chuckled and flipped through the book, smearing one of the pages with ketchup. "Yeah, so have you gotten to this section yet?"

"Uh, no…"

"Good, cause this part will throw you for an absolute loop. If you look here," Ed pointed to a complex series of interlocking lines, "you'll see the way he tries to shore up the expected reverb."

"Uh huh," I said, even though I had little idea what my roommate was talking about.

"Well, it all looks perfectly simple on paper, but in the real world it's anything but. You try to get those lines right—without crossing them, or throwing off the whole sigil—then come talk to me." Ed shoved a few more of my fries in his mouth.

"How do you know all this, Ed?"

My roommate took another oversized bite of his burger. "Huh?"

"I mean, you aren't a Magician. You've said as much countless times. But you seem to know more about this stuff than anyone I've ever met."

"Mom," Ed said through a mouthful of burger meat and ketchup.

"Your Mom taught you all this?"

Ed nodded, then set his food down to smoother it in ketchup a second time.

"Why would your mom teach you all this Magick when—"

"When I'm not a Magician?"

I could sense there was a frustration in Ed's voice, one he'd gone out of his way to hide throughout the time I'd known him, but it peeked its head up now to sniff the air.

"Because she loves me, that's why."

"I see."

Ed's frustration faded away, skittering back in its hole like a groundhog that had seen its shadow.

"It's a long story. I'll explain it to you one day, but Mom is a Magician's Magician. She's got more smarts in her pinky than I have in my whole body. She taught me stuff that would have made old Jacobean jealous."

"I believe it. Listen, Ed, can I ask you something about how Magicians are raised?"

My roommate frowned at his burger. "Yeah, sure. I'm not a Magician though."

"I know, but your mom is."

"One of the smartest I've ever met."

I nodded, sliding the book back to my side of the table and flipping it closed. "Do you know if there are, like... challenges?"

"Huh?"

More students had filed into the dining hall, and a few of them were busy working the remote for a distant wall-mounted television.

"Hmm, how do I put this another way? Uh, you know how a mama bird will push the baby bird from its nest?"

"Not firsthand I don't, but I've heard of the concept." My roommate tilted his head at the squawking of the distant television. "What are you getting at?"

I didn't know why, but for some reason I didn't feel comfortable telling Ed about the Withering directly. "I'm just wondering if your mom was ever, like, pushed into using her Magick or have something terrible happen to her."

"If she was, she never told me."

I frowned. "And I assume your mom never did anything like that to you?"

Ed hesitated, but before he could respond, the television's volume jumped dramatically. The reporter's clipped tone cut over the din of the dining hall.

"What can you tell us, Steve?"

Ed set his burger down and turned around. "Isn't that University Avenue, Gene?"

It was.

The camera panned over a taped-off crime scene just off campus, catching the bloody top of a bus stop bench before swinging away. A single pink carnation lay crumpled on the seat.

Oh, no. No, no, no!

"Do we have an identity of the individual?"

The camera swung back to the reporter, his perfect hair unmoving in the early evening's light breeze. "Yes, a witness says his name was David Singer, a local preacher known for his enthusiastic street-corner sermons."

"Was there any indication why he would have killed himself?"

A photo of David Singer popped up on the screen, a younger and far happier version of the man Morgan and I had met earlier today.

Morgan, what did you do?

"That's a shame," Ed said, turning back around in his seat. "The guy was a jerk most days, but he did do some great volunteer work."

They flashed another picture up. This one showing a younger David passing out bowls of soup, a joyful grin on his face. My stomach churned at the grainy picture. The food in my gut rolled over uncomfortably.

"Gene, you okay?" Ed asked, taking the last of my fries.

"No, I've got to go."

"Why? What's wrong?"

"I need to talk to Morgan, now." I grabbed the book and

shoved it under my arm, leaving a confused Ed at the table. Mental pictures of a bloody-faced David Singer played on repeat in my head.

20

CONFRONTATION

*D*avid Singer's face and the twisting carnation wore a groove in my head so deep it was all but impossible to crawl out of. I shot across the street and took one of Ed's many shortcuts toward Morgan's dorm.

It can't be. There's no way she did that to him, right?

Tall grass between the buildings swayed gently in the early evening air, while tiny wildflowers turned up their petaled faces at the coming dusk.

You felt the Magick.

Dinner sat uncomfortably in my gut, the frics churning in the monster-sized acid wash the preacher's face had drummed up.

That doesn't mean it was her.

I emerged from the alley and stepped out onto the plaza in front of the library. The grassy field was awash in students enjoying the cool evening.

Listen to yourself. Morgan gave him a flower, that's it. He didn't kill himself because of a flower. Did he?

The library's brick walls loomed in the distance, jutting up from beyond the plaza's ancient oaks to carve out a chunk of the fading pink sky.

David Singer, local preacher commits suicide...

Carnation pink shifted to red behind the massive building, and in that colorful sky I found the preacher's dead eyes staring back at me. My stomach rolled again and I placed a hand on it.

Dead of an apparently self-inflicted gunshot wound...

I fought down those thoughts and crossed the wide plaza, walking beneath the oaken canopy. Spanish moss drifted in the breeze, swaying like a kite's tail, and bringing with it more memories.

If Morgan had been willing to risk me at the hands of a Withering...

Dark faces appeared in those tree's thick bark, only to fade away when I looked again.

Just take a deep breath and focus.

My mind was little comfort—it was far too focused on pink carnations and the bloody face of David Singer.

She said she was making the world a better place.

I shook the offending thought from my head and scampered out from beneath the plaza's trees. My feet hesitated on the distant sidewalk, forcing me to turn back and take in the great brick walls of the imposing building. The breeze shifted just enough for me to make out the tiny windows beyond the trees. Dark shapes moved behind those windows, formless and hungry. I blinked my eyes and the bright orange windows once again contained only the faces of tired students.

Focus, Gene.

I stepped off the sidewalk and away from the library, but I couldn't escape the feeling that it was watching me.

Honk!

Lost in thought, I almost became a hood ornament on the narrow street beyond the library. Emergency services vehicles raced past, their flashing lights throwing great splashes of color on the surrounding buildings.

University Avenue wasn't far away, and neither was the spot where it had all happened. I shook that thought away and turned down another shortcut between the buildings. There was nothing for me there. Only one person had the answers I needed.

Morgan.

I emerged from the gap between the buildings in front of her dorm. The sun had sunk beneath the distant horizon, shrouding the brick and concrete structure in a cloak of mystery. Street-lamps sprung to life and cast their hazy orange light through wiry and grasping branches. Jagged and angry shadows played across the steps. The sidewalk was empty, and no cars lined the street. I slipped across beneath the lamp light to stand on the dorm's steps.

I need answers.

A large wooden door blocked my way inside. It was sure to be locked, but that wasn't about to stop me. I placed a hand on the heavy wood and reached for my Magick. The cosmic power was frustrated and angry, much like me. It wanted out and it wanted answers—now.

"Gene, what are you doing here?"

The Magician's voice shattered my concentration and released the tenuous grasp I had on my Magick. The power swirled disappointedly in my chest.

"Morgan." I swung around ready to make demands and get answers, only to find her half-carrying a clearly intoxicated redhead up the stairs. "What?"

"Unlock the door," she said, ignoring my question and tossing me her keys.

"Is she okay?"

"I hope so." Morgan paused and motioned for me to take the girl's other shoulder. "I found her like this around the corner."

"Is that Jess?" I asked, my nose wrinkling at the strong smell of alcohol.

"It is. Help me get her up the stairs."

Don't lose sight of why you're here, Gene. Don't let her distract you!

"Gene, are you going to help me or not?"

I took Jess's other arm, and we half-dragged and half-carried the largely incoherent girl to her dorm room. Morgan knocked on the door a few times, but got no answer.

"Reserare," she said, and with what seemed like zero effort, Morgan's Magick unlocked the door.

Click.

She guided me into the darkened room and motioned to a narrow bed. "Let's put her there."

I nodded, the sounds of distant conversation drifting into the room from down the hall.

It took a few seconds to maneuver Jess into her bed. Once we got her there, Morgan went right to work in taking off the girl's shoes and pulling up her blanket before ushering me outside. "She'll be fine," Morgan said, gently closing the door behind her.

The television reporter's voice echoed in the hallway. It bounced off the hard floors. "If you're just joining us, tonight's breaking news is a tragic story—"

Morgan ignored the community room television. "What are you doing here, Gene? I mean, not that I don't appreciate the surprise."

The TV responded before I could. "David Singer, local preacher and community volunteer, died this evening by an apparent self-inflicted gunshot wound."

Morgan froze. "Gene... You didn't come here to talk about The Jacobean Prefect, did you?"

"No."

Morgan pushed past me and headed down the hall, stopping

at the open door to the community room. A large television hung from the wall, surrounded by other girls on the hall. Many of them in tears.

"Morgan," I whispered, quiet enough for my voice to slip beneath the blaring broadcast un-noticed. "What did you do to him?"

Morgan's shoulders tensed up, and her knuckles whitened against already pale fingers. She grabbed my hand and pulled me toward her dorm room. "It's not safe. Come with me."

"No," I said, yanking my hand back once we were far enough away from the community room to not draw attention. "I'm not going anywhere until you tell me what's going on."

Morgan's eyes pleaded with me. "Gene, it's not safe. I will tell you everything once we are in my room. Please!"

I shook my head. "No. You're the only one that put me in danger here. You shoved me into that Withering."

A tear slid down Morgan's cheek. "Gene, if it came for David, then it'll come for you. I can't protect you out here."

"Protect me from what?"

Morgan reached for my hand, but I pulled it back. "No, damn it. I want to know what you're protecting me from. So far you've been the most dangerous thing in my life—by a wide margin."

More tears fell from my girlfriend's worried eyes. "Please, Gene. Don't make me say it. That only brings more attention."

"Attention from what, Morgan?"

My girlfriend ignored me and spun around, racing to the door of her room and grabbing the handle, only to discover I still had her keys.

"Keys, Gene! Give me my keys."

I fished the chain out of my pocket and squeezed them, the cut metal biting at my fingers. "Tell me, Morgan. Tell me what you are so afraid of."

Boom!

Lights flickered at the sound of a distant electrical transformer going down.

"That," Morgan cried, pointing at the dimming lights. "Please, Gene. You know me. We've been together. If I'd ever wanted to hurt you I could have a hundred times, but I didn't and I wouldn't. Please you have to believe me. Give me the keys and come inside the room before something worse happens."

The lights dimmed and the distant community-room TV buzzed.

"Please, Gene!" Morgan clutched at the door. "Please, before it's too late."

I tossed her the keys and she snapped them out of the air. Morgan's hands shook as she slammed the right one home.

Click.

She pushed the door open and raced back to me, her eyes frantic. "Please, Gene. I promise I will explain it all, but I can't lose you, I just can't. You are my world. You are my everything."

"I want answers."

Morgan nodded, dragging me toward the open door. "And you'll get them, I promise. Just please get inside."

I gave up and let her take my hand. Together, we disappeared into the dark unknown of her room.

SWEAR WORDS

*M*organ shot across the room and pulled the curtains shut. "Close the door."

"You promised me answers."

"And you'll get them, but only after the door is closed."

I let the heavy door slam behind me. Morgan wasted no time completing the lines of a confusing pattern in the dust of the door.

Click.

Like the tumblers of a complex lock, Morgan's Magick spun with expert precision. The door sealed against the frame, and a faintly glowing sigil on the inside told me it would stay that way until she deemed otherwise.

"Now, Morgan," I said, crossing my arms. "I want my answers, now."

My girlfriend nodded, her shoulders drooping. "The Reaver was my doing."

"What?!"

She pointed to her desk, where a small lamp beamed golden-yellow light down on a partially disassembled Rubik's Cube not much bigger than the palm of my hand. It sat in a complex arrangement of interlocking lines traced into the paper that had been blank before.

"Not on purpose, mind you, but it was my fault just the same."

"I don't understand."

Morgan ran her fingers along the complex sigil that held the tiny toy. I'd seen that design before; it was on the paper that had fallen from her shelf, and a similar one had graced the inside of Marcy's arm. What was it Ed had said?

"Ten Spins..." The words tumbled from my lips.

"Yes, but you have to understand. I did it to protect you. I did it to protect all of you."

Chaotic Magick swirled within the seal, a power both violent and vicious, it ramped up against the invisible walls of Ten Spins' sigil.

"What? You did what?"

Morgan threw herself down on the bed, her hands on her face. Tears returned to those sparkling eyes. "I thought it was over."

It was hard to keep her on track, and the conversation kept shifting. "No, Morgan. We aren't doing this again. You're going to tell me what happened to David Singer. I want to believe you had nothing to do with it, but the timing—"

"I'm not a murderer," Morgan cried between her tears. I didn't use Magick to make him kill himself. Do you believe me?"

I hesitated, and that hesitation was enough for Morgan to wilt before my eyes. "You don't."

"I want to," I said, scrambling in spite of myself. "I want to believe you, but your Magick is so powerful and I—"

"Powerful? Gene, of the two of us you are the only one in this room capable of that level of Magick."

"Me?"

Morgan pointed a finger at my chest. "You overpowered a

Reaver and still had enough strength to walk me home. A Reaver! And you still don't even understand what that means. My God, Gene, you took a Yaga Doll in the face and walked away."

Shorty...

My mind drifted back to the other night. Those green eyes were still clearly visible when I closed my own.

"But the flower—"

"It was a flower, Gene."

I shook my head. "No way, I felt the Magick. That was not just some flower. You did something. What was it? The petals of Bella?"

"Look—" Morgan jumped up from her bed and ripped a book off the shelf, then flipped through the pages. "Here," she said pushing the text in my face.

"The Petals of Belladonna?"

"Yes, I told you that before. Read it if you want. It's a simple bit of Magick."

I skimmed the complex diagrams and dense Latin. It might have been straightforward, but Morgan understood this so much better than I did.

"What does it do?"

"Beautiful woman."

"Huh?" I closed the book and handed it back to her.

"I simply wanted him to treat women a little better, is that asking too much?"

I threw my hands in the air. "He shot himself in the head!"

"I didn't do that."

"Well, if you didn't, then who did?"

Morgan slumped back onto her bed, ruffling the reasonably crisp sheets. "It's not a who, Gene."

"I don't understand."

"You wouldn't even if I told you," Morgan said, her head in her hands.

Feeling pretty smart, eh Gene? You've made her cry and accused her of being a murderer. Any other brilliant moves up your sleeves?

I pulled her desk chair out and spun it around till its back was to her, then straddled the seat. "If you tell me, I promise to try and understand. I have almost gotten through Jacobean's Prefect. I'm not you, but I'm getting there."

Please work.

Morgan sighed, her shoulders shaking with each breath. "I don't have Ten Spins' sigils on my desk because I'm strong, I have it because I'm weak."

"You aren't weak."

Morgan wiped her eyes with her loose-flowing sleeve. "I am. I might seem tough to you, but there are things out there that want me, things I'm afraid of."

"What sort of things?"

Morgan pulled her legs up into her chest. "Things that cannot pass that lock on my door."

Even in the bright light of the room I suddenly felt cold and exposed. "I didn't know."

"How could you? It's not like I walk around broadcasting it."

"What is it?"

Morgan hugged her legs. "Honestly, Gene, the less you know the better."

We sat in silence for a few moments; I had no idea what to do or say. I opened my mouth to speak, but before I could make much more of a fool out of myself Morgan snapped up from her bed. "I'm sorry for David, I'm truly sorry that happened to him. The things that are coming after me, they have no problem with collateral damage. I should have known that." She walked past me and reached for the door. "I've burdened you with enough of my issues. I need you to leave before you become a target too."

"Morgan, wait I—"

"No, Gene. I'm not going to let something happen to you. I couldn't live with myself if it did, and you aren't ready to defend yourself yet. You are an amazingly gifted Magician—amazingly gifted—but not ready for this."

I stopped at her door, not willing to walk through it and out of her life all together just yet. "No, I'm not, but what if we work together?"

"No, it's too dangerous," Morgan shook her head, "I couldn't stand to see you hurt."

"But you said it yourself, I'm powerful."

"Raw power isn't the same, Gene. You might be able to throw wild haymakers, they're just that, wild. You lack precision, accuracy, or anything remotely similar."

I stepped into the hallway, then stopped and placed a foot against her door. "With you teaching me I could get there."

Morgan's red-rimmed eyes stared at me. "I don't have nearly that much time, and I'm not going to risk your safety in the process. Your focus is all over the map…"

"But yours isn't. You are as lethal as a pit viper when it comes to complex Magick—isn't there something you can do? Together I'm certain we can stop whatever is coming after you."

Morgan bit her lip and hesitated.

"Come on," I said, my voice practically pleading. "What have you got to lose?"

"You." She took my hand.

I answered her instantly and without thinking. "I'm not going anywhere."

Morgan shook her head. "Not good enough."

"What do you want me to—"

She cut me off and pulled a black steel ring from one of her desk drawers.

"What's that?"

"You lack focus, Gene. I can't give you focus overnight, but I can give you this." She placed the cold steel band in my palm.

I held up the muted black ring and tried to make out the

small symbols etched into the steel surface too tiny to read. "And this is?"

"Dead Man's Tongue."

"What?" I said, practically dropping the ring.

"It's just a name, Gene. It's not really a tongue. Think of this as a way to help you focus, to cut through the noise." Morgan removed an identical ring from the drawer. There was Magick in those rings, but I couldn't put my finger on what it did.

It sat heavy in the palm of my hand. "This doesn't mean we're married, right?"

Morgan giggled and wiped her eyes. "No, we aren't married, Gene, but this is what I mean when I say focus."

She slipped a ring on her finger and pointed to mine.

I pushed the Dead Man's Tongue on my pinky—it was the only finger it fit.

Morgan slipped her arms around my neck and drew me in for a deep and salty kiss. "Thank you, Eugene Law. I never thought I'd find someone to help me face down my monsters.

"What are we up against?" I asked, kissing her back and enjoying the taste of her lips.

Morgan let me go and grabbed a jacket out of her closet. "I'll explain it all soon, but first we need to take these for a test run."

Chaotic Magick swirled around the tiny cube on Morgan's desk.

"What about that?"

"It's coming with me." Morgan reached into the sigil and twisted the cube, its Magick vanishing like a candle in the wind. "You can never be too careful. Are you ready to go?"

The Dead Man's Tongue tingled on my finger. "I am."

Morgan kissed me again, but this time I was ready for it.

22

NEGATIVE NELLY

*W*e slipped out of Morgan's dorm under the cover of darkness. The sun had set, and the sky was awash in twinkling stars.

"Where are we going?"

Morgan hesitated on the street's edge. Her eyes remained fixed on the distant library, its brick top peeking out above the plaza's ancient trees.

"No more trees, I hope?" I tried to make a joke, but Morgan was clearly not in the joking mood.

"No." She grabbed my hand and took me down a shortcut between the historic dorm buildings.

"Where are we going?"

"You'll see."

We exited the narrow alley and marched past a small pond. Much of this a path very similar to the one Ed and I had taken just the other night.

"Business college?" I asked, guessing at our destination, but Morgan appeared to be on a mission and afforded me no response.

We emerged from her shortcut in front of a stodgy brick

building I had more than a passing familiarity with—it was the same place Ed and I had stared down a horde of Shades and chaotic Wild Magick.

The accounting building.

Morgan didn't go inside. The brick structure was sure to be locked on a Saturday night. She guided me around to a courtyard on the far side. During the day, this brick paver patio was a great spot for eating lunch, or catching up on all things beancounting, but right now it was devoid of life and light. A gloomy dark hung over the circular yard. Large oaks surrounded the paved clearing and pressed in upon us, their branches swaying gently in the cool wind.

"This will work," Morgan said, pulling a piece of chalk from a tiny pocket in her tight-fitting pants. "There's still a residue."

"A residue?"

Morgan made a mark on the ground, then counted out a few steps the other direction before making a second chalk mark.

"A residue of what, Morgan?"

The cool night air cut through my simple jacket, ruffling my shirt and prickling at the hairs on my chest.

"Morgan?"

"I need to concentrate, Gene. Could you please not say anything for a minute? The Velcurses Conundrum is difficult on even the best of days," she said, then paused and tossed the chalk to me. "Second thought. You know Velcurses, right?"

"Yeah, but it's—"

"Show me."

I fumbled with the chalk in my fingers. "I don't remember exactly—"

"You've got this, Gene. I believe in you." Morgan held up her hand. The dark ring of muted steel shined even in the gloom. "Focus."

I took a deep breath and tried to bring up The Velcurses

Conundrum in my mind. Morgan hadn't lied: it was a complex seal, and it was going to take time.

"What are you going to do?" I asked, drawing the initial whorls in powdery chalk.

Morgan walked to the edge of the courtyard, her eyes focused on the horizon beyond the tall trees. "Just focus on the seal, Gene."

I did what she asked, and found the complex design coming to me readily. The Dead Man's Tongue tingled on my finger, and as it did, the intricate Magick seemed to flow from my mind with ease.

"Hey, this is helping." I twisted my hand to complete another turn in the complicated symbol. "Morgan?"

My girlfriend stood at the edge of the courtyard, her back to me, and her hands raised. Her green hair and jacket sides caught the breeze. "Are you almost done, Gene?"

"Just about. This is really a lot easier with the ring."

"Good."

I hopped over a line to avoid smudging it and started a fresh set of spirals on the other side. "Almost there. What are you doing?"

The wind picked up, rustling the branches and flapping the edges of my own thin jacket. Morgan's Magick drifted over me. It turned like the gears of an enormous and invisible machine, grooves within grooves, and whirred away to some unforeseen end.

"Morgan?"

"Finish it now, Gene."

A chattering sound bubbled up from beyond the clearing—a sound I'd heard before. It grated on my ears and shriveled my soul.

Shades!

Like hundreds of pairs of jagged teeth clicking against each other, the chattering noise filled the dark branches.

The chalk fumbled in my fingers. "Morgan, what are you doing?"

"Is it done?"

"No, but this is The Velcurses Conundrum. Ed says it can't be used against negative-energy—"

Morgan raised her hands high, her hair whipping in the strengthening wind. "I don't care what Ed says. Is it done?"

Red eyes sprung up throughout the dark branches, cold and hungry, and they glared down at us from all sides. I fumbled with the chalk, suddenly unable to remember how to complete the seal.

"Gene?"

"Uh, almost there."

Morgan's Magick rolled like a great belt and gear in the cold night air, while all around us hungry eyes seemed to multiply.

"What are you doing?" I cried, my hands shaking to complete the seal.

"I told you that to stay with me was dangerous, and now you see why. The library is hungry, Gene."

"Huh?"

Branches shifted, creating an opening wide enough to see the distant brick building. The angry glow of its porthole windows joined the Shades' eyes in hungry malevolence.

"Each and every time I touch my Magick it claws out for me. The library's Shades are what pushed David Singer to suicide; they come for me, and anyone I care about. They are its guardians—the first line of defense."

"I don't understand," I said, cutting a chalk line through Velcurses' confusing pattern and completing the Magickal seal.

"There's nothing to understand." Dark and shadowy shapes flitted between the branches behind Morgan. "There is only focus."

I stepped back inside the seal, then extended a hand for her. "But Ed said—"

"Edwin Lovely is wrong." Morgan raised her hands to the sky. "Get ready…"

The cold wind picked up and sent the wagging beards of spanish moss twisting in the looming dark of the trees. "Get ready for what?"

"We're going to channel all that Magick and focus into Velcurses Conundrum."

"But I've seen it, Morgan, it just pumps the Shades full of power."

Black and shadowy claws appeared along the edge of the branches, while behind them, twisted mouths chattered in the gloomy half-light.

"You didn't have me," she said, taking a cautious step back. "Together we won't fail."

Shades dropped down out of the trees like vultures. Wispy bodies advanced on us undisturbed by the wind. Eyes like burning coals stared right through me.

"Are you ready, Gene?" Morgan took another step backward toward me.

"Ready to do what? Morgan, I'm telling you, if I send Magick into this seal it's going to—"

"You let me worry about that. You just do what you do best. It's time for you to swing yard, Eugene Law, swing as hard as you can, hold nothing back. You understand?"

Hiss!

Hungry shadows, like shapeless patches of inky midnight, clawed their way across the brick courtyard toward us.

"Morgan!"

My girlfriend swung her head around, her hair flying wildly in the wind. "Stop asking questions, stop talking, and stop worrying. Be a Magician, damn it. Use that power, and I'll take care of the rest," Morgan held up her fist, the muted steel ring cutting a void across her finger.

I crouched down inside The Velcurses Conundrum, its

complex lines and whorls twisting around me. The seal was too difficult to understand, I didn't have Morgan's focus.

Or do I?

The Dead Man's Tongue tingled on my finger.

"Now, Gene!"

I slammed my palms against the cold brick, closing my eyes and reaching deep for the power. The Magick roared up like a boiling cauldron of cosmic energy. It surged through my hands and into the seal, rolling down the lines and dancing across the whorls. Just like before, the Shades surged, their bodies billowing up with the negative energy that flowed from The Velcurses Conundrum.

"Morgan!"

Shades clawed at my girlfriend, but still her Magick churned. "More, Gene, stop holding back!"

I dug deeper, pulling in whatever I could and sending all of it into the confusing seal. Negative energy swelled, and with it the Shades.

"Morgan, what are we—"

Boom!

With a sound like thunder, Morgan's engine kicked into high gear. What her Magick lacked in power, it more than made up with in cunning precision. Negative energy swirled out of the shadowy creatures like you'd wring out a wet towel. The steel ring burned white-hot against my finger, but I dared not touch it. Morgan's hair whipped in a frenzy, the wind and Magick twisting it like a tiny vortex.

She slammed her hands together in a powerful clap and the power vanished—along with the Shades and the wind.

"Morgan!"

23

TRUTH AND LIES

"Are you okay?" I jumped the chalk seal to get to Morgan. "Does this mean it's over?"

Morgan took a deep breath, her eyes practically shining. The Dead Man's Tongue on her hand glowed in the courtyard's gloom.

"Hardly." She shook out her hair and flexed her fingers. "This is only the beginning."

"But I thought—what the hell?"

A tiny moth crawled out from beneath the seam of my jacket, rubbing its diminutive legs together before launching itself into the air.

Morgan glared at the tiny insect. "Gene, we need to go."

"Why?"

"Because I'm here to tell you what she's really doing." My roommate stepped out of the shadows on the edge of the courtyard, a small matchbox in his hand.

"Ed?"

The moth landed in the open box and beat its wings in a rapid-fire pattern.

"Exactly what I thought. Thank you, Bono," Ed said, patting the tiny moth on its head before gently closing the box.

"A Tattlewing? Really? You used a Tattlewing on your own roommate?" Morgan shook her head, taking a step back from the Demon Hunter and his fishing vest full of artifacts.

"I didn't want to, but you left me no choice."

Morgan frowned. "Well, the bug will tell you the same thing Gene will: I'm innocent."

Ed pulled a crumpled-up paper out of his vest, and held it up in the moonlight. While it was impossible to read the lettering, the symbol in the center brought back immediate memories. That was the symbol I'd seen the other day.

Ten Spins...

"You broke into my room," Morgan said, positioning herself next to me.

Ed shook his head, then patted at a keychain hooked to his vest. "I didn't break anything."

"So your roommate has no problem letting himself into my dorm room and sneaking through my things. How do you feel about that, Gene?"

My stomach rolled and the first hints of adrenaline set my heart racing. "I don't like it."

"Gene, don't you understand? I had to. The moment she used Ten Spins' Soul Push on me I knew she was trouble."

Morgan grabbed my hand and her soft fingers intertwined mine. "Gene, you of all people should know Magick isn't evil. It's a tool, nothing more and nothing less. I did what I had to do to stay alive—to protect us."

Ed waved the paper in the air. "Do you know what this is? Of course you don't, so let me tell you."

Blood pounded between my ears and my shoulders tightened. "Ed—"

"No, you seem to be clueless about more than half of this stuff. I'll explain it to you. This is one of Ten Spins' specialties, violent and chaotic Magick. You want to bring Reavers like a moth to the flame, you do it with this."

Morgan squeezed my hand. "All of Magick is chaos, it comes from the Void. Yes, I found a scrap of Ten Spins' Magick, so what? Have you felt the power that runs through this place?"

Ed frowned.

"Of course you haven't, because you aren't a Magician. For all that knowledge in your head you have no power, nothing. You can't truly feel the energy that swirls around this place. Gene feels it, and he understands it at a level you'll never touch."

"Don't try to explain to Gene what he feels."

My mind drifted back to the Wild Magick and the chaos that ensued. "I do feel it," I said. "I felt it that night. I told you as much. That was no Poltergeist, that was Wild Magick. This place is swimming in it."

Morgan nodded, pushing her body against mine. "And I trap that chaos. If you understood Magick, you'd understand what that sigil really does. But you aren't a Magician, so you couldn't know."

Ed huffed. "I may not be a Magician, but I have forgotten more about Magick than you've ever learned."

Morgan's Magick hummed. "Gene, you feel it, don't you? You're a true Magician, you can feel my Magick. What is it like? Is it chaos? Is it the wild and violent actions of a Reaver?"

"No."

"Tell him," she cried, tears appearing in the edges of her eyes. "Tell your roommate. He's not a Magician, he can't understand us, he can't really know Magick. Tell him, Gene. Tell him what my Magick feels like." Morgan pulled my hand up against her chest, her heart beating against our intertwined fingers. "Tell him who the woman you love really is."

Morgan's eyes sparkled even in the dark courtyard, her tears catching what little light slipped through the dense trees.

I turned to face my roommate. "That's not Morgan. Her Magick is not chaotic."

"Gene, with all due respect—"

"No, Ed. You're going to listen to me." Morgan's fingers squeezed mine and her hair brushed my cheek. "We're the Magicians here, not you. So, I think you need to just shut the hell up and let me explain something to *you*."

My roommate opened his mouth, and then closed it again. It was clear he didn't quite know how to respond.

"Good," I said, puffing out my chest with confidence. "I've felt Morgan's Magick many times, just like I'm feeling it now. She's the exact opposite of chaos or confusion."

Ed threw his hands in the air. "Damn it, Gene. That doesn't matter. She's manipulating you, can't you see that? Everything she does is a manipulation. She's using you."

Morgan wiped her eyes. "I'm not manipulating him. I'm in love with him. Why can't you see that?"

My heart caught in chest.

What?

"This is an amazing production, really, but it doesn't change the fact you are leading him on. You don't love Gene."

Morgan's lip quivered, and her Magick flickered. "I'm sorry things aren't working out with you and Porter, but that doesn't mean either of you get to ruin what we have."

Ed's mouth fell open. "What are you—"

"The rumors are flying around, Ed. Everybody in the dorm knows it. You and Porter were never going to work out anyway. You're too volatile. One minute you're up and the next you are down. You want chaos, Ed? You should look in the mirror. It's no surprise Porter has been dating other guys."

Veins protruded from the sides of my roommate's neck. "I don't… she hasn't…"

"But she has, Ed. In fact, I found her this morning having coffee with Gene. Did you know that?"

"Is this true?" Ed asked, the color draining from his face.

"We had coffee, but that's it."

Morgan shook her head. "Gene's too modest, or he's too much of a man to say otherwise, but Porter is sweet on him. Any woman can tell."

"Gene!" Ed took a menacing step toward us.

"I didn't do anything." I held up my hand. "I promise. She invited me out for coffee on her way to work on Saturday. We went to Perks. Honestly, Ed, I'm telling you the truth."

"He is," Morgan said, her hip pressed against mine. "Of all the men here, Gene's the real deal. He doesn't cheat on his girlfriend. He stands up for her. He believes in her, and because he believes in her, she sticks with him. She sticks with him through everything. You could learn a lot from Gene."

Ed took another step forward and his hand drifted to one of the many pockets of his vest.

"Stop," I said. "Don't even think about it."

"Gene." Ed shook his head slowly, his hand not moving away from the vest. "You can't see clearly. She's doing something to you. I promise I can help you see it, just let me."

"I think you need to go home, Ed."

Morgan's ring clinked against mine. "Better yet, I think you need to check on Porter. I'm guessing she's getting ready to head out to meet someone shortly. If the rumors are true, he's a jock—you might have more than a little trouble."

"You're lying."

Morgan shook her head slowly. "If that's what you want to believe, Ed. Neither Gene nor I will stop you, but what if you're wrong? What if she's laughing and holding the hand of someone else right now? Someone strong... someone powerful... someone not you?"

Ed's shoulders crumpled before our eyes. He dropped his hand away from his vest, his face drooping in the gloomy dark.

"Is this the person you want to be with, Gene? Think about that…"

My roommate stormed off into the dark. He left me alone with Morgan and a heart full of doubt.

EYES ON THE PRIZE

*M*organ pulled open the heavy door to her dorm building and motioned me inside. "Come on, Gene. There's no time to waste. Those Shades are going to regroup and we need to get you a lay of the land before we make our attempt to get inside."

Ed's bike sat propped up against one of the trees outside her dorm. Somewhere in that building my roommate was sure to be confronting Porter.

"Why did you say that?" I asked, stopping on the front steps.

"Say what, Gene? You're going to have to be a lot more specific." Morgan's eyes shone in the orange glow of the flickering gas lamps that hung beside the door.

"Why did you tell Ed that Porter is cheating on him? Is she dating someone else?"

Morgan tilted her head as if trying to slide the memories of what she'd said into position in her mind. "Huh?"

"You told him Porter was cheating on him. Is that true? Is she cheating on him?"

Morgan motioned me inside. "Of course it's true. I mean, how could it not be?"

"And you've seen this?"

My girlfriend sighed and again directed me to come inside. "Not directly. It's not like I have a Tattlewing I send after people —that's Ed's specialty."

The thought of that moth's tiny feet on my neck made me shiver. "So you don't know for sure? You just made it up?"

Morgan let the door close and came back down a step. "Gene, I'm a woman, I know women. I've seen how the two of them interact. What's worse, I saw how she interacted with you."

"We got coffee." I threw my hands in the air. "We just got coffee."

My girlfriend smiled and shook her head slowly. "There are times your ignorance is just so damn cute, but this is *not* one of them." She paused to point toward the distant library. "We only have so much time, Gene. We can't spend all of it outside gabbing about your roommate and his soon-to-be ex-girlfriend. We've got work to do."

I shook my head. "No, don't change the subject. Porter wasn't coming on to me."

Morgan grabbed my hand. "God, I don't know what's worse, the fact that you didn't notice, or that fact that you are so adamant about making sure I know that. I guess on the one hand it's sweet that you didn't notice, but on the other, it's also dangerous."

I frowned. "Dangerous?"

Morgan nodded, gently pulling me toward her. "People like Porter and Ed only exist to tear us apart. They're afraid of what we could become, of what we represent."

"I don't—"

"You don't have to understand," Morgan said, giving me that same crooked smile I'd witnessed before. "You just have to believe. Believe in me, believe in you, but most of all, believe in us. Did you see what we just did?" An excited Morgan turned me around to face the trees, and the distant walls of the library beyond them.

"The Shades..."

"You were amazing, Gene. Tell me, did you feel the focus? Did you feel what it was like to command your Magick and not have it command you?"

Truth be told, I had felt it, but I wasn't sure how I felt about the rest of what went down.

"It was nice..."

Morgan laughed, her voice soft in the gathering gloom. "Nice? Oh, Gene. It was far more than nice. It was proof of just how amazing you are, and how amazing you can become."

My mind drifted back to the Magick, and to the power that roared like a tidal force in my chest. It was there, and it would always be there—but with Morgan it could be so much more. I wouldn't be a slave to that cosmic energy; with Morgan I would be its master.

The Dead Man's Tongue tingled on my finger, and I was lost in the visual of powerful Magick when Morgan waved her hand and pulled me back to the present.

"I know it's exciting, Gene. I know because I'm excited too, but we can't get complacent now. We can't let people like Ed and Porter distract us from our mission. We are too close to give up now—real power awaits us."

Morgan's words caught me off guard. "Real power? I thought we were protecting you."

My girlfriend tensed up and her fingers tightened against mine ever so slightly.

"We are protecting me—and you as well, remember—from the horrors of that place, but there's more at stake now, so much more."

"What do you mean?"

Morgan sighed and her muted steel ring clinked against mine. "Gene, the best way to fight fire is with fire. You may think I have immense Magickal knowledge, but I can assure you, it's nothing compared to what exists inside those walls. The library you know isn't the one I know. To you it's a simple repository of books on normal and boring things—but I know the secrets it doesn't share. I know the way inside the true library." Morgan let her words hang uncomfortably in the air.

"But the Shades..." I said, the distant library no longer looking quite so boring.

Morgan dismissed me with a wave of her hand. "Just the tip of the spear, Gene. There are far worse things that roam the halls of that evil place. Can you feel it? Close your eyes and reach out with your Magick."

The Dead Man's Tongue tickled at my finger.

"Do it, Gene," Morgan said, closing her own eyes. "Let your Magick expand..."

I did what she said, the steel ring guiding my thoughts and tightening my focus. My Magick bubbled up like a hungry brook. It spilled out of me and over the steps.

"Reach, Gene. Reach for it, see that vile place for what it really is..."

I opened my eyes to find a soft coating of ash and soot covering the bare branches like snow. Beyond them, the library stood defiant. Dark and fluttering shapes shifted around it like tattered flags in an invisible wind. Something cried out in that unnatural twilight, and the vision vanished.

"That is the true face of the library," Morgan whispered, gently pulling me back to the present and helping my Magick dissipate.

"What is it?" I asked, blinking away that dark visual.

"A repository for the most powerful Magick. It's been all but forgotten, but I found it." Morgan beamed with pride. "I found the scraps hinting to it—the hidden wisdom your roommate thought was wrong to possess. He doesn't understand, Gene. He'll never understand. Ed isn't a Magician." She put her hand on my chest. "He doesn't have this, and he never will. If you can't feel the power swirling in your chest, then you shouldn't be the one to tell others what they can and can't do with it."

She's right...

"The library is hungry, Gene. It wants me, and now you, because you're with me." Morgan held up my hand, the Dead Man's Tongue catching the flickering lamp light. "But now you aren't easy pickings. We're together, and the two of us are making it nervous."

A cool breeze caused the oak branches to sway and give us a better view of the distant library. Gone were the dark shapes and malevolent walls. The treetops that had been covered in ash and soot were now a muted green of healthy oak leaves.

"Why can't I see it now?"

"Because it's the perfect disguise," Morgan said, following my eyes and reading my thoughts.

"What do you mean?"

"The library—it's a perfect disguise. Students and faculty walk in and out of there every day, their heads mired in thought, never knowing something far darker swirls around them just out of sight."

"I don't understand."

"That's because you haven't seen the Gloom. I promise you once you have all of this will make so much more sense."

At the mention of the Gloom my chest tightened. "The Gloom?"

The negative plane—a dark, cold, and inescapable place.

"I know what your roommate has said, but don't let Ed's words scare you." Morgan's eyes sparkled like bright gemstones in the flickering lamp light. "The Gloom is dangerous, but it isn't unbeatable."

I swallowed back at the bile rising in my throat, while Morgan guided me toward the dorm door. A cold wind at my back pushed me forward and into an uncertain future.

25

SLIP AND SEAL

*M*organ pulled me into her room and immediately flipped the light on. The papers on her desk were a mess, and someone had clearly been through her bookshelf.

Ed.

I closed the door behind us. "Do you want to lock it?"

"Huh?" Morgan said, picking up papers and stacking books.

"The lock on your door. The sigil you used before, remember?"

Morgan shoved a few books into my hands. "Oh, right. No, it's not necessary. We handled those Shades, so there's nothing to worry about for the moment."

"Oh…"

Morgan directed my attention to the shelf. I started stacking the missing volumes back where they went. "I'm sorry Ed did this."

My girlfriend nodded and pulled more papers out from under the bed. "I'm not. It shows you just what kind of person he is. You don't want people like that in your life, Gene—trust me. He's controlling and manipulative. My father was like that.

You don't need that in your head. It changes you..." Morgan turned her attention back to the desk and the mess my roommate had left for her there.

Is that really who Ed is?

My mind drifted back to the fun times with Ed Lovely—the hours we'd spent watching *Gulfwatch* and commenting on the quality casting and undersized swimwear. I chuckled at the time we'd exorcised that restless spirit in the Rec Center.

I didn't know you could do that with a squash racquet, and I'm pretty sure Ed didn't either...

My stomach bottomed out at the thought of where our friendship was now.

What happened to us?

Morgan grabbed my arm and shook me out of my haze. "Gene, can you give me a hand with this?"

"Huh?"

My girlfriend pointed to the large area rug that covered the polished concrete floor of her tiny single room. "I need to roll it up."

"Oh, sure," I said, stepping off the woven carpet to come around and help her curl its heavy fibers.

Morgan and I twisted the heavy rug into a thick roll, then pushed that carpet burrito up against her bed.

"Whoa..."

The floor beneath Morgan's rug was stunning. It held an expertly etched sigil that appeared to have been scored directly into the polished concrete. Lines twisting within lines, the symbol was unlike anything I'd ever seen before.

"What is that?"

"That," Morgan said, leaving the cigar-roll of rug to join me beside the powerful design, "is the Seal of Ariadne."

"Ariadne?"

Morgan nodded, lightly tracing her fingers along the etched

lines. "No one really knows if she was simply legend, or actually real, but the sigil bears her name just the same."

"What does it do?"

Morgan flashed a crooked smile. "Do you know the myth of the minotaur?"

"Uh..."

My girlfriend shook her head. "I'm going to take that as a no. The legend goes that the minotaur was trapped in a great labyrinth, which was too confusing for any mortal to comprehend. Ariadne's boyfriend, Theseus, was sent into that maze thanks to her jealous father. Certainly something I can appreciate. Still, being the crafty person she was, Ariadne gave her man a ball of string and a sword. The string or thread is why the sigil has been associated with her today. The Seal of Ariadne is like an inexhaustible thread between your body and the spirit you project into the Gloom."

The Gloom...

"What has Ed told you about the Gloom, Gene?"

"Not much."

Morgan shook her head. "That's not surprising, but it doesn't matter. It's for the best that I'm the one explaining it to you anyway, since we'll be on the inside shortly. You need to know what it's like."

My already hesitant stomach twisted in on itself again. "Uh, inside?"

Morgan got up and searched the top of her dresser for a hairband. "Yes, inside. We can't very well get the information we need out here. We need to see the library on its home turf."

"The library exists in the Gloom?"

Morgan pulled her hair tight and wrapped the black band around it, her green tips poking out like feather-light blades of grass. "Almost everything exists in the Gloom in one way or another. It's a broken copy, a twisted shadow of the original. Everything here exists there, but it's dark, warped, and twisted."

"Sounds lovely."

Morgan frowned. "It isn't—it's a mess."

"And we are going inside this mess?"

"No," she said, fixing her hair in the mirror.

"Oh, thank—"

"At least not in person this time," Morgan replied as if she'd been talking about a trip to the grocery store.

"This time?"

Morgan got down on her knees and crawled along the edge of the sigil. She inspected the entire design meticulously, confirming each junction and tracing each spiral with her fingers. Her nail caught on a particularly stubborn piece of dirt that had wedged itself in the paint and she picked at it until it broke free. "The Seal of Ariadne is a projection gate. It's going to let us visit the Gloom in spirit."

"Isn't that still—"

"Insanely dangerous?" Morgan flicked the dirt away. "Yes, but we'll be together and I don't anticipate too much trouble here in the dorm."

"What do you mean 'here in the dorm'?"

Apparently satisfied the sigil was intact Morgan took a seat in the center of it, then folded her legs comfortably beneath her butt. "The Gloom mirrors our world, Gene. Everything we see here," she gestured to the surrounding room, "in the Gloom it will be broken, burnt, and shadowy."

"Right…"

"And there's more," she said, relaxing her shoulders with practiced ease. "Sometimes intense emotions and feelings bleed over into the Gloom, and that brings bottom feeders."

Her words coaxed just a little more bile into my already unhappy stomach. "Feeders?"

"You ever own fish?"

"No."

"My uncle had fish." Morgan took off her jacket and tossed it on the bed. "When we were little, he bought a bottom feeder to keep the tank clean."

"Did it work?"

Morgan nodded. "In the beginning it did. That little creepy-crawly would scour its way along the bottom of the aquarium and suck up all manner of crap."

I sat outside the seal, admiring its design, but still quite leery of getting inside of it. "Then what happened?"

Morgan placed her hands one inside the other like some meditative pose. She closed her eyes and let the air out of her lungs slowly. "It got hungry."

I swallowed back at the bile in my throat. "I'm guessing this story doesn't end with your uncle's bottom feeder starving to death."

"No."

"So," I said, suddenly feeling unprotected and exposed in Morgan's room for the second time. "You think we'll run into a bottom feeder in the Gloom?"

Morgan opened her eyes and tilted her head to one side. "Just one would be fine by me. I can deal with just one. It's when there are dozens that I start to get concerned."

"Dozens?"

"Maybe more," she said, rolling her neck like an athlete prepping for the big game. "But you need to stop worrying and start focusing. I need you at your best on the inside. We can't mess around. Now, give me your hands."

Morgan held out a hand toward me.

"Wait," I said, still not quite ready for whatever she was planning. "I'm not following why it is we are going to the Gloom in the first place. I mean, I'm rather partial to this plane—it's where I keep all my stuff."

"Come on, Gene."

"How about I just watch your back here?"

Morgan shook her head. "No, that's what you are going to

do there. Remember how you promised to help stop the library from hurting me, or others? What about David Singer? You don't want more people to end up like him, do you?"

I don't.

"Fine." I carefully crawled over the edge of the ornate design to take a seat opposite her. "Let's just get this over and done with and not turn it into an elaborate sight-seeing visit."

Morgan nodded her head slowly, taking my hands inside hers. "We are on a mission, Gene."

My legs twisted beneath me, and I wondered how she could stand pressing her ankles against the hard concrete like this. I tried to push that thought out of my head and comfort myself with the knowledge that I wouldn't be doing it for long.

Especially if your spirit gets eaten by a bottom feeder.

Morgan took my hands in hers. "Are you ready, Gene?"

No.

"Yes."

"Close your eyes and focus your Magick. Small amounts, Gene. Don't push it, just let the Seal direct your energy. Don't overload the sigil, it wasn't designed for two people."

"Wait! Is this safe?"

"Not in the slightest," Morgan said, her hands squeezing mine. "You aren't backing out now are you, sexy?"

I took a deep breath, and for an instant I wondered just how much of my decision making had been delegated to the wrong organ.

"Okay, now wha—"

26

SHROUDED

*W*alls darkened and paint peeled. Morgan's formerly bright room faded in a haze of gloom and ash. Her perfectly made bed crumpled like burnt paper, while all around the tight space small piles of soot collected like dirty snowdrifts.

"Morgan?" I spun around, my body floating free and turning end over end in the eternal twilight of the Gloom. "Morgan!"

"I'm right here, Gene," my girlfriend said, her own spirit-like form drifting gently in the enveloping dark.

"Is this it?"

Morgan nodded, then twirled an ephemeral cord in her translucent fingers. "Welcome to the Gloom, Eugene Law."

"Is that Ariadne's Thread?"

"Yes."

I twisted left and right trying to find my own silvery cord. "I should have one of those, right? I can't seem to—"

Morgan's hand shot out and yanked at something behind my back. She twisted a second silvery cord in her fingers like the carnation she'd given David, and my heart beat just a little faster than I might have wanted it to.

"Hey, I need that."

"You do need this. Otherwise things could go very badly for you." Morgan frowned at my gently pulsing cord.

"What's... bad?"

Morgan put a hand out to my face and directed my attention to the floor beneath us. We hovered above the swirling sigil, bobbing like parade balloons tethered to our bodies by a pair of spaghetti-like strands.

"You want to end up stuck here? Or worse?"

I shook my head.

"Good," she placed my cord in my hand, "then don't let this get cut. Ever."

"Got it," I said, taking the still-pulsing cord and consciously winding it around my fingers. "Where are we?"

"We are in my dorm room." Morgan pointed to our motion-less bodies below. "But our spirits are in the Gloom."

Ariadne's Thread pulsed brighter in my hand. "Why is it doing that?"

Morgan moved her translucent hand to my shoulder. "It's doing that because you are getting nervous."

"Well, I'm free falling in the Gloom. Can't a guy be a little nervous about that?"

The cord pulsed again, bright and angry.

"Stop it now, Eugenc Law," Morgan hissed. Her soft fingers pinched my ghostly shoulder and solicited my full attention in the process. "Take a deep breath and count to ten. Unless, of course, you want to keep ringing the dinner bell."

Morgan's previous story concerning bottom feeders made calming down a tall order, but I tried just the same. I closed my eyes and counted down, doing my best not to imagine what might be lurking in the dark corners of the dorm.

"There you go." Morgan let go of my shoulder and gave it a light slap. "Nice work, sexy."

I opened my eyes again and found Ariadne's Thread no longer flashing like a strand of broken Christmas lights.

"It's dark in here."

Morgan rolled her ghostly eyes. "Dark? It's the Gloom, Gene. Did you expect it to be Rainbow Brite?"

It would have helped.

"No, I guess not." A soft clicking sound set my heart racing. "What was that?"

Morgan placed a translucent finger to her lips, then took my hand. Her spiritual body sailed through the door, dragging me behind it. From what little I understood about ghostly movement it was all about willpower, and Morgan possessed that in spades.

We floated gently in the narrow dorm hallway, where dozens of closed doors punctuated the concrete in either direction. The same soot and ash from her room covered the floor here, laying in dark piles against the unwashed concrete. Morgan dragged me to the end of the hall where a wide window looked out upon the campus.

"Where is everybody?" I whispered, finding it odd there were relatively few students crisscrossing the fields or traversing the sidewalks.

"Not everyone appears in the Gloom," Morgan said, drifting softly beside me. "I'm not exactly sure why, but I believe it has something to do with soul and passion."

Translucent cars and bright flashing headlights appeared in brief bursts along the narrow road that ran next to the building. It was like watching an old movie that had half the frames taken out—one moment the car would be there, then in the next moment it wasn't.

"Look." Morgan pointed past the street and beyond the mist-shrouded trees. "That is the library."

Dark and ominous, the brick building peeked above the

trees. Sections of it were covered in a thick blanket of what looked like black and gray fabric.

"What's all over it?"

"Umbraling webs," Morgan said, her hands absently squeezing the silvery cord binding her to her body.

"Umbralings?"

"Do you like spiders, Gene?"

Somewhere back in Morgan's room, my real life stomach clenched up at the mere mention of the word. "No."

"Neither do I." Morgan's bright eyes never wavered from the distant building.

A flash of glowing yellow, startling in the dark monotone of the Gloom, caught my attention. A pair of people exited the dorm beneath us.

"Ed?"

It was him, but he wasn't alone. He had a fellow vibrant soul chasing after him.

Porter.

"Is that Porter?"

Morgan nodded. "Yes, it's your roommate and his girlfriend. We don't have time to waste, Gene. The longer we stay here, the greater the chances of things taking notice. There are more than bottom feeders in the Gloom."

From our perch, it was impossible to make out what they were saying, but their body language spoke volumes. Porter had her hands on her hips, occasionally taking one off to point at Ed, or his bike, or both. For his part, my roommate remained nonplussed. He shrugged and said something back, then turned to leave.

"Gene," Morgan said, her hands subtly directing my attention back toward the library. "We need a plan of attack. This isn't the time to catch up on your favorite soap opera. The library is defended by…"

Morgan kept talking, but I was too transfixed on the scene playing out below me to pay much attention to her words.

Ed was on his bike now, but Porter had blocked his path. By this point they were both gesticulating like crazy, and it appeared they were cruising right past civility and into a full-on fight.

"What do you think, Gene?"

"Huh?"

Morgan's thread pulsed angrily. "Pay attention! I asked you a question."

"I'm sorry."

Morgan grabbed my face and pointed it back toward the library's dark tower. "I asked if we should try…"

Again her words faded as I found myself unable to tear my focus away from Porter and Ed. He'd found a way to get past her and was pumping hard toward the street's edge. Something dark, like a black sheet flapping in the wind, appeared above one of the vanishing cars.

Morgan must have seen it too, because she stopped talking abruptly.

"What is that?"

"We have to go," Morgan said, unraveling the cord she'd twisted around her fingers.

Ed's bike skipped along the sidewalk seams, kicking up loose gravel en route to the street.

I pointed at the black and tattered bedsheet fluttering between the vanishing cars. "Wait, what is that?"

"Death Shroud." Morgan dropped the rest of Ariadne's Thread from her hand. "Time to go back. Pull the cord now."

"Wait…"

The Death Shroud appeared again. Like clothes left on the line in a strong wind, it slapped and cracked along the top of one of the here-and-gone-again cars.

"No, Gene," Morgan said, trying to unravel my own cord.

"We don't mess with Death Shrouds. We go back to our bodies now. We can try again another time. Right now, we let nature take its course."

Ed turned back to yell something to Porter, his head facing away from the Death Shrouded car currently on a collision course with his bike.

"Ed!" My thread pulsed like a Christmas tree.

Morgan grabbed my shoulder. "Stop! You're going to get us killed."

My roommate's front wheel slipped on one of the roots, launching him over the handlebars and into the street.

The clicking sounds I'd heard earlier suddenly reappeared, followed by Morgan's screams.

Black and bulbous spider-like creatures emerged from individual dorm doors, their front legs, like feelers, clawing at the stuffy air.

Morgan frantically grabbed at her cord. "Umbralings! Come on, Gene. We have to go! Now!"

Had I known more about travel in the Gloom I would have understood what came next, but I didn't; all I knew was my roommate was in danger. In one instant I was standing next to Morgan, and in the next I was on the sidewalk, an airborne Ed tumbling face-forward past me.

"Ed!" Porter shouted, her voice echoing in the unceasing twilight.

The Death-Shroud-encased car appeared again, barreling toward my roommate at break-neck speed.

"Ed!" Porter shouted again, racing down the narrow sidewalk—but I knew she wouldn't make it in time. Ed Lovely hit the street hard, his head bounced against the ash-covered ground. The Death Shroud expanded, its inky blackness filling the misty air.

I lunged into the street behind him. "Ed, get up," I cried, my hands passing through him. I wasn't really here. I was still in Morgan's dorm room sitting in the Seal of Ariadne.

Ed lay unconscious on the street in front of me, seconds away from certain death, and I was helpless to do anything about it. My only companion was the silvery thread that now pulsed gently in my hand.

The thread!

I may not have known what to do in the Gloom, nor had any clue what a Death Shroud was, but I knew predators. I stepped in front of Ed and held my thread up high, then put every ounce of panic I could into that silvery string.

Turns out, I can freak out like the best of them.

Ariadne's Thread lit up like the Fourth of July, sending waves of bright white light out across the Gloom and letting any and everything in the immediate vicinity know there was something tasty to snack on.

Come and get it!

IN YOUR EYES

*L*ike the megawatt flashbulb from the world's largest camera, Ariadne's Thread flooded the street with a powerful burst of light.

Screech!

The car barreling toward Ed swerved to the side, narrowly missing my fallen roommate before jumping the opposite curb, cutting across the sidewalk, and coming to a stop against a distant light pole.

Malevolent laundry fluttered off the car like a lost tarp on the highway. It caught the non-existent wind and swelled. The tattered and worn edges of that black blanket snapped and twisted in the dark of the gloom.

"Morgan." I turned back to the dorm to find more milky-white eyes appearing like hungry mice along the edges of the ash-covered building.

Bad, bad, bad!

Porter shot through me and off the curb. Oblivious to my presence, she raced to Ed's side and lifted his head gently. "Eddie, are you okay? Eddie!" Her voice was a distant and muffled version of its normal self.

Sirens wailed in the distance.

More good Samaritans poured out of the surrounding buildings and off the sidewalk. Like the strobe lights of a cheap haunted house, they popped in and out in various states of help and concern, while against that backdrop, the Death Shroud swelled. It filled the space beyond them with a worn and threadbare darkness.

The pull of that evil bedsheet was strong. I twisted Ariadne's Thread in my hand, slowly backing away from the ever-expanding Shroud.

Crap, crap, crap! Wait, the Thread, pull the Thread!

With my fingers looped through the glowing string, I readied my hand for a pull.

Here we go, one, two—

"Gene?"

"Ed?!"

My roommate's spirit drifted out of his body like the last wisps of smoke from a faded campfire. A faint and barely visible thread dangled behind him.

My ghostly roommate rubbed a translucent hand across his face, and then froze. His eyes were wide and unwilling to tear themselves away from his ghostly fingers.

"Ed, what the hell are you doing here?"

The Demon Hunter held up a bloody hand. It glowed bright against the swelling blackness of the Death Shroud behind him. "I was hoping you could explain that to me…"

Flashes of people appeared and disappeared around my roommate's body. Porter's whimpering cries turned his attention to the scene playing out beneath him.

"That's… me? I have blood all over my favorite shirt. Why is there blood all over my favorite shirt?" Sudden realization played out across Ed's shimmering face. "Gene, am I dead?"

The swelling darkness of the Death Shroud behind Ed drifted closer. Like a soundless blanket of inky midnight, the black cloth sent its tendril-like edges snaking around my room-mate's ghostly legs.

"Ed, you've got to pull your cord!"

My roommate turned his attention away from the commotion around his body. "Am I dead, Gene?"

"No, but you might be in a second. You need to pull that cord!"

Ariadne's Thread drifted gently behind my roommate, only to be sucked up like spaghetti by the tattered black flag.

An ambulance pulled up just past us. Its paint looked faded and chipped in the misty darkness of the Gloom.

"Pull your cord, Ed," I cried, pointing to the rapidly vanishing string behind him. "Pull it before—"

Snap!

The faded edge of Ed's slivery thread vanished into the Death Shroud.

"Ed!"

Color drained from my roommate's face. His already transparent body started unraveling into the black hole of the malevolent laundry. Ed's faded hands reached for me, his spirit coming apart before my eyes.

"I got you." I grabbed for his hands, only to have my arm yanked back by Morgan's translucent fingers holding my sleeve.

"No! I'm not losing you to that thing. Your roommate is gone."

EMTs appeared and disappeared. Afterimages of them popped in and out of the Gloom as they loaded Ed's unconscious body onto a gurney.

"We're losing him," one of the paramedics said, his muffled voice barely registering in the shadowy darkness.

Ed's ghostly face cried out in a silent scream as he unraveled into the Death Shroud's yawning blackness.

My cord flashed wildly. "What do we do?"

Morgan pulled me back and shook her head. "We leave—now. Ed's caught in the Death Shroud's embrace."

"No," I pulled my hand back, "I'm not leaving him."

Below us the gurney rolled into the back of a pale and muted ambulance. Porter climbed in beside it.

Ed's soul unwound like a spinning top, his legs vanishing into the void.

"You don't have a choice. I told you not to get involved, but you ignored me. You should have let him die, but you didn't. If it was his time you have upset the balance. Now Ed's soul is disintegrating because of you."

Morgan's words hit me like a pile-driver.

Did I do this?

Alien cries split the twilight got my girlfriend's attention. "Now, Gene."

Morgan grabbed my arm again and pulled me back, away from Ed's soul, and the soon to be departing ambulance.

"No! If I did this to him I'm going to undo it."

"You can't undo it," Morgan said, her face focused and resolute. "There are things you can't undo, and this is one of them. You don't come back from a Death Shroud, no one does. We've got to get clear before we pull our cords." Morgan dragged me toward the dorm.

"But what about Ed?"

We floated up past the steps, my roommate's ghostly body gone beneath the waist. "There's nothing we can do for him now," Morgan said, pulling me up and away from the quickly fading scene. "Nothing short of a minor miracle can save him now."

Short... Shorty!

I yanked my arm free of Morgan's grasp and propelled myself through the chipped paint and bent metal of the departing ambulance.

"Gene!" Morgan cried.

Come on, Shorty. Ed needs you.

The inside of the ambulance was orchestrated chaos. EMTs worked on my roommate, cutting off his fishing vest and tossing it aside. Porter gripped the gurney's steel edge, her fingers white.

The vest!

The broken remains of Shorty's top knot and head tumbled out across the rubbery floor.

"Shorty." My hands passed through the broken and shriveled flesh. "Shorty, wake up!"

The ambulance engine rumbled to life.

I shoved my shimmering fingers into the shriveled head. "Damn it, Shorty. I need you!"

"Gene, is that you?" A ghostly version of Ed's latest toy tumbled into my hands. His glowing head was restored to its former glory. "It smells like you." The tiny Yaga Doll's stitched lids searched for me.

Emergency personnel worked feverishly on my bloodied roommate's body. Porter hovered over him, tears streaking her cheeks.

Hold on, buddy. I'll fix this. I promise.

I clutched Shorty to my chest and jumped out of the van, landing on the ash-covered ground as the vehicle rolled off into the faded dark of the Gloom.

"No time to talk, Shorty. Ed's in trouble."

The diminutive ghostly head sniffed the air like a dog hot on the trail. "Death Shroud!" Shorty's voice wasn't quite as confident as it had been only moments earlier.

I stumbled to my feet. The great black Shroud flapped in a non-existent wind in front of me. Ed's soul unwound even faster than before.

The Yaga Doll shuddered in my hand, if he'd had shoulders I was sure he would have been shaking them.

Morgan hovered above the sidewalk, the bright tips of her

hair streaming out like a flickering flame. "Gene, what are you doing?"

Ed...

My roommate continued to unravel before my eyes. Like someone was vacuuming up an infinite spool of yarn, Ed's soul was being consumed by the black Shroud. His arms and legs were gone, and in seconds he'd lose his chest as well.

"Can you smell it, Shorty?"

"Yes," the tiny head said, sniffing the air. "I can, and much more. Gene, you are in grave danger. You should not be here."

Ed's chest slipped away, lost to the yawning void. All that remained of my roommate's spirit was his head, drifting almost serene in the ashen twilight.

"Tell me about it." I pried at the stitches on his eyes. "Just like last time, I'm going to point you at the monster and try to stay out of the blast radius."

"Yaga Doll." Morgan scrambled backward toward the dorm. "Do not unravel his eyes in the Gloom! A Yaga Doll was never meant to be brought here—there's no telling what will happen when you open its eyes. Drop the Doll and pull your cord now!"

"She's right, boss," Shorty said, keeping his lids closed even as I pried off the last of the stitching. "I shouldn't be here; none of you should."

"Shorty, I don't give a damn. Will you do your thing, or not?"

The Yaga Doll broke into a wide grin, its teeth shining in the bright glow. "Happy to..."

"Don't do it, Gene—" Morgan's words vanished in the rush of green flame.

28

GOODBYE, SHORTY

*A*wash in brilliant green fire, the Yaga Doll was like a roaring comet on the end of a string. Twin laser-like eye beams pierced the Gloom. Their unholy light cut a path of destruction across the shadowy dark. A stray shot lanced through the billowing Death Shroud, only to slide off and scorch a line through the sidewalk.

"Stay on target, Shorty!" I shouted, trying to keep the bouncing Yaga Doll from consuming my roommate, or anyone else that might happen to end up in his gaze.

The tiny head laughed, his voice deep and resonating. "I make no promises."

Shorty's eyes cut back across the hazy dark and slammed into the Death Shroud. The bright laser-light bore a hole through the tattered beast. The monster twisted like a giant gym towel and released Ed, then turned its attention to me. My roommate's head floated like the top of wayward dandelion above the twisting Death Shroud.

"Get him, Morgan... Morgan?"

She was gone.

The malevolent bed sheet swelled, black and tattered wisps of fabric reaching for my arms and legs.

"Over here, Shorty. " I tried to adjust the bouncing head like an off-balance lantern.

The Yaga Doll's eye beams rocketed past the Shroud and rained righteous fire down on the street. They kicked up ash and deep grooves in the shadowy pavement before burning away the hazy mist of the Gloom itself.

"On the Shroud, Shorty! On the Shroud!"

The soul-munching black flag of evil billowed up and consumed the space in front of me, yet still Shorty found ways to miss it.

"I need more Magick," the tiny Yaga Doll said, its voice booming.

My roommate's head twisted in the shadowy twilight above the Shroud, his color slowly returning, along with a faint silvery cord.

He's alive!

The Death Shroud extended a tendril-like edge of its rippling cloth toward my twisting roommate's head.

Not so fast!

I grabbed the bouncing Shorty with my hand and pointed him directly at the Shroud. "Now, Shorty! Full power."

The eye beams tore through the Death Shroud and it pulled back from my roommate like a shrinking violet.

"Keep it up." I advanced on the cowering Gloom-beast. Shorty's head was an unholy lantern of fiery power. The Yaga Doll's eyes erupted in a bright flash, then flickered and stopped. The bright green lasers vanished like a child's toy when the batteries run out.

Crap.

"Shorty!"

The Death Shroud hesitated, then sprung back to life, swelling like a sail in high wind and reaching for my roommate.

"Ed!"

The Demon Hunter's eyes fluttered open. His disembodied head spun in the strange gravity of the Gloom. "Hey, Gene," he said, his lips smacking as if he'd just woken up from a long nap. "You know something? I just had the craziest dream. I dreamt I was at the beach. I hate the beach, but anyway, I was bobbing in the ocean and..." Ed looked down. "Gene, where are my arms?"

I furiously smacked the Yaga Doll against my palm like a TV remote. "Working on that."

The Shroud's undulating arms of tattered cloth wove through the air like tentacles on a mission and closed in on my roommate's drifting head.

"Can you work faster?" Ed's noggin asked as it continued to spin into the ether. His frantic eyes followed me with each turn.

"I'm trying." I shook the doll then turned it around to face me.

"Gene, don't look it in the—"

Ed's words were lost in a brilliant flash of green light. Shorty's eyes sprung back to life and bathed me in their fiery glow. "It's time, Gene..."

What?

Fire raced down my arms and consumed my chest. The Yaga Doll's power pulled on my Magick, siphoning it away like the end of a great vacuum hose. I pointed Shorty's eyes back at the Shroud, but I lost control in the burst of power. Bright green light cut across the brick walls of the dorm building, shattering windows and sending hordes of Umbralings streaming out onto the lawn.

"Umbralings, Gene!"

"I see them." I tried to direct the barely contained Yaga Doll toward the skittering spider-like beasts. "There are too many."

Umbralings surged out of the dorm like ants from a toppled ant-hill. They skittered over the broken ground in an angry wave.

Ed's head spun higher in the perpetual twilight. "The Shroud!"

I spun back around, the Yaga Doll held high, and poured everything into the billowing Shroud. Brilliant and unholy fire tore through the fluttering Gloom-beast, burning open one hole and then another. Tattered pieces of the Shroud ripped away beneath Shorty's withering gaze like dust in the wind.

Morgan appeared on the other side of the torn Shroud. "Gene, there are more coming. I'll get your roommate's head, but we have to get out of here, now!" Shorty's gaze ionized the air around Morgan, forcing her to dive out of the way and grab Ed's tattered cord in the process. "Turn that thing off and let's go!"

"You heard her, Shorty," I said, doing my best to keep those death-lasers off my girlfriend and her bobbing head-shaped balloon. "Kill the high-beams."

Shorty's light show cut through trees and sliced the tops off parked cars. "No."

"Shorty!"

Death Shrouds erupted into the distant sky from atop the library. Like a murder of noxious crows, they filled the twilight with billowing and inky darkness.

"Hurry, Gene!" Morgan shouted, yanking Ed's cord and wrapping it around her hand. "Just drop the damn doll and let's go."

The milky-white eyes of Umbralings filled the oak branches behind my girlfriend, their hairy legs hungry and tasting the air.

I tried to throw the Yaga Doll away, but once again found him stuck to my fingers.

Morgan tucked Ed's head under her arm and my roommate's eyes suddenly went wide. "Gene, your Thread!"

Umbralings skittered along my silvery cord like a macabre circus act, their spindly legs carrying them straight toward me. I tugged at the glowing thread, but the agile beasts held on tight.

Crap!

Morgan sprung up and out of the way of a lunging Umbraling's fangs. "You've got to turn it off."

I could only think of one way to do that.

Be in control of your Magick, or it will control you.

"Gene!" Morgan's voice felt distant and garbled. "What are you—"

I turned the doll around and stared directly into its eyes. Magick surged through me, rocketing down Ariadne's Thread like electricity down Ben Franklin's kite. Cosmic power popped bulbous bodies like blisters in the sun. Shorty's fire burned away her words, but I didn't dare look away. I was locked in a battle of wills, a staring contest that could only have one winner. The Yaga Doll's voice boomed in my head.

Your power will be your undoing.

What had started as roaring flames became something more. Shorty's gaze wasn't simply a manifestation of burning Magick, there was something else moving in the twisting green flames—me.

Eugene Law: the friend, the roommate, the Magician. That image didn't last. It shifted and darkened in the Yaga Doll's fury. There was an uncertain future hidden in those eyes: a future that spoke of bad decisions and dark paths. Was it a future cast in stone? Did I still have a chance to choose a better way, and was there even a better one to choose?

Show me, Shorty.

The eyes swirled and brought with them more visions: tall grass that swayed beneath a brilliant sun, tiny black buttons tumbling like rain from my fingers, and my own dark and shadowy face.

I'm sorry, boss. A long and dangerous road awaits you.

A final burst of flames surged from the Yaga Doll's eyes, burning away those visions and melting the Yaga Doll itself. Shorty left me lost in a sea of green and black. I felt myself falling backward, twisting in the weightless twilight of the Gloom.

Morgan shouted something, but again her voice was distant and lost in my mental haze. Strong fingers grabbed my arm, while tips of green hair fluttered in the twilight above me.

"Take your cord..."

My cord? Ariadne's Thread hung limp in the ruddy dark of the Gloom.

"Gene! Take your cord!"

My hands moved without precision, clumsily reaching for a string that seemed at times to be so large and yet so elusive. Billowing shapes filled the sky and snapped like flags on the high seas. For an instant I found Morgan's face inches from my own.

"Grab your God-damn cord or we all die in the Gloom!"

Ariadne's Thread...

I hooked my fingers around the fading string, willing my exhausted eyes to stay open.

Morgan pulled me toward her. "Do it!"

The black and spindly legs of a hungry Umbraling appeared on her shoulder. Sharp fangs shone beneath its milky-white eyes.

"Morgan, your shoulder." I tried to speak but my voice felt distant and remote, a part of me, yet at the same time not.

The Umbraling's fang sunk deep into translucent flesh. Her scream jolted me from my haze.

Morgan!

My roommate's disembodied head tumbled into my lap. "Gene, pull the Thread before before we all get unmade!"

My fingers tightened around that silver cord even as the sky filled with an uncountable number of Death Shrouds.

Morgan tore at the Umbraling. "Now!"

I thought about Morgan's dorm room.

"Gene," Ed said, his mouth muffled against my legs.

I thought about the Seal of Ariadne painted on that cold concrete.

"Do it!" Morgan screamed.

Most of all, though, I thought about my roommate, his missing body and the ambulance it had left in.

I just want to go home.

29

GETTING AHEAD

"Gene..." Morgan's voice was raw and tired.

"Ugh." I blinked my eyes in the dim light of her room. "What the hell happened?"

"You didn't listen to me. That's what happened." Morgan yanked her hands out of mine and pushed herself up.

"I didn't have a choice. Ed was—"

"Your roommate was as good as dead—in fact, I'd argue he still is. His head is somewhere in the Gloom, while the rest of his body is barely hanging on in the ER."

"Uh, actually, I'm right here."

My heart skipped a beat as the floating head of Ed Lovely appeared above us. It bobbed along gently like a half-spent party balloon running low on helium.

"Any chance one of you could get me down?"

"Ed, where the hell is your cord?" Morgan asked, reaching for Ariadne's Thread but finding it missing.

The Demon Hunter's head whooshed up to bump against the popcorn ceiling. "Ouch!"

Morgan frowned and climbed out of the seal. "Gene, give me a hand." She pulled books off her shelf and handed them to me.

"But his cord…"

My roommate's face turned away from the spiky ceiling. "Is gone, and that's going to be a problem. What were you two doing in the Gloom? Heck, what was I doing in the Gloom?"

"You don't remember?" Morgan asked, looking up from the book in her hands."

Ed rolled across the lumpy ceiling. Small pieces of dust and grit lodged themselves in his translucent face. "I… No. I don't remember. Have I been here before?"

"Ed?"

My roommate smiled. "Howdy, partner. Have we met?"

"Morgan, what's happening to him?"

My girlfriend shoved another book in my hands. "He's disintegrating, Gene. If you want to save him we have to hurry."

My roommate furrowed his brows while the rest of his head rolled back and forth across the speckled ceiling. "Hey, you two, does the 'Plycene Construct' mean anything to you?"

"Morgan?"

My girlfriend shook her head. "No, he's missing more than eighty percent of his soul. He wouldn't get past the first step."

"Oh, right," Ed's eyes traced the path where the rest of his body should have been. "Would someone please tell me where the rest of my soul went?"

"You don't remember that either?"

My roommate shook his head which sent him bouncing toward the corner.

I closed my eyes to blot out the spectacle. "It was—"

Morgan interrupted me before I could finish. "It's not important. What is important, is finding a way to get you back to your body before you disintegrate—or something worse…"

"There's something worse?" I asked.

Morgan ignored me and continued to flip through her books.

"You know, you'd think a guy could remember how he lost

his body," Ed said, pursing his lips. "I mean, it's not something you just misplace on the street corner."

"Your body is at the hospital."

"What?!" My roommate's voice jumped two octaves and a couple dozen decibels. "What the hell is it doing at the hospital?"

"Your body is in the hospital because you hit the curb wrong and ended up in the street," I said, flipping through one of Morgan's books.

"I did? That doesn't sound like me."

I nodded. "You were arguing with Porter at the time."

My roommate smirked. "*That* sounds like me. Wait, who's Porter?"

"Are you two finished?" Morgan tossed a book to the side to open another one.

Ed's eyes opened wide. "Gorbel Conjecture! Wait, what is that?"

Morgan again shook her head, this time following it up with rapid hand movements. "You don't have enough soul for the Gorbel."

"Are you sure?" I asked, handing the book back to Morgan.

"I'm certain." She slammed the volume down on her shelf. "We can't use the Plycene, or the Gorbel, and while I'm at it, Meejinks and the Twenty-Nine Tongues is off limits too."

The library...

"What about the library?" I asked, trying hard not to think back to dark brick building nestled deep the heart of the Gloom.

Morgan smiled. "You're right! There are secrets in there far beyond what either you or I are aware of."

"Hey, you guys... something's happening—" Ed's voice faltered as his face contorted in pain.

"What's wrong with him?"

Morgan grabbed two markers off her desk and tossed one to me. "Remember the Jacobean Prefect?"

"Sort of…"

"Then get to work!"

Morgan pointed me toward a bare patch of concrete away from the Seal of Ariadne, and together we went to work covering the floor with the complex sigil. I traced the lines, cutting and intersecting each junction of Jacobean's infuriating prefect, while Morgan completed the swirling whorls and spirals.

"Closer, they need to be tighter," Morgan said, pointing to the edges of the last set of lines. "Hurry, Gene."

Above us Ed Lovely continued to gurgle. It was as if he were choking on his own blood, except he had no blood to choke on. "What's happening to him?"

"His soul is disintegrating."

Shit.

I traced the lines faster, cutting edges and smearing corners. "Hold on, Ed. I'm coming."

Morgan worked her way around the circle, her own marker matching mine stroke for stroke.

Ed's gurgles slowed, and I looked up to find him fading from view altogether. "Morgan!"

"I see it, keep tracing!"

The Jacobean Prefect slowly came into view beneath us while, hovering above us, Ed Lovely fought to hold on to what remained of his soul.

"It's done," Morgan said and tossed aside her marker. "Time for you to light it up, Gene."

"What?"

Morgan grabbed my hand and slammed it down in the center of the circle. "Give it some juice before you lose your friend all together."

I let the Magick course through my body, willing it into the complex circle. The Dead Man's Tongue tingled against my finger. Thanks to the newfound focus, my mind traced the lines and expanded at the intersections, drifting through the sigil until it reached the edges. I'd become one with the Jacobean Prefect, and for the first time I understood it.

Pop!

The Magick circle snapped to life, and like a magnet sucking up iron filings, it drew Ed Lovely's head into the center.

"Amazing," Morgan said, her words soft yet sultry. "You have grown so much, Gene. See what a little focus can do?"

What was left of my roommate floated precariously in the circle, held aloft by my Magick and Jacobean's nigh-insane calculations.

"Ed?"

Morgan shook her head and stood. "He can't hear you. He's in a form of stasis now; that should buy us enough time to reach the library and find what we need to put him back together."

"We're going to project ourselves into the Gloom again," I asked, taking a wary look at the Seal of Ariadne.

"No," Morgan said, brushing the dust from her knees. "There will be no more projecting."

"So how do we—"

Morgan pulled aside the curtain that served as her closet door and removed a thick leather jacket from the rack. Rich cowhide shone in the light, but there was something else twinkling among the jet-black fabric.

Sigils?

Morgan held the jacket up, and sure enough, thousands of tiny sigils sparkled like motes of glitter. Painstakingly designed, each one had to have represented hours of work. The jacket itself was a masterwork of Magick from cuffs to collar.

"What is it?"

Morgan gently placed the warm leather in my hands. "It's how you're going to survive inside the Gloom."

"Inside?"

Morgan nodded, then retrieved a smaller jacket of her own. "I've been working on these for a while, Gene. Ever since the night we met—I knew you'd be the one."

I examined the complex sigils, stunned at their detailed design. "The one?"

"Yes, Gene. The one to see me past the guardians. The only one strong enough to take us all the way."

"All the way to where?"

Morgan slipped her arms into the sleeves of her jacket then shook out her hair. "To the heart of the library."

"What if I don't wan—"

"Then your friend will die a terrible and painful death. The Jacobean Prefect can't last forever. His soul will eventually disintegrate. Piece by piece, Ed will fall away until, in the end, there is nothing left but the echo of his torment to fill the Gloom's void."

"Morgan..."

She took my jacket and helped me pull my suddenly tired arms through the sleeves. Even though the coat was warm, an icy-cold wave of fear tingled my spine.

"Shh, Gene. Let the Magick work."

I gave in and let Morgan's sigils weave her complex power around me. The symbols pulled at my skin, tingling my hairs and generally making me feel more than a little uncomfortable.

"Come on," she said, leaving Ed's head to float gently, trapped inside the Jacobean Prefect. "Now's our time."

My poor roommate's face hung there, frozen in a mask of pain and frustration, and for a moment I wondered if my own head would be next.

30

WELCOME TO THE GLOOM

*M*organ rifled through a number of items from her room, then stuffed them in a small bag before yanking my arm out the door. We found the accident scene clearing outside. Ed's banged-up bike had been moved over by the trees, and the sight of it was more than a little unsettling. I hadn't had have a chance to take back those things I'd said, and now I wasn't sure I ever would.

I'm sorry, Ed.

Morgan grabbed my hand. "We'll do it, Gene. We'll get him back, but we can't stop now." She dragged me past the scored pavement and down one of the narrow alleys between the buildings. The library loomed above the distant tree tops, quiet, but no doubt waiting like a hungry predator.

"Stop." I pulled my hand back.

"What is it? You're wasting time, Gene, time Ed doesn't have."

"This is all happening too fast," I said, taking a moment to hold my head and lean against the wall.

"I know you took a Yaga Doll at close range, and even though that didn't seem to faze you, it had to have taken a toll." Morgan's voice softened. "But your friend is counting on us."

"I don't know."

"Gene," Morgan placed a hand on my shoulder, her eyes sparkling beneath the wide moon. "Ed is in bad shape, and I can tell you for certain that if we don't go to the library right now…"

"What?"

Morgan hesitated as if choosing her words carefully. "Then there is no chance he'll make it."

The library…

The dark brick building peeked out from behind passing clouds.

It was watching and waiting.

"It's been about the library all along, hasn't it."

"Excuse me?" Morgan pulled her hand back sharply.

"All of this. The Magick, the secrets, the books," I held up my finger, "even this ring. Every single step in this process has just been you getting what you wanted: power."

Morgan glared at me, holding up her own Dead Man's Tongue; the dark steel caught what little light there was in the narrow alley. "Has your Magick improved?"

"That's not—"

"It is a simple question, Eugene Law. Are you a better Magician today than you were yesterday?"

My mind drifted back to Jacobean Prefect, the last time I'd called upon my Magick, and the smooth control with which I'd directed it.

"Yes," I said, my voice nearly inaudible.

"I'm sorry, I can't hear you?" Morgan placed a hand on her ear. "Would you mind repeating that?"

"Yes, all right? Are you happy? Yes, I am a better Magician because of you."

Morgan sighed, cupping my cheeks in her hands. "And that's

all I've ever really wanted to hear. You mean the world to me, Eugene Law, the absolute world."

"This is dangerous, isn't it?"

Morgan nodded, her eyes locked with mine. "It is immensely dangerous, but I know you can do it. I know because I've seen what you are capable of."

"You mean like getting stuck in a Withering?"

Morgan's eyes narrowed. "You have come a long way in a short time, Gene." She let go of my face and held up my hand, the Dead Man's Tongue wrapped around my finger. "You're a focusing machine now. The Magick obeys your commands, not the other way around."

I hesitated, leaning against the narrow alley's brick wall while I got lost in thought. Visions of my roommate's head twisted in my own.

I'm sorry, Ed.

I shook away those unpleasant thoughts. Morgan was right —Ed wouldn't survive without our help, without my help. The library's glowing orange windows shone through the distant trees like the eyes of hungry predator. I couldn't help but glare back at them.

I'm not afraid.

"Well, Gene? What's it going to be?" Morgan held out her hand.

"You promise we can save him?"

She shook her head. "No."

"But—"

"But—" Morgan grabbed my hand and pulled me close—"I will promise you that the only chance we have is beyond those walls. Isn't that better than doing nothing?"

"It is. Let's do this."

My girlfriend smiled, but this time it was her eyes and not the library that held a predatory hue.

~

"Stop!" Morgan hissed just before we reached the wide sidewalk that surrounded the plaza. There were no students out this evening, at least none that we could see. The library's ominous brick crested above the dense oak trees that covered the field outside. I was leery of those oak trees, and for good reason. I had no interest in becoming one of them any time soon.

"We cannot cross the sidewalk before we enter the Gloom. We'd be detected immediately. Come on," Morgan said, pulling me down a side street just past the plaza.

"Where are we going?"

Morgan gestured for me to keep my voice down. "I've been walking through this for weeks."

"Weeks?"

She nodded. "Just about every night at ten-thirty. Now, there's a weak spot on the far side. It's not much, but the lock is soft there, and that entrance isn't heavily guarded."

Ten-thirty...

My mind brought back visions of the Wild Magick in the accounting building what felt like a lifetime ago. "What do you mean weak spot?"

"It takes more Magick than I can muster to even begin to break into the library. In fact, every time I've tried there's been a burst of Wild Magick blowback—and Shades, lots of Shades."

"Shades?" My stomach churned.

"Yes, but you've already handled that for us. Now come on." Morgan dragged me down the side street, past park benches and empty bike racks before stopping in front of a rusted metal door around the far side of the building. The door sat at the top of a small set of steps that lay adjacent to the narrow loading dock. The steep-pitched concrete driveway was empty this evening, along with the small garage door above it.

I had only placed a foot on the driveway before Morgan yanked me back. "Not yet. Zip up your jacket."

I fumbled with the zipper; my hands shaking in the cool evening.

Morgan did not have the same problem.

"This is a Sojourner's Jacket, Gene. I spent countless hours making it. Each sigil has been chosen for a reason, and together they form a web of Magick that will keep your heart beating and your brain working even in the dark of the Gloom," Morgan said, pulling my zipper tight. "Whatever you do, do not take the jacket off until we're out. Without it you'd have only minutes in the infernal twilight."

I willed my hands to stop shaking. "Okay."

Morgan let go of the zipper and held my fingers tight. "We are so close—so very close—to completing something I've only ever dreamed about."

"And saving Ed."

"Yes," Morgan said, appearing to catch herself. "And saving Ed. I'm all but certain what we need to save him exists inside."

I took a deep breath and exhaled.

For Ed.

"I'm ready."

Morgan smiled and kissed me on the cheek. Her normally fiery lips felt strangely cold against my skin. "Let's do this." She fished a small piece of green chalk from her bag. It was the same chalk we'd used to draw The Velcurses Conundrum.

I let Morgan guide me to an open space on the pale concrete. "What are we doing?"

"Ten Spins' Bent Key, Gene."

"Wait. Didn't Ed warn us about his Magick?"

Morgan crouched down and set to work inscribing a complex symbol along the pavement beneath us. Swirling lines crisscrossed and intersected within that circle. Lines within lines and each one fighting for control. Chaos seethed within the seal, barely controlled and pushing at the edges. Morgan continued to draw, the chalk becoming an extension of her fingers and the ticking mind that drove it. The sigil grew until it encompassed both of us within its confining circle.

Morgan stepped outside of the design and paced like a proctor on exam day. Her eyes never wavered from the violent pattern. "Perfection."

She snapped a hair band off her wrist and tucked up her hair into a tight ponytail. "Are you ready?"

Not in the slightest.

"Yes," I said, tamping down on my own concerns.

Morgan grabbed my hand and guided me into the complex sigil. "Push your Magick into the seal, Gene."

I reached for the power boiling inside me and directed it down into the complex swirls of Ten Spins' Bent Key. I sent it into the swirling lines and through the complex intersections, guiding it in a way that would never have been possible before Morgan.

"It's going to be a little cold." She checked her zipper and then mine. "Just be ready for it."

I nodded, shoving my other hand in my pocket.

The chaotic power of the Bent Key hit me like a spring-loaded gut punch. Morgan's last words took the wind out of my sails before they scrambled into an indecipherable jumble of static and white noise.

"Welcome to the Gloom, Eugene Law."

31

SOOT AND ASH

*T*he cold hit me first. It was an icy slap that clawed at the air in my lungs. I opened my eyes, unaware that I'd closed them, only to find myself alone beneath the library's darkened walls. Soot and ash fell like snow around me, kicked up by a gentle breeze and spun into tiny eddies. The glowing orange porthole-like windows were now dark, an inky blackness that lay like hole punches in a curtain of scorched brick.

Cold.

"Morgan?" I croaked, my voice rough and muted in the shadowy twilight of the Gloom.

No response—Ten Spins' Bent Key was empty except for me.

The seal's complex and violent lines remained muted, plain, and no longer glowing. Still, a quiet power waited beneath them.

"Morgan?"

My breath vanished in the chilling mist and the icy air worked my lungs like a bellows. Morgan had been right, it was like standing in a freezer. I pulled the jacket's zipper up tighter and flexed my fingers a few times inside the coat's lined pockets, trying to force some feeling back into them. Stagnant and dense, the air in the Gloom was like breathing through a straw, and I had to suppress the sudden urge to panic.

The Bent Key got us in, but what about getting us out?

I pushed that thought out of my head and sucked up what amounted to a deep breath in the chilling twilight.

Focus, Gene. Where the hell is Morgan?

Soft ash fell from an overcast sky. It clumped in powdery piles at my feet. I carefully brushed them aside, making certain not to not smudge the masterwork sigil in the process.

"Morgan?" My muffled voice bunched up again—it was almost as if I were talking through a snorkel, unable to project my words, and what volume I did have didn't make it very far.

You're going to have to leave the sigil, Gene.

I picked up my foot, then put it back down again.

In order to leave the sigil you have to take your foot and step outside *of said sigil.*

I picked up my foot again, but before I could put it back down, the library's side door opened slightly, creaking in the chilled air.

"Morgan?"

Only darkness lay beyond that door—a thin sliver of inky blackness against the rusted steel.

"Morgan, is that you?"

Creak...

The door opened farther, gently swinging on unhappy hinges.

I took a cautious step forward, careful to keep my feet inside the lines of Ten Spins' Bent Key, though I wasn't entirely sure what good that would do me.

Something shifted beyond the door. "Morgan, is that you?"

Bang!

A hailstorm of bat-like creatures exploded from the narrow gap. Not thinking, I jumped out of the Bent Key and landed in a nearby pile of ash, the soft soot cushioning my fall.

Snake bodies carried on thin black wings shot over me and up into the eternal half-light of the Gloom. They spun like a startled flock before vanishing into the overcast sky. I laid motionless in the soot and took a few more chilling breaths, letting the stragglers fade away before sitting up.

"Gene?"

"Morgan!"

My girlfriend's head stuck out from the dark of the library, still very much attached to her body.

"Morgan, how did you get—"

"Transmission error. You arrived," she looked at her watch, "twenty minutes after me."

"How did that—"

"I didn't adjust for your weight," Morgan said, leaning out from the door's edge to check the surrounding area. "Too many beers with Ed. Come on, we have a long way to go."

I pushed myself up, but I hadn't gone a few feet before Morgan's sharp voice stopped me cold.

"Do not move."

I froze—my hands and arms locked in position and my feet still deep in the piling ash.

"I need you to stay very still," Morgan said, slowly creeping out of the library's dark. "Do not move a muscle."

My butt cheeks reflexively clenched together. I hoped that didn't count.

"What is it, Morgan?" I asked through gritted teeth.

She crept closer, her hands out and ready. "I think it's best if I don't tell you."

By now my heart rate was steadily climbing, and in the stark cold of the Gloom I could feel the blood pulling away from my extremities.

"Is it on my—"

"It's on your back, Gene. Just above your shoulder."

I started to turn my head.

"Stop! What did I say about moving?"

Gah!

Morgan's eyes followed something on my shoulder, but I didn't dare look.

"It's moving toward your neck," she said, inching closer. "It's going to be cold, very, very cold. Do not move."

"Morgan," I hissed. "Just get rid of it!"

"Remember when we talked about bottom feeders?" Morgan asked, now only a few feet away.

"Yes..."

"You have one on your neck."

My mind immediately went to the Umbraling with its spider-like legs. I imagined the creature poised to strike, its fangs held high and ready to pierce my soft flesh.

Morgan must have been reading my mind. "Not an Umbraling. Which is a shame, because that would have been easier."

"Easier?!"

"Yes, they aren't nearly as small and don't move quite so fast."

"Morgan..."

"You're moving, Gene. Stop."

She was right. In my frustration I'd tilted my head, and now whatever had developed an interest in my neck was more than happy to start to exploring the back of my head.

"We just need to stop it before it reaches your ear."

"My ear?"

My stomach churned at the thought of anything from the Gloom reaching my ear. Finding an earwig in your bed as a kid can leave a powerful and lasting impression.

"Yes, your ear."

My patience had just about run thin, and coupled with the intense cold of the Gloom I wasn't sure how much longer I'd be able to remain in one place.

"Can you hurry, please?"

"I'm going to count to three," Morgan said, her eyes never wavering from my head. "And when I reach three, you are going to look that way." She pointed off to the side. "One."

"Wait!"

"What?" Morgan asked, her hands on her hips.

"On three, or after three?" I said, willing my neck to remain as still as possible.

"Huh?"

"You know. Is it like one, two, three, and we go, or one, two, three, and we go on the word three."

A sharp spike of bone-chilling cold hit my cheek.

"Three!" Morgan shouted, and I turned my head to the side as quickly as I could.

Her hand snapped out like the crack of a whip and ripped off whatever was crawling along my face. She threw it to the ground, where it landed with a hard, wet slap.

The slug-like thing hissed and spit, twitching in the soot and picking up a light dusting of ash in the process.

"What the hell?"

Morgan rammed her heel down on the beast, crushing it into the broken pavement like day old fish.

"Thanks," I said, rubbing the still burning side of my face. "Any idea what that was?"

"None, but it's not the first one I've run into since I got here. Except when I ran into mine I didn't have anyone to help me," Morgan said, pointing to a burn mark on her own neck.

"Did you find anything to help Ed?"

Morgan shook her head. "No, it's a maze inside, but there are two of us now."

"You aren't suggesting we split up, are you?"

Morgan smiled. "No. You wouldn't last ten minutes."

She took my hand and led me to the door. The yawning darkness on the other side was stifling and oppressive. It was impossible to see beyond the narrow frame of the door, and I thought for sure I heard something clicking in the distance.

"Umbralings?"

Morgan nodded. "But they're the least of our worries, Gene."

Crack!

Something rustled in the mist-shrouded oaks behind us. Alien and large, it snapped branches and sent leaves falling to the ground in dense clumps.

"Come on," Morgan said, returning to the dark of the library and beckoning me to follow.

I hesitated, my feet once again not quite sure they wanted to move.

Morgan vanished in the darkness. The sound of her feet the only indicator of her presence.

The oak tree shuddered again. A second something joined the first, and their combined screeches set my heart on overdrive. "Wait for me."

I turned back briefly to get one last look at Ten Spins' Bent Key. The faint chalk had all but faded beneath a blanket of soot and ash. I may not have been very keen on Ten Spins or his Magick, but in that moment I hoped to God I saw that one again.

UNDER THE TABLE AND FEELING

We'd had a garage growing up.

It would have been a perfect place to keep cars out of the elements; except, we hadn't kept cars in there— we couldn't. The Law family garage collected junk, and it, along with my parents, had been extremely good at it.

The few times I'd had to go in there and search for something I'd always had to stumble around feeling for the light bulb string. Our garage had no windows, and that impenetrable dark was a minefield of toe-stubbing goodness without a cheap bulb to guide the way.

The Gloom-version of the library wasn't much different than my childhood garage, except that in here the things that could stub your toe preferred eating it instead.

"Morgan, I can't see anything."

There was a faint sigh followed by the subtle whirring of Morgan's Magick. "Lux," she whispered, unlocking the secrets woven into my jacket and hers. The small stitched sigils across our arms and chest glowed in tandem.

"Thanks." I held up my sleeve and wondered just how long it would take me to master something that detailed.

Too long.

The dim glimmer of the Sojourner's sigils lit up both Morgan's face and the finger placed against her lips. Satisfied she had my attention, she pointed at the ceiling. The jacket's light didn't extend far, but it was able to reach the bulbous bodies of dozens of Umbralings clinging to the high ceiling. The chitinous, spider-like creatures crawled along thick black webbing, slipping in and out of narrow holes, their feelers occasionally out and testing the air. Spindly legs clicked against each other with each pass above our heads. Even though they were out of reach, I couldn't help but duck down.

Handling the Umbraling-induced fear far better than me, Morgan guided us past broken chairs and overturned tables, many of which I remembered from their real-world counterparts the few times I'd been inside in the actual library. Tapping legs and the dull scrape of feelers rubbing together consumed my thoughts—so I wasn't ready for Morgan's sudden stop.

Bump!

"Hey," I whispered, before clamping a hand over my mouth.

A lone Umbraling twisted in the air in front of us, its pupilless eyes shining in the faint glow of Morgan's Sojourner Jacket. The creature's feelers slid over one another like kitchen knives, brushing at the soft ash that coated them. I choked back at the bile rising up in my throat. Umbraling fangs slid out from a hidden place within its jaws, and I immediately reached for my Magick.

Morgan's hand shot out and grabbed my sleeve, and I froze. More Umbralings descended on thin, web-like strands around us. The bulbous creatures had figured out something was up and come to investigate.

Morgan ran two fingers down her jacket sleeve, sending the sigil's faint glow to nearly nothing.

Thump!

My own jacket still held enough light to see with, though I

wasn't sure I wanted to. The table behind us now held an equally large and impressive Umbraling. These weren't the same as the tiny versions that I'd seen in the dorm; these Umbralings must have come from a better feeding ground, they were large, aggressive, and fearless.

Thump! Thump! Thump!

More Umbralings rappelled down on thin strands of black webbing. The retriever-sized creatures landed on tables and knocked over chairs.

"Morg—"

She yanked my sleeve and pulled me under the closest table. Her sudden movement kicked off a surge of activity. The Umbralings must have sensed blood in the water and sprang into action.

Click, click, click.

The sounds of spindly legs on the hard concrete set my stomach churning. Magick boiled up in my chest and prepared for a massive burst. Morgan shook her head and dimmed the luminosity of my jacket as well, leaving us in the faint halo of a terrifying half-light that didn't extend past the four legs of the tiny table.

"What do I—"

Again Morgan glared at me and I bit my tongue.

White and hazy eyes appeared along the table's edge like a row of dusty ping-pong balls. Morgan unzipped her jacket halfway and it was my turn to glare, and I did as much while grabbing her hand.

You said not to unzip the jacket!

Morgan gently pushed me away and reached inside the folds of her Sojourner's Coat, coming back with a small plastic squeeze bottle of what looked like ketchup.

What the hell are you doing? You better not be seasoning us!

Umbraling legs kneaded the shadowy dark at the farthest reaches of our light. Morgan zipped her jacket up slowly, and each soft pop of the zipper set my already exhausted nerves on edge.

Shrick...

Hairy feelers traced the burned underside of our table, sliding along the jagged wood and giving us an eye full of the monster's impressive fangs.

Morgan started to pop the cap, but stopped, her eyes never wavering from the spidery creature. A second set of fangs joined the first as another spidery Gloom-beast crawled beneath our makeshift shelter.

Morgan!

Instead of popping the loud bottle top, my girlfriend twisted the lid off slowly, then placed it on the ground.

What is she doing?

More legs peeked beneath the table's edge like hairy fingers. They slid down the bent legs and tickled at the air around Morgan's head.

Whatever you're doing, you better do it now!

My Magick screamed out to be used. It bubbled and boiled in my chest, fighting to escape, and it took all I had to clamp down on it.

Spindly arms danced above Morgan's face. The fangs beneath them quivered in the dim glow of the Sojourner's Jacket —mere inches separated my girlfriend from those terrifying teeth.

Come on!

I reached for my Magick again, this time sure I was going to unleash hell on the creatures, no matter what Morgan wanted. She'd thank me later when she didn't have eight inches of fangs embedded in her cheek, but before I could release even a drop of that cosmic power, Morgan went to work. Like a bomb squad professional, she upturned the small plastic bottle and dumped its contents in thick globs into her palm.

Umbraling's slowed, softly probing the shadows and reaching for her face.

This is it, Gene. Sink or swim... What are you waiting for? Do it!

Before I could unload what would have been a barely controlled burst of Magick, Morgan applied the ichorous jelly on her face, smearing it around like some foul-smelling night mask. She shoved the bottle into my hand moments before the Umbraling feelers brushed across her smothered skin. Hairy, segmented fingers picked up the gel and immediately retracted, rubbing themselves together as if struggling to understand the implications of just what it was it had found.

I followed suit, dumping when remained of the bottle into my hand as quietly as I could, then slapping it against my face. The revolting slime oozed over my skin and smelled of rotting meat, but I didn't dare hesitate.

Please work, please work...

Umbraling arms traced their way across my jacket, stopping briefly to fiddle with the zipper line above my chest. It took all I could to stay still. I had only half my face covered, but to move now risked discovery.

After touching the gel, those hairy fingers pulled back slowly, dragging across the soft leather and catching at the sigils woven into the fabric. Magick surged in my chest; the fight-or-flight reflex was kicking into high gear, and coupled with my shaky hands I didn't know how much longer I could hold it back.

Morgan's eyes shone in the dark.

Do not move!

The Umbraling testing Morgan backed away from her face slowly, then turned its attention to me. I wanted to spread more of her rotten meat sauce of my skin, but to do so now would most assuredly have been suicide. I could only lay there while the Gloom beasts worked their legs over my exposed body.

I didn't dare close my eyes, but I also didn't know how much longer I could stare at those sightless orbs before I lost it myself.

The second set of narrow arms gently drifted through the sheen of slime I'd hastily applied to my cheeks. The creature paused briefly, then retracted its fangs in favor of rubbing those feelers together.

My heart pounded in my chest, and the urge to both retch and lash out came in equal measure. Morgan's eyes pleaded with me to remain still. Deep breaths were off the table, so I settled for shallow puffs of air, hoping they wouldn't be enough to get the Umbraling's attention.

The larger of the two creatures tapped legs with the other, and there appeared to be an exchange of information—fangs retracted and I let out a thin sigh of relief.

The Umbralings backed slowly out from under the table, their narrow legs clicking on the hard concrete.

We did it.

Morgan's eyes shared my excitement—at least right until the plastic bottle slipped out of my fingers and clattered on the hard concrete.

Crap.

DEAD MAN'S TONGUE

*P*ale white eyes, too many to count, emerged from the darkness. Hungry fangs quivered in the dim light of the Sojourner's Jacket.

"Gene, don't—"

I lost Morgan's words in the surge of Magick. Held back for too long, the cosmic power trapped in my chest overflowed its damns with the force of a crushing wave. Her voice faded beneath the crashing wave—set free and without limits—the unstoppable power tore apart Umbralings by the dozens, their bodies bursting like water balloons in the tumult of unbridled Magick.

Snap!

The zipper on my Sojourner's Jacket popped. Unable to withstand the torrent of destructive energy, the sides flapped wildly.

"Stop, Gene," Morgan cried, grabbing my wrist. "You've got to stop!"

She was right, I needed to stop, but I didn't know how. I'd held the Magick down for so long that the rush of adrenaline had set it on overdrive. It had a will of its own and was more than happy to do what it pleased. I grabbed my lapels and tried to squeeze the jacket shut, hoping to hold back the flow of a power no longer interested in listening to me. It didn't work. Magick overturned tables and tossed aside chairs. It raced up the distant walls and crushed the bodies of Umbralings by the dozens.

"Stop, Gene!" Morgan shouted again, but I was no closer to getting a handle on that firehose than I had been only moments before. The room was awash in the uncontrollable fire of Wild Magick, and that power wanted more.

"I can't!"

Empty shelves toppled over, crashed to the ground, and filled the air with great clouds of soot and ash. Morgan tried to pull my jacket shut, but the power was too much for her. It singed her fingers and forced her to yank them back before she lost them.

Strange cries echoed in the distance, and Morgan's face told me what I didn't want to hear.

We're about to have company.

More Umbralings exploded against the ceiling, sending a light mist of Gloom-beast gore raining down on us.

"If you don't stop, Ed won't survive the night!"

I wanted to listen to her. I wanted to rein my power in. I wanted it under the kind of control Morgan had, but I didn't have her precision—my power directed me.

"I'm trying!"

Morgan grabbed her Dead Man's Tongue, and while it was hard to feel above the catastrophe swirling around me, her Magick was doing something. It was subtle at first, but in no time the sharp sting of my own ring became my overwhelming thought. The Dead Man's Tongue on my finger tingled, then burned, quickly becoming hot enough for me to claw at it. The power in my chest ebbed, the infernal ring siphoning away more than my attention.

It took my Magick.

The flow of cosmic energy shuddered to a halt, lost to the muted steel of the Dead Man's Tongue and the deceptive subtly of Morgan's Magick. I pulled the two flaps of my jacket together, hoping the lone button at the top and the not completely-detached-zipper would be enough to keep me alive in the Gloom.

Morgan clutched at her ring. It glowed with a brilliant orange sparkle.

"Are you okay?" I asked, not sure if I was, but worried about Morgan and her ring. I contemplated collapsing on the ash-covered floor, but then remembered the slug-like thing and thought better of it.

Morgan nodded and took a few shallow breaths in the stirred-up air. "You walk around with this much power?" The words had barely escaped her lips before she clutched at the ring again.

"What do you mean?"

Morgan got to her feet and dragged me up with her. "That was no big deal for you wasn't it?"

I shrugged my shoulders, not exactly sure what the right answer was. "I guess."

Morgan shook her hand like she'd touched a live-wire or accidentally placed her fingers on a hot stove. "I underestimated you, Gene."

Thwump!

A dead and barely recognizable Umbraling crashed onto an upturned table near us—the Gloom beast's melted eyes startled me far more than I cared to admit.

"If we'd had the element of surprise," Morgan said, her own eyes on the ceiling, "we've lost it for certain."

As if to confirm her suspicions, a new and distinctly frightening cry echoed from one of the floors above us.

"What was that?" I asked, equally concerned with keeping the intense cold out of my Sojourner's Jacket.

"I don't plan to hang around and find out." Morgan pointed to a narrow set of spiral stairs in the corner of the room. "Come on."

I followed her to the stairs, carefully stepping around the still-smoldering bodies of ashen Umbralings. "What was that you had me rub on my face?"

"Dead Umbraling," she said, grabbing the railing and taking the steps two at a time.

"How did you get that?"

Morgan didn't answer me, but judging by her relative comfort walking and talking in the dark heart of the library it wasn't hard to speculate.

She's been in here before.

WE REACHED the top of the stairs and stepped off the narrow metal landing into a literal maze of tall shelves. Morgan brought the glow of her jacket up a few notches, then turned to do the same to mine.

"Thanks," I said, my fingers tugging on the suddenly stubborn ring. "Why can't I take this off?"

Morgan didn't look at me, instead, she focused all her attention on the rows of shelves just beyond the dim halo of the jacket's light. "I've activated it—it's for your own good," she said, counting off the rows with her fingers.

"Activated?"

"That burst of Wild Magick could have easily gotten us killed. Magick doesn't work the same in the library. Think of it like this, you know how they say don't smoke a cigarette while filling your gas tank?"

I nodded, still absently fingering the steel ring.

"Well, this is worse. That's why your outburst was so hard to control—the library makes Magick do strange things. That's why the Sojourner's Jacket is so important. These sigils do more than act like a nightlight."

"You've done this before, haven't you."

Morgan's eyes sparkled in the faint light, but again she didn't answer my question. She turned her attention back to the rows of ash-covered books. "This is the Floor of Unresolved Fears," she said, taking a single step off the metal landing and into the wide room.

"You didn't answer my question."

"And I'm not going to. I'm going to keep you alive. This is an easy place to get lost, and once you do, it's next to impossible to get back out again."

As if to illustrate her point, Morgan directed my attention to what appeared to be a person-shaped lump halfway down one of the rows.

"What happened to them?"

Morgan didn't answer me.

"Morgan?"

My girlfriend held up a hand. "I need to confirm something. Do not move."

I stayed on the platform, listening for the phantom click of Umbraling legs echo in the distant halls as Morgan counted off the rows one at a time.

"Okay, it's right—" She stopped abruptly as she appeared to catch sight of something farther down one of the narrow rows.

"What is it?"

She stepped into the row and disappeared from sight. Her hard soles clacked on the concrete for a few seconds, then stopped.

I waited on the landing, still listening to my own heartbeat. It was after what felt like a few minutes of contemplation that I started to wonder what had happened to her.

"Morgan?"

No answer.

I cautiously stepped off the landing, my shoes all but silent on the soot-covered ground.

"Morgan?"

I took a few more cautious steps, turning back to the landing frequently to make sure it was still there.

"Morgan?"

Still no answer. In fact, my only companion appeared to be the rabid pounding in my own chest. I reached the opening of the row and turned back again, still comforted to find the landing exactly where I'd left it.

"Morgan?"

The narrow row of shelves seemed to expand into infinity, while an unceasing row of books stacked into the darkness above me. In fact, it wasn't what I saw that concerned me; rather, it was what I didn't see that set my blood pressure pumping.

There was no Morgan.

STARING INTO THE VOID

I took a few tentative steps toward the narrow aisle, then stopped, and quickly returned to the relative safety of the landing.

The spindly click of Umbraling legs echoed in the stairwell below. The sound confirmed what I'd already expected—there would be more coming.

No doubt agitated and hungry.

I fiddled with the Sojourner's Jacket. Whatever Morgan had done to make the sigils glow, I wasn't up to the same task. In fact, my Magick didn't appear up to any task. I reached into that swirling cauldron of power and found it strangely muted. It hadn't vanished completely, but like a mostly empty jug, very little circled gingerly at the bottom.

Is it the ring?

I fingered the Dead Man's Tongue. Its cold steel bit at my finger and still refused let go.

What are you doing?

The dark metal didn't respond.

I tugged on the lapels of my jacket, pulling them closed against the busted zipper. The soul-chilling cold of the Gloom still found a way through. It clawed at my shirt and sent the meager hairs on my chest on full alert.

Where the hell are you, Morgan?

She'd gone out of her way to tell me not to move, but now she was gone, vanished down one of the seemingly endless aisles, and I didn't know what to do.

I thought briefly about retreating down those steps and out to Ten Spins' Bent Key, but if I did I knew Ed would never survive.

She's been here before...

I shook that thought out of my head. I didn't know that for certain. Images of my roommate bubbled up in my mind. Ed's soul had been consumed by a Death Shroud and his body was certain to be clinging to life on some hospital bed. I thought back to the last words we'd had before it happened, words I'd wished I could take back.

You can't let him go out like that.

I stood on the landing and took turns inspecting each of the aisles closest to me. Of the four I could see down, including the one Morgan had disappeared into, only one held anything beyond the stacks of books.

The body... If it even is a body...

It was too far down the aisle to see clearly. It might have been a person slouching against the shelf, and it also might have been just a stack of books creating a near-perfect optical illusion.

I took a few cautious steps away from the landing to the edge of the narrow aisle that held our mystery person.

"Hello?"

My voice echoed uncomfortably between the high shelves.

I got no response.

Crap.

I was stuck.

Either I was going to man up and go down that aisle, or I

was going to stay here indefinitely. The longer I stood there the colder I got. Morgan was right, having my Sojourner's Jacket open wasn't helping me much at all.

It beats freezing to death.

I took a cautious step down the aisle, then stopped and immediately checked the landing behind me.

Still there.

I shook my head. If I had any chance of surviving this or finding whatever it was we needed to save Ed, I had to get it in gear. I pulled my jacket tight and approached the sitting form.

"Hello?"

Again I received no response, but the closer I got it became easier to see why. It was not a stack of books, or some optical illusion. It was a person, or at least what remained of them. Burned beyond recognition, their body was nothing but ash and slowly disintegrating black limbs.

Holy crap.

A scorched head bent uncomfortably to one side, its sightless eye holes staring forever at the ground. There was nothing to be gained from this exercise. Whoever this was, they weren't going to provide me with any solid intel on how to find Morgan or get out of here.

"Well, they won't if you don't ask them."

The sound of a new voice caused me to jump and yelp in equal measure.

It was a voice I'd heard many times before. He'd worked in the cafeteria and had made me breakfast more often than I could recall and rarely, if ever, charged me.

"Willie?"

"You could say that," the line cook said, leaning against the shelves behind me and absently flipping through a book. "You humans make Magick so damn complicated. Jacobean's Prefect?" He held up thick vellum pages. "It's kind of like virgins talking about sex."

"Willie, how are you… what are…"

The older man slammed his book closed and tossed it on the ground behind him. "Right. I knew this day was coming, but I had really hoped it would be when you were older. It's going to be hard enough for you to wrap your head around this as it is."

"I don't—"

Willie waved me off with his hand. "You don't understand. Well, why would you?" He gestured to the shelves around me. "You've been filling your head with monstrously complicated formulas. How on earth could there be room for anything else in there?"

Morgan said this was the Floor of—

I didn't think it was possible, but Willie cut me off mid-thought. "Yeah, yeah. The Floor of Unresolved Fears!" he said, swinging his hands like a first-year drama student. "Humans make everything so complicated."

"So you aren't—"

"An Unresolved Fear? No. I'm not. Listen, maybe I've shown up too early for your underdeveloped brain, but I sort of needed to. You aren't long for this plane of existence if you don't get your stuff together, Eugene Law."

"I don't believe you," I said, taking a step back from whatever it was pretending to be Willie.

My favorite breakfast chef sighed and ran a tired hand over his face. "Would it help if I looked like this?"

Willie's color drained away and his body shrank—arms shortened and his skin puckered up like an overripe fruit. In a few dizzying seconds he'd gone from Willie to David Singer, complete with the preacher's bullhorn.

"Singer?"

The preacher nodded, breaking out into a wolfish grin. "We can do this all night, Gene. But it doesn't matter. Here's what *does* matter. You are only minutes away from ending up like the crispy critter there behind you."

My heart beat faster and the familiar churning in my stomach returned. "How?"

"Good! See, now you've changed tactics. You realize that it doesn't matter who I look like, or what I am. What matters is your survival. I've got a lot riding on you, Eugene Law." David Singer picked at a small stain on his shirt.

"Thanks, I guess."

The hellfire-and-brimstone preacher nodded. "Sure thing. Don't worry, you'll have a chance to pay me back. We'll make sure to keep those scales nice and even."

"What do I do?"

Mr. Singer pointed past me down the infinite row of books. "Well, for starters you don't go that way."

"Why not?"

The middle-aged man pulled a book off the shelf. "Good grief! The Gorbel Conjecture? Now that guy was a complete moron. This won't be missed." David threw the book over my head. It had only just reached the burned corpse when it burst into flames. The pages went up like flash paper and the cover curled up in an invisible heat.

"That's why."

"Shit."

Singer smiled, pushing back the thick glasses that had slid down his nose. "Exactly."

"So I go back," I said, walking toward the cantankerous preacher. He graciously stepped aside to show me an aisle behind him that stretched out to infinity.

"Son of a bitch."

Honk!

Singer pressed a button on the bullhorn as if to point out the obvious, then placed a boney hand on my shoulder. In sharp contrast to the rest of the gloom, his hand was warm and inviting. "Sure is, Gene. I may not like how complex humans make their Magick, but you have to give credit where credit is due.

Velcurses knew how to make a maze. This could have been because he was basically insane—a lot of the great ones were—but not all of them."

"Are you sure?"

David nodded. "You aren't insane, Gene."

"I don't know about that." I carefully stepped out from under the preacher's hand. "I'm talking to a dead person who couldn't possibly be here. If I'm not crazy, then I'd say the bar for insanity might be a little too high."

"I'm here, Gene. Just not in the sense you understand yet. It's going to take more time for you to come around to all this. All of which is why I would have preferred to wait, but I can't have my star pupil going off plan, especially when they show so much promise."

"I can't go back?"

Singer shook his head. "No, I'd recommend against that."

"And I can't go forward?"

"Not unless you want to resemble human charcoal like Samantha there," the preacher said, pointing to the ashen corpse.

"Well then what's left?"

Honk!

David placed the bullhorn down and gently scooped up my hand. I wanted to yank it back, but his fingers were deceptively strong. "How about we take this governor off and find out?"

"Huh?"

Singer placed a single finger on the Dead Man's Tongue. "Time to start being who you were meant to be, Eugene Law, and not who someone else wants you to be. Let Morgan find her own battery."

35

CHAOS

"*M*organ's battery?"

The preacher nodded. "As descriptions go, it's not entirely wrong."

"But she said—"

"Morgan Crowley says a lot of things." Singer held my hand up to his face. "I don't suppose you can take this off?"

I yanked my hand back and tugged at the cold steel. "No."

"That's not surprising. I'm going to take a wild stab and say you agreed to wear it willingly?"

'It'll help you focus, Gene.'

"Yeah."

David Singer scrunched up his face. "Weren't thinking with the right organ, eh? Maybe you should have listened to the sermons?"

Even in the cold of the Gloom I felt my face flush. "I did it—"

"Because you care for her. Right, right, that's all well and good, but Gene, that's Dead Man's Tongue. You'd think you'd at least have looked it up."

I suddenly found myself feeling very uncomfortable.

"Let's see," the skinny man said, pulling pulling books off the shelves. "There's got to be something here... Five Stripes of Ferrius? What a load of crap!" He held the book up for me. "I mean, like he was the first person to think to draw five angled lines at one time. So what?"

"Um, this isn't helping me."

Singer slammed the book shut. "You're right. It's not. I don't think you really want to take that ring off."

"I do!"

"Nope, I get the sense you still believe in Morgan. I think you still care about her—" the hellfire preacher pushed a finger into my chest—"in here."

"I don't know what to think."

The skinny man clapped. "Human ethics and emotions are so amazingly complex—layers within layers."

"Listen, if you aren't going to help me," I said, looking past him and wondering if that nifty flaming book trick had been just that: a trick. Morgan had called this the Floor of Unresolved Fears for a reason. I pushed my way past the dead preacher and walked back to the ashen body.

"Whoa, Gene! Let's not get hasty. Maybe it would help if you had some background. A little context goes a long way."

"What are you—"

I froze. The girl's empty sockets now contained bright blue eyes.

"Give her a minute, Gene," David said, crouching down to brush fallen soot off the girl's face. "It's tough when you've been dead for a year. The poor girl isn't Lazarus, you know."

"A year?" I said.

The corpse coughed, newly restored lungs ejecting wet globs of black on the hard ground.

"Oh yeah, it's been at least a year. Hasn't it, Samantha?"

Bright eyes glared with an anger so intense I took a step back.

The preacher tugged at the girl's ashen face like a grandmother pinching the cheeks of a favorite grandchild. "There you go, sweetheart. You can so do this. I know it hurts like a mother, but you can blame Gene here for that. He's the one that didn't believe me—maybe he'll believe you."

"Screw you..."

"Now, now. We don't need that," David said, squeezing the girl's face tighter. "It's not his fault he fell for Morgan's charms. I seem to recall another sweet young thing falling for the same tricks."

The girl's low growl was almost inhuman.

"Yes, I get it, you don't appreciate coming back from where it was you ended up just to hold a conversation with me of all things. But—and I mean this, Samantha—this is for your own good. It's your chance to do something beneficial for the grand plan. Wouldn't you like that? Wouldn't it feel good to be a little useful with your afterlife?"

The girl coughed again and the ash of her face fell away to reveal gentle porcelain skin. "I... hate you."

"Excellent! Now we're making some real progress. That's what I wanted to hear. How's that pain?"

Samantha's jaws clenched, and I swore I could hear what remained of her molars grinding together. "Unbearable."

My old neighbor nodded. "Well, that's to be expected. I mean, you were scorched beyond recognition by Chaos Magick."

"Chaos Magick?"

"Oh yes, Morgan's been working on unlocking Chaos Magick and summoning Reavers for the last few years. Isn't that right, Samantha?"

The ashen girl nodded, her spine popping like bubble wrap. "Yes."

"Ah ha! See, Gene? I told you Morgan can't be trusted."

Samantha grabbed my hand. Her burned fingers were cold

as ice. "Neither can this thing. Don't listen to what it promises. Whatever you do, do not agree to its help."

"Oh, Samantha," David stood and placed a hand on top of her head, "don't get jealous just because you aren't the favored child anymore."

Samantha didn't let go of my hand—instead, she clung to it tighter. Her bright blue eyes locked on mine. "They're all lying to you. All of them. That's all they are—liars. Morgan doesn't love you and she never will. She doesn't understand love. It's not in her nature. But as bad as Morgan is, this thing is infinitely worse—"

"Now, Samantha…" Singer's boney fingers clamped down on what remained of the girl's head.

Tiny cracks appeared along her skull, but still she didn't stop. "Please! Please promise me you won't accept its help. Promise me you won't become a slave to the V—"

Samantha's head shattered in a burst of soot and ash, and her bright blue eyes tumbled down her broken chest and rolled like marbles across the floor before coming to a stop at my feet.

"Oh my! Will you look at that? The dead can be so flimsy sometimes. It's like one little squeeze and poof, dust again."

Samantha's body crumpled into a loose pile at my feet.

"What did you do?"

The preacher dusted his hands off. "Me? I've only done everything I could to get you out of trouble. Who paid your bills after your parents were gone? Who got you that scholarship? Who kept you from going off the rails? Who made sure you got into college?"

"You? But why? Who are you?"

My old neighbor shook his head. "Everything in due time, Eugene Law, everything in due time. The thing you need to figure out now is what you're going to do about the Chaos Magick swelling up at the end of the aisle."

"What?!"

Singer wasn't lying. The red light of a swirling cloud of Chaos Magick washed over both of us.

"Well, I've done enough interfering for now. I figure you got this, but if you don't, please do be a dear and sit down like Samantha did. Who knows, some future kid might need me to revive you and get some life lessons answered in the process. Do them a favor and at least try to plan out some useful words of wisdom and not all that melodrama Samantha spouted. All right?"

I turned away from the red glow and found David Singer gone.

"Shit."

Chaos Magick twisted and turned like a malevolent cloud, its bright light making it harder to see. I contemplated turning around and running, but then I remembered Morgan's words.

You can get lost in here forever.

There was nothing left to do but stand and fight. I tugged at the ring again, but still the ring refused to let go.

"God damn it, Morgan."

The mist of chaotic Magick swelled and set my hands shaking.

Come on, Gene. You've got to stay focused. You've got Magick. Use it!

I ran through the constructs in my head. Thanks to Morgan I'd learned so many, but in the heat of the moment they'd become a jumble in my mind.

Humans make Magick so complicated.

What did he mean by that?

The Magick reached Samantha's remains, burning them away like yesterday's news.

Whatever you are going to do, you better do it soon...

I reached into the power in my chest. It was still diminished because of the ring, but it would have to be enough.

"Come and get me," I said, my useless fists out in front of me. "I'm not afraid of you."

"Gene!"

Morgan!

My girlfriend's hand shot through one of the shelves and grabbed my raised fist. "Stop, it's not real."

"What's not real?"

Fiery and chaotic Magick licked at the spines of the surrounding books.

"None of it is real. It's me. Stop!"

36

REAL OR IMAGINED

"Gene," Morgan's voice cut above the swirling cloud of chaotic Magick, "you've got to snap out of it."

I pulled back on my hand. "Who's Samantha?"

"I have no idea who you're talking about. You've been speaking gibberish since I found you. Snap out of it before you get us both killed. Without me you can't get out of here, and I'm the only one that knows the way home. Think about Ed—he doesn't have much time."

"But the burned girl… she told me…"

Chaotic Magick licked at the edges of my shoes.

"What girl? Gene, you aren't making any sense. What are you seeing?"

"It's Wild Magick, Morgan. Chaotic and violent. I don't—"

"It's not there!"

I shook my head. "You care to come over here and make that claim?"

"Listen to me," she cried, but I couldn't. I was too busy backing away from the swirling display of powerful Magick.

"Damn it, Gene. If there's Magick there, reach for it."

"What?!"

Morgan's eyes sparkled from the other side of the shelf. "Do it, reach for the Wild Magick!"

"Are you—"

"Do it!"

I extended a hand toward the angry cloud of cosmic energy. My fingers brushed the edge, and I tensed up, half expecting to lose them in the process.

Nothing.

There was no heat, only cold, a cold the Sojourner's Jacket was barely making a dent in fighting.

"I don't..."

Morgan's hand pulled me back against the shelf. "You don't feel anything because it isn't there. You need to stop. This is what the library does to you. This is why it's so important you believe me. You'll never survive in this place without me. Let your Magick go and take my other hand."

Morgan's hand extended through the gap between the dense volumes.

"Take it, Gene!" she shouted.

Chaotic Magick twisted and churned just inches from my face.

I don't know what to believe.

Samatha's ashen face appeared in my mind. "Don't let her consume you, Gene."

The dead girl's words struck a chord, but I hesitated.

Was she even real?

Something flashed in the pile of ash that had once been Samantha's remains.

A ring!

The steel edges of a second, smaller Dead Man's Tongue glinted in the chaotic Magick.

"Gene, take my hand!"

I scooped up the steel ring and shoved it in my pocket. The twisting Magick reached for me, bent and crooked tendrils of violent power clawing at the thick air.

"Gene!"

Morgan's hand flailed to get my attention, while Samantha's harsh words echoed in my head.

'Take her hand, but don't forget her teeth. She doesn't care about you, she only cares about your Magick.'

"Gene!"

I grabbed Morgan's hand and my world went white.

"Where are we?" I asked, blinking my eyes in the dim light.

Morgan smiled and her crooked grin was accompanied by a hug that threatened to squeeze all the air from my lungs. "You made it!"

"Huh?" I rubbed my head.

"I found you on the landing. Somehow you made your way across. I don't know how you did it, but you survived the second floor."

Morgan let go, and I pushed myself up to a seated position, then pulled the jacket tight against me. Stairs rose up in front of us, twisting into a hazy darkness before vanishing into the floor above. This wasn't the landing I remembered.

"How?" I asked, fighting with a zipper that might never work right again.

"I have no idea. You shouldn't have found your way through on your own. The second floor claims everyone—everyone, Gene. You are the first."

"Aside from you?"

Morgan hesitated. "Right. I mean, aside from me, you are the first one to have made it to the far side intact."

I shoved a hand in the jacket pocket and used the other to pull myself up. "Crazy. So you're saying all that wasn't real?"

Morgan nodded. "But it felt real, didn't it?"

I shook my head slowly. "Yeah."

"That's how the floor always wins: the fear. It can be crippling, but somehow you survived it."

I had help. David Singer, or was that something else? What was it Samatha told me? Don't accept its help?

"How did you survive it?" I asked, still coming to grips with this sudden reversal of fortune.

Morgan fished a small plastic compass ring out of her pocket.

"This," she said, showing me the unwavering arrow. "I tried to come back and find you, but you were already gone. You can imagine my surprise when I found you here on the *other side* of the floor. It took all my Magick just to make it here, and I had help." She held up the ring. "Yet you made it without any of that. I hope one day you can remember enough to tell me how you did it. Who knows, maybe these shelves will hold books full of *your* Magick." Morgan snickered and shoved the tiny compass back in her pocket.

"Yeah, who knows."

"All right," she said, grabbing the stair rail. "The third floor awaits, Master Magician. Are you ready?"

"Wait," I said, a vision rattling around in my head. "Who is Samantha?"

"Samantha?" Morgan tilted her head to one side. "I don't know any Samantha."

"Are you sure?"

Morgan nodded. "Completely. Is this something from your visions?"

"I guess. It just seemed so real."

Morgan pointed to the broken zipper of my Sojourner's Jacket. "Gene, your jacket has been half-open for a long time. It's the Gloom getting to you. All the more reason for us to pickup the pace. I'm not going to lose you again."

I nodded. "Right, that's got to be it."

Morgan took a few tentative steps up the twisting stair, then stopped when she noticed I wasn't right behind her. "Is there something else, Gene?"

"It's nothing. I'm just trying to understand all of this."

Morgan shook her head. "Don't. They're called unresolved fears for a reason. It's not something you're going to figure out standing in the Gloom."

"I guess."

"I don't have to guess—I know," Morgan said, leaning against the railing, excitement in her eyes. "You were right. This isn't my first trip inside, but this is the farthest I've ever come. No one has been able to make it past the second floor. The last time I barely survived myself, but here we are. You made it. You're standing on the landing and only steps away from the third floor. Do you know what's up there, Gene?"

"More fears?"

"No!" Morgan practically jumped out of her skin. "The secrets of the universe. Don't you get it? That's what it's been about since the beginning. All my Magick amounts to parlor tricks compared to what waits for us on the third floor."

"Will we be able to save Ed?"

Morgan's eyes glossed over. "Huh?"

"Ed, you know, my roommate? The guy who is nothing but a disembodied head?"

Morgan blinked away what must have been visions of grandeur. "Ed... Yes, of course. Gene, there's unbelievable power just a scant few seconds away. I'm sure we'll find something to save your roommate. The greatest minds in Magick have stored their secrets on that floor, and we are only seconds away from reaching them. Can't you feel it?"

I reached out with my Magick, but found it strangely muted,

like trying to breathe through a narrow straw. Even with that blockage, Morgan was right. There was a power above us, an alien and ancient power; however, unlike her, I wasn't nearly as excited to venture into it.

"Come on, Gene. It'll all make sense soon. There's only a little way further to go. You can do it. You've already come so far. Just a few more steps and we'll be there."

I placed a tentative foot on the first step. Morgan took that as success and bounded up the next few two at a time, her heels echoing on the hard stairs.

Her giddiness was difficult to ignore, and soon I found myself running along behind her. I switched hands, pulling my cold fingers out of my pocket and placing them on the railing, then shoved my other hand in the opposite pocket to warm it up.

What's this?

My fingers traced something round and metal inside that pocket.

I stopped, fished it out, and held it up in the dim light. Morgan's feet continued to pound their way up the stairs. If she was still worried about drawing attention, her excitement at having made it to the third floor had overtaken that fear.

It was a ring. A narrow-band steel ring with a complex set of interlocking symbols traced down the sides.

I held it up to my own ring—they were a match.

"Come on, Gene!" Morgan shouted, her voice fading on the distant steps above me.

A vision of Samantha's burned face appeared filled my mind, her skin peeling and those piercing blue eyes locking me in their unwavering gaze.

'Don't trust her. Morgan only cares for one thing, power, and she'll destroy you and anyone you care about to get to it.'

Were you real?

Samantha's skin burned away until all that was left were her eyes.

'Do not trust her...'

Morgan vanished into the dark above me, and soon even her hard footsteps became a faint echo in the ash and soot of the Gloom.

37

SMALL, GREEN, AND RUBBERY

*T*he spiral staircase came to an abrupt stop not far above us, unceremoniously dropping Morgan and I on the landing of the mysterious third floor. In truth, it didn't look anything like I'd expected it to, but I had very little in the way of expectations to go on. Just like the floor below us, books lined narrow rows of shelves, but unlike the Floor of Unresolved Fears, this level was open and spacious, with an almost inviting set of tables and chairs. High above, clouds swirled past the hazy glass of broken sky lights. A faint dusting of soft ash piled loosely across the tabletops.

"This is it, Gene," Morgan said, her voice resuming its hushed tone. "We've reached the third floor. The book has got to be here…"

"Book? You mean the book with a way to saving Ed?"

Morgan nodded. "Yes, I'm sure of if—that and so much more."

The excitement in her voice was palpable, and it was hard not to get caught up in it myself. We'd come so far: we'd traveled to the Gloom, passed the front steps, and fought our way through a hive of Umbralings. The Floor of Unresolved Fears hadn't done us in, and all of that meant we'd earned the chance to stand here, mere feet from the power necessary to put my friend back together.

"Well, what are we waiting for?"

Morgan held me back. "There's no way we've come this far to face nothing. Something's here—I just know it."

We stood on the platform and let our eyes adjust to the faint light that trickled in through the broken glass above. Nothing moved in the shadows of the third floor, nothing but the occasional mote of falling soot.

"Whose books are these?" I asked, trying to make out the distant spines.

"They're the combined wisdom of untold Magicians through the ages. In the eighteen hundreds, when the university was formed from the last vestiges of the East Florida Seminary, the books were brought here, to the Gloom. It's no surprise the library was built on this spot." Morgan stepped off the landing carefully, and gently brushed the small piles of ash away with her foot. "Follow me and do not touch anything unless I say to."

I nodded, keeping my footsteps in line with hers, my feet falling into the grooves she left behind.

Morgan's eyes traced the nearest row of spines and she rattled off their names: "Wugerlin's Paradox, The Pycidean Cyclone, The Keplinger Obstinate…"

I reached for one of the books and Morgan slapped at my hand. "I said don't touch, and I meant it. Those are not what we're after."

"But one of these might have something to help Ed, right?"

"No." Morgan walked past the tantalizing volumes.

"How do you know?"

She didn't answer me, and instead directed my attention to a large table in the center of the room. A single volume book lay open on the table, its pages fluttering softly in the open skylight's faint breeze. "That's it."

"How do you—"

Morgan placed a soft finger on my lips and squeezed the sides of my jacket together. "I know, because I've been looking for it a long time. I know because the same man who wrote it designed the sigil we used to get in here."

"Ten Spins?"

"Yes, and there's no way that book would be left out in the open without something guarding it," Morgan said, her ticking Magick slowly filling the room. "Revelare!"

Bright flashes of light sprung up around the large room, hidden sigils appearing beneath the piles of ash and soot.

"What are—"

"Human Phase Knots." Morgan pointed at the nearest sigil. "Think of them like bear traps designed to catch and hold a human being."

"And if we stepped in one?"

Morgan snapped her hands together like a gator's jaws.

"Oh."

"Come on. Follow me."

The pulsing sigils shone like dark-red taillights beneath the piles of soot and ash. They were stacked on top of each other, configured in a monstrously complex pattern throughout the room. There was no direct path to the book that wouldn't have led us into any number of them—Morgan had no option other than to concoct a circuitous path around the large room. We hadn't gone ten paces before she stopped to fold her arms across her chest.

"What's wrong?"

She shook her head. "I'm thinking, just give me a minute."

I crouched down to get a better look at the sigils she was hellbent on avoiding. Their complex patterns were nothing I was familiar with, but that came as no surprise—there were a lot of things I wasn't familiar with.

The pulsing symbols had a rather magnetic-like pull to them, and I found myself strangely mesmerized by their twisting lines.

Morgan put a hand on my shoulder and yanked me back. "Pay attention!" she snapped. "You almost fell in. Come on, I think I have a path."

I shook my head and followed Morgan deeper into the room, Ten Spins' distant volume never completely out of sight.

We'd walked the length of the floor at least three times, no closer to reaching the frustrating volume. Time in the Gloom was hard to measure, but I was all but certain we'd spent close to an hour tracking and backtracking our path around the frustrating floor—an hour Ed didn't have.

"Damn it," Morgan said, crossing her arms again. "This is pointless. We need the book to come to us."

I reached for my Magick, but Morgan stopped me. "No, the Phase Knots might distort it. It's too risky. We need help."

"Help?"

Morgan nodded and unzipped her jacket, then removed a large chocolate bar. It was one of those king-size candies I'd always hoped to get at Halloween as a kid. Needless to say, I'd never actually gotten one—I was the kid that ended up with raisins or apples.

"What's that for?" I asked as she broke the bar into smaller pieces.

"We are close to the Hells. Cosmologically speaking, the Gloom isn't far from them."

"The Hells? There's more than one?"

Morgan nodded, crouching on a bare patch of ash-streaked floor and laying out the pieces of chocolate. "It's best if you don't try to study this sigil."

"Why?"

Morgan removed the chalk from her jacket. "Conjuring sigils are hard on the eyes and on the brain. If you've never done them before there's a good chance it'll be too much for you."

"How so?"

Morgan pointed a finger at her head and spun it in a tight circle, the universal symbol for crazy. "It's like those hidden pictures. You know, those things you stare at to see the 3D image?"

"Yeah."

"Well, with these, the hidden image gets imprinted on your brain."

That didn't sound like something I wanted any part of.

"Morgan, what are you conjuring?"

Once again, Morgan's selective hearing returned and she ignored me.

"Morgan?"

My girlfriend completed the spiraling design, and I did my best to not focus on it, but she was right—what little I saw was enough to make my eyes want to cross.

"Stay back," she said, gently pushing me away from the sigil. "There are three rules for what's coming. First, do not give it a name—that's my job. Second, do not trust it, and third?"

"Yes."

"Don't fight the ring."

"What do you—"

Morgan spun around to face the complex pattern and held out her hands. "Kilgore the Unsettling, Bringer of the Infinite Tortures, hear my cry and deliver me!"

Morgan's Magick whirred and the Dead Man's Tongue on my finger burned. My Magick unwillingly joined hers and together they entered fractured lines of the sigil. Something green and blurry appeared in the confines of the twisting spiral.

"More power, Gene," Morgan whispered.

The Dead Man's Tongue scorched my hand. I wanted to fight her, but the ring was too strong.

"Argh!"

"Almost there…" she whispered.

The green blur sharpened into a wiry ball of leather wings and sharp talons.

Pop!

The sigil's edges curled and a brief puff of sulfurous smoke signaled the end of the conjuring. The demonic shape inside stretched out its bat-like wings. Bright green and almost rubbery in appearance, the tiny creature rubbed coal-black eyes that perched above a bulbous nose. A long tail snaked out behind it, twisting back and forth like an angry feline. Its high-pitched voice spoke in a language I didn't understand.

"English," Morgan barked at the small creature.

"Crap." The green monster stretched out like a cat in the scorched sigil. "The Gloom? Humans summoned me to the Gloom. Of all the places—"

Morgan stomped her foot. "Silence!"

"Oh well, there's a silver lining. It is humans after all, they *always* screw things up. So at least there's that."

"What is it?" I asked, finally finding my voice again.

"It," Morgan said, picking up a small piece of chocolate and holding it out like an offering, "is an Imp, a Minor Demon."

"Hey!" The Imp puffed out his tiny chest. "Who you calling Minor?"

38

KNOTS

*M*organ dismissed the diminutive Demon with a wave of her hand. "I said silence."

"Yeah, and your conjuring sigil indicates I don't have to listen to that request. You missed a whorl."

My girlfriend's eyes flashed in frustration. "What?!"

"Yeah, the ninth one." The Minor Demon pointed to a line in the confusing sigil. "Listen, what is it that you want?" As if to prove his point, the winged monster jumped out of the burnt seal and snapped the candy bar from Morgan's outstretched fingers. "I'm not keen on spending any more time in the Gloom than I have to."

Morgan regained her composure and crossed her arms. "This room is full of Human Phase Knots."

The tiny Imp's wings folded and unfolded gently in the shadowy twilight as he panned the large room. "Hey, will you look at that? They listened to me. I said humans would be the ones to try to get in here. Told em, 'Velcurses, you are a crazy dude, but you need to put some Human Phase Knots in here.' I didn't think he was paying attention—on account of most of his face missing from a Blackheart incident in the—"

"Enough!" Morgan shouted, cutting off the Minor Demon.

I caught movement in the broken glass of the skylight above, but when I turned to look it was gone.

The Imp bit into the chocolate bar with more gusto than I expected, his lips smacking between mouthfuls of nougat.

"Morgan," I whispered, grabbing her shoulder and pointing to the broken window above. "I think I saw something moving up there."

She dismissed me much like she had the Imp.

"Kilgore the Unsettling. I have named you and bound you to me. By the rules of the—"

"Ugh!" the Imp said, his wings pushing him into the air. "Just tell me what it is you want."

Morgan pointed to Ten Spins' volume on the distant table. "Bring me that book."

The Imp twirled gently in the shadowy twilight. "Right, so you need to poison the—Wait. What? You want me to get a book?"

"Yes."

The Imp furrowed his rubbery little brow. "Uh, that's a little underwhelming. I mean the room is full of books."

"That book." Morgan pointed to the large volume on the center table. "Bring me *that* book."

Another flicker of movement in the window above drew my attention. Something was out there, but what?

The Imp spun slowly, letting his wings catch a gentle updraft. "The one on the table?"

"Yes," Morgan said, frustration showing in her tone.

"That's Ten Spins' design," the Imp said, drifting toward the open book.

"Yes, bring it to me!"

Kilgore landed on the table and folded his wings in. "How about we get you another book? There are quite a few here to choose from. I know! There's some really crazy, sexy, fun Magick in the Jillian Jumble—"

"Bring me Ten Spins' book!" Morgan shouted, her voice booming in the shadowy twilight.

The Imp's shoulder's slumped. "What about you?" he said, turning his attention to me. "You sure you want this book? I mean, let me tell you, the Jillian Jumble is full of some pretty awesome stuff. I mean, you know what they said about Caligula?"

"Uh, no?"

The Imp slapped his forehead. "Come on, kid, work with me. Can't you at least pretend?"

"Okay..." I replied, completely confused.

"Good. So, like I was saying," the Imp's tail snaked under the cover of Ten Spins' book and pushed it closed, "the Jumble makes Caligula look like Mr. Rogers."

"Ignore him," Morgan said, her fingers twitching. "Bring me the book, Kilgore."

The tiny Demon leaned against the closed volume. "You sure? Last chance. As humans go, you two aren't bad looking. We could totally get a little Jillian going..."

"The book."

The Imp sighed, climbing onto the monstrous tome and digging the claws of his feet into the binding. "Oh man, this is one of his human-skin-covered works. Ugh."

"Bring me the—"

"Yeah, yeah, yeah," the Demon said, cutting Morgan off and flapping his wings. "Bring me the book. I command you, blah, blah, blah. You really got yourself a winner here, man." The Imp's wings pumped harder and he rose into the air, but only just barely, the book weighing him down considerably. He added his tiny hands to the book's cover, dragging the hardback toward Morgan. "You... You do know what this guy was all about, right?"

"No," I said, unable to tear my eyes away from the Imp's labored flight.

"Ignore him, Gene." Morgan's hands reached out for the book. "He's trying to confuse and distract you. That's what Imps do."

The Minor Demon adjusted his grip. Bright green hands clutched the spine to keep the volume from falling into the Human Phase Knots below him. "Meh. Whatever. You're the one that summoned me. I had a really great spot with a view of the Tower of Unceasing Torment. Do you know how hard it is to get a spot like that? I bet you don't. But I gave it up to come here." The Imp's claws slipped again, this time his recovery forced him to adjust his trajectory. He fought to get the over-sized load under control. "You know what they told me? 'Don't do it, Kilgore. You just picked out a great spot. The New Dead roast is starting soon—you'll miss it.' I said, 'It's a human summoning, guys, and I haven't had chocolate in years. I'm going!'"

The Demon shook his rubbery head, those wide ears flapping against his skull. "I'm an idiot." He dropped the oversized volume into Morgan's outstretched hands.

Morgan's hands caressed the revolting cover. "Ten Spins' Infernal Constructs."

The Imp plopped down on one of the other tables near me, his body clearly exhausted. "Oh, it's *that* one, eh? Well listen, Magician," he said, shaking out his fingers. "It's been nice knowing you. I would have gone with the Jumble, but that's just me."

"What's he talking about, Morgan?" I asked, backing away from the Minor Demon, though I stopped just short of walking into a Human Phase Knot.

Morgan opened the book and rapidly flipped through the pages, clearly looking for something.

"She ain't going to answer you," the Imp said, sitting up and stretching out his wings.

"Huh?"

"You don't have to be a Major Demon to understand what your woman has planned. Besides, I'd argue they wouldn't understand, anyway. They're all hellfire and brimstone, but nothing between the ears, you get me?"

Morgan's eyes lit up—whatever she was looking for she'd found it.

"What is it? What did you find Morgan?"

The Imp pointed at the ring on my pinky. "Dead Man's Tongue, eh? You put that on willingly?" He scratched his head. "Huh, maybe she doesn't need the Jillian Jumble to get you to do what she wants."

"Morgan!"

My girlfriend pushed ash aside and cleared a spot on the closest table, then laid the book in an open spot. "Knot him."

"Huh?" I said.

The Imp's shoulder's slumped. "But he's the only interesting one here."

"Do it!"

I raised my hands. "Wait, what are you talking about?"

"Sorry, kid. At least you've been fun to talk to." The Minor Demon shot off the table like he'd been launched from a catapult. The tiny monster hit me full on in the chest, knocking me backwards and directly into the center of a Human Phase Knot.

I wanted to shout, to lash out, to do basically anything, but I couldn't. The sigil's Magick held me fast like hardened epoxy, my hands extended and locked in a futile attempt to dislodge the rubbery Imp. Kilgore the Unsettling flapped his wings and soared into the air above me before slipping outside my newly restricted field of vision.

Morgan removed the Rubik's Cube from her jacket and placed it on the table next to Ten Spin's book. The Imp drifted down to land next to it, cautiously sniffing the small plastic toy. "Shit on me and call it a sundae. You built one. I gotta say, Magician, that's damn impressive."

Morgan ignored the Imp and instead twisted the cube into a different position.

"You know they want out," the Demon said, his tail twisting in and out of the shadows. "You've got skills, I'll give you that, but you lack the power to open the main doors. Velcurses, Eldero, even Gorbel never got those doors to so much as budge. What makes you think you'll be able to?"

Morgan acknowledged the Imp for the first time since receiving the book. She used a finger to trace a line around his oversized belly. "Because I'm not going to—he is."

The ring?!

The Imp chuckled, his laughter decidedly sadistic. "I figured as much. You got a big enough battery to do it though? He looks pretty scrawny to me."

Morgan twisted the companion ring on her finger and Magick rumbled in my chest. "Oh yeah, trust me. He hits like a dump truck."

MAGNETIC PERSONALITY

I fought the Phase Knot's Magick, but for all my fury it didn't budge, and neither did I.

"Oh, Gene. Don't look at me like that," Morgan said, turning a page in Ten Spins' book. "I needed you to stand still and let me do what I came here to do."

I wanted to shout, flail, anything, but the sigil's locking Magick held me tight.

"He looks pretty pissed," the Imp said, lifting off the table and flapping his wings to hover just inches from my face.

Morgan dismissively traced a finger down the book's page. "He'll get over it. When I free the old Magicians locked inside this prison, they'll reward me, and in turn I'll reward Gene."

The Imp tilted his head to one side. "You think he'll survive?"

Morgan flipped a page back and forth. "He's stronger than he looks."

"Really? He seems a little soft." The Imp tugged on the loose skin of my cheeks.

"Leave him alone." Morgan looked up from the book. "Wait. On second thought, in the Phase Knot he's relatively safe, but if he finds a way out I could be in trouble. Take off his coat."

"What do I look like? A hostess?"

Morgan's eyes glared from the book's edge.

The Imp sighed. "Right, right, take off the jacket. I command thee, blah, blah, blah."

Morgan placed the book down on the table and picked up her Rubik's Cube. "I can't believe we've made it here, Gene."

The Imp's claws caught the broken zipper and yanked it down the rest of the way, opening my Sojourner's Jacket. Morgan had been right, the Phase Knot kept me from freezing to death. All I could do was glare at her, and that wasn't having much of an effect.

"Come on, you couldn't figure this out from the beginning? Did you really believe a Reaver just happened to show up on my sidewalk and bust out of Marcy?" Morgan twisted the tiny cube, then referred to the book again. "Or that there just happened to be an Illickthid there? I'll admit, I wasn't certain who would win, but I had a contingency plan regardless of the outcome."

The Imp flapped his wings and dragged one side of the heavy jacket off my shoulder.

"I'd planned it all, but I couldn't anticipate everything. I had no idea you'd show up, or your idiot roommate and his Yaga Doll."

The diminutive Demon tugged at my sleeve. "Yaga Doll? That's not good."

Morgan waved off the tiny monster's concerns. "It's gone. This guy brought its spirit into the Gloom and unleashed it on a Death Shroud."

"Impressive." The Imp crawled up my arm and pushed at the heavy fabric. "Stupid, but impressive. So, Doll's gone?"

"Completely."

My jacket sleeve slipped off and dragged across the floor.

Morgan twisted the cube again, her complex Magick ramping up. "Almost there, Gene. You know, something's been bothering me. How did you find out about Samantha? You, the same guy that didn't bother reading about the Petals of Belladonna? You know if you had you'd have found out exactly why that preacher blew his brains out, or why Jess appeared so intoxicated. You didn't even question it, you just dove right in to help." Morgan shrugged her shoulders. "I mean, hell, I even told you the ring was Dead Man's Tongue. Did you bother to look that up? I could have said it was anything, but I didn't. I told you exactly what I handed you and you still put it on your finger."

I trusted you.

Morgan shook her head. "Samantha wasn't even half as strong as you, but she was a hell of a lot smarter. I had to hide so many things from her. That girl would take even the tiniest hint, and I'd never hear the end of it. I had to make up so many things with her around, but not with you. It's amazing what a little sexy time does to a guy—didn't have the same effect on Samantha."

The Imp grabbed my opposite sleeve and pulled it toward the ground.

A shadow flashed across Morgan and Ten Spins' book, and she paused to look up at the broken skylight. "The natives are getting restless. Let's get this done, Kilgore. Once the masters are here, they'll be no threat."

"Almost got it..." the Imp said, yanking off the last of my heavy sleeve and sending the Sojourner's Jacket crashing down on him in a heap. "Ugh."

"Excellent. Any residual protections in those woven sigils won't help you now, Gene. I could lie and tell you this won't hurt a bit, but I know how much you treasure honesty, so I'm going to lay it out for you." Morgan twisted the tiny cube and sent her Magick out into the wide room. "I'm going to use as much of your Magick as it takes to unlock the prison and release the Magicians entombed inside. The library is more than just a repository of their works locked in the Gloom. It's a prison, and thanks to you we're about to have a good old-fashioned jailbreak."

The Dead Man's Tongue on my finger burned, and the Magick in my chest bubbled in anticipation.

"Hey," the Minor Demon unburied himself from the heap of enchanted fabric. "Check this out."

Morgan ignored him and instead focused all of her attention on the Cube and the Magick she was pulling in. "Thanks to Ten Spins' book, I know what I need to finish the Cube, and thanks to Gene I'll have enough juice to do it."

What started as a trickle quickly swelled to a raging river as my Magick roared out the ring in a burst of white-hot pain.

Morgan!

"That's where you come in. The man who looks a Yaga Doll in the face and lives, there's enough power in you to blow this prison to splinters, and soon that power be mine."

The Imp flapped his wings and rose up between us. "Did you know he had a second one?"

"Huh?" Morgan tilted her head, concentration and Magick wavering.

The Imp produced a steel ring. The same steel ring that had been in my coat pocket—the same ring that had graced Samantha's dead hand.

"Don't let that hit the sigil!" Morgan shouted, dropping her Magick and releasing me from the throes of the Dead Man's Tongue burning against my finger.

"Gah!" The Imp jumped, startled by her excited response. The narrow band slipped from his claws and tumbled end over end.

Pling!

The muted steel hit the hard concrete, sending up a puff of ash before rebounding back up into the air.

"Get it!" Morgan cried.

The Imp's claws missed the little band, and his wings made it impossible for Morgan to reach the ring in time.

The steel spun and twisted before landing in a Phase Knot next to mine.

"Shit!"

Hum...

The swirling Magick of that trapping sigil buzzed in my ears. Feedback raised the hairs on my arms like being caught in a magnetic field.

Pop!

The other Phase Knot vanished, its symbol burning out in a flash of light.

"They aren't connected, are they?" Morgan asked.

The Imp shrugged his shoulders.

Pop! Pop! Pop!

Phase Knots throughout the room winked out—including the one I was standing in.

The blast of cold hit me the instant the confining Magick vanished. I was standing in the Gloom, in the flesh, and without the protective Magick of the Sojourner's Jacket.

Morgan leapt for the Cube, and in the process ramped her Magick back up, filling the room with the whirring clicks power. I fumbled for the jacket, but in the burning cold my frozen fingers were reduced to semi-useless oven mitts.

More shadows passed overhead and frightful moans filtered through the ash-filled haze.

"Death Shrouds," the Imp cried, springing into the air while his wings flapped furiously.

Morgan twisted the Cube and turned up the heat on the Dead Man's Tongue again. "It doesn't matter. Once the doors are open nothing will stop me."

I clawed for the Jacket, my fingers hooking the heavy leather sleeve. No sooner had I grabbed that saving coat than the remaining glass in the overhead skylight shattered, and a whirl-wind of hellish dish rags poured into the room.

Death Shrouds.

40

ON THE LINE

he black wave of malevolent laundry crashed into Morgan, knocking her into the table and sending both the Rubik's Cube and Ten Spins' Infernal Constructs sliding to the ground. The swirling monsters kicked ash and soot into the air, quickly making it impossible to see.

Morgan screamed, her voice a mixture of fear and frustration. I forced my freezing hands into the Sojourner's sleeves, and had the coat half on when a small pair of hands helped me pull the other end around.

"Come on, kid, we're getting out of here. I'm not hanging around to meet the neighbors," the Imp said, his rubbery face obscured by the whipping ash.

"Gene," Morgan cried, her voice raw and distant. "Help me!"

The Dead Man's Tongue pulled at the Magick churning in my chest. The Imp shook his tiny head. "You want to leave?"

"Yeah…" I said, my mouth barely forming words.

"Me too. Here's the deal, Magician. You get me out of here, and I'll get that ring off your finger."

Morgan pulled on my Magick again, the sheer force of her

will yanking my knees out from under me and missing the Imp by mere inches.

"As long as I get to keep the finger," I said, clutching at the offending digit's burning ring.

The Imp opened his mouth, then snapped it shut. "You aren't making this easy, Magician."

Morgan's face appeared behind a whirling column of Death Shrouds, the green ends of her hair spinning wildly. She snapped a hand out and grabbed onto one of fluttering creatures, pulling it in and draining more of my Magick in the process.

The Imp grabbed my hand and dragged it toward a nearby Phase Knot. "It's a long shot, but I want the hell out of here. You ready?"

"What are you doing?"

The Imp held my hand above the spent Phase Knot and picked up Samantha's ring. "Either I'm saving my meal ticket, or I'm about to really screw myself over." The Minor Demon slid the smaller ring on my finger until it touched mine.

Clink!

Morgan's stranglehold on my Magick snapped, and in the process my power restored the Phase Knot beneath my hand.

Crack!

The Imp pulled my hand back before it could become tethered to the confining power. "We need to go, now!"

Phase Knots erupted to life around the room, including one beneath Morgan.

"Gene!" she screamed, but the rest of her words were cut off by the frustrating sigil. The Death Shrouds swirled around her, pressing in on the Phase Knot and passing just above the discarded volume.

The book! I can't go back empty handed!

I lunged for Ten Spin's Infernal Constructs, even as more

Phase Knots sprung back to life around me. The Imp took to the air, wringing his claws in frustration. "What are you doing?"

I scooped up the volume and drew the attention of a quilt-sized Death Shroud in the process.

Ah, hell.

"Right, let's go!"

I made a mad dash for the distant steps. The Imp flapped furiously behind me. I hit the landing hard and took the steps two at a time, practically falling forward into the Floor of Unresolved Fears with reckless abandon.

"Where do we go now?"

Imp slammed into my back. "Ugh! You mean you don't know?"

The moaning whispers of Death Shrouds drifted down the steps behind us.

"You're a Demon, right?"

"Last I checked."

I dashed down one of the confusing floor's many aisles. "Well, can't you do something?"

The tiny monster dug his clawed feet into my shoulder like he was steering a horse. "Here goes nothing. Turn right!" The Imp's sharp talons directed me out of that aisle and into another one.

We hadn't traveled more than a few hundred feet when he dug into my shoulder again. "Wait, that's not right. I mean, that was *right*, as in you took a right, but I'm not sure if that was the right direction, navigationally."

Somewhere a few shelves over a bright swirl of chaotic Magick lit up the gaps between the books.

"Whoa—are you sure that's an 'unresolved' fear?"

"Make up your mind!" I shouted, wincing at the bastard's sharp claws.

"Left, now!"

I grabbed the edge of the shelving and used my sore hand like a whip to slingshot us around the next corner.

"This is just like those old westerns I used to watch," the Imp said, straddling the back of my head and grabbing onto my ears like reins. "Hi ho, Silver!"

By now my lungs had warmed up enough to get the air flowing reasonably well, but it was my legs that were showing signs of wear.

I know, I know. I need to start running. Damn it, Ed, as soon as I finish saving your ass we'll go for a run.

I'd have carried this Imp another mile if it meant avoiding the Death Shrouds swirling through the shelves behind us.

"So, anything else we should be looking for?" the Imp asked, pulling my right ear and dragging me down a different aisle.

"Huh?"

"It's the Floor of Unresolved Fears. Is there anything I should be on the lookout for?"

"No, I think I resolved all of my fears so far," I said, my lungs burning.

"Hmm," the Imp tugged on my left ear, "that's interesting. I'm guessing you don't get out much."

We turned another corner and the spiral staircase landing down to the lower level came into view. "There it is!"

"Nope," the Imp smacked my head with his tail, "that's a fake set."

"No it's not."

"Look again," he said, directing my head. Sure enough, an open hole was all that remained of the once massive landing.

"Holy shi—"

The Imp slapped my face. "I'll have none of the 'H word' around me, thank you very much."

Before I could respond again, he swiveled my head the other direction. "Look! There are your stairs to the first floor."

We hadn't made it past the first steps when the clicking legs and hiss of the Umbralings sent the Imp into a tizzy.

"Umbralings?! Who thought it was a good idea to fill the lower level with Umbralings?" His tiny fingers gripped my head like a vise, the rest of his diminutive body now solidly planted on my scalp. "How many would you say there are down there?"

"Hundreds, maybe thousands."

The tiny Imp's wings beat a few times then sucked in as close as they could.

"If you can fly," I said, trying to see past the darkness below. "Then I suggest you do so."

"And get caught in their damn webs? Oh, hell no."

A brief flapping of tattered cloth behind me provided all the motivation I needed. "Umbralings are bad, but I've seen what a Death Shroud can do in person."

The Imp's tail looped its way around my neck a few times. "Ah, the old soul suck, eh? That's a bugger of a problem to deal with."

"You'll have to tell me all about it on the other side. Are you ready?"

The Imp's small claws dug into my scalp. "Go!"

I raced down the steps and into what remained of the Umbraling nest. Thick webs hung like macabre streamers from the walls, scorched in places from my Magick—a moment that felt like days ago at this point.

"Duck!" the Imp screamed, his toes clawing at my neck. I followed his lead and pushed my head down just in time to avoid the glistening fangs of a falling Umbraling.

Hiss!

"You did all this?" the Imp asked as we jockeyed between the upturned tables.

"Yeah, but it was an accident."

"Impressive."

The side door wasn't far off, but a dense clump of Umbralings had taken up a position in front of it. Webs spiraled out in all directions from the center of that opening, ensuring we'd be trapped the moment we hit it.

"The window!" the Imp yelled, his tiny claws once again directing me like a plow horse. "There!"

The partially broken glass wasn't big enough for both of us.

"See you on the other side." He launched his tiny body off my head like a diving board and out the shattered panes.

Damn it.

I tucked my chin against my chest and hoped to hell I had enough momentum to make it out.

Boom!

Unlike the movies would have you believe, jumping through a broken window hurts like hell, even in the Gloom. I landed in a reasonably soft pile of ash, but when something slug-like moved under me I was back up and limping as fast as I could away from the building.

"The Bent Key," I cried, unable to find the complex sigil beneath a blanket of fallen ash.

"You used Ten Spins' Magick to get in here?" the Imp asked, floating gently in the air just above me.

"Yes! But I can't find it."

The Imp beat his tiny wings, sending tumbling piles of ash rolling away, and revealing the edge of the chalk.

"There it is," I said, practically jumping into the complex sigil.

The Imp landed next to me, carefully folding in his wings and then taking a few seconds to admire Morgan's chalk work. "It's not bad. I would have done a little more here. Maybe fixed that whorl there just a bit, but all in all, it'll do."

The wailing moan of a Death Shroud set my hairs on edge. A flock of them streamed out of the library and I froze.

Morgan...

The Imp slapped my cheek, quickly turning my attention back to the present. "What are you waiting for?"

I took a deep breath and sent every last drop of my Magick into the Bent Key, hoping it would work and that whatever was in this book had been worth it.

Hold on, Ed!

PART III
CAST OUT

41

DEALS

"Hey? You okay?"

I blinked my eyes in the bright afternoon sun. "Huh?"

"Bro, you're like a ninja," the hazy blue-and-green blob said, his voice a mixture of confusion and awe. "Like, one second I'm getting some lunch from the Hare Krishnas on the plaza and then I turn around and 'poof,' crazy jacket dude."

Jacket?

The Sojourner's Jacket felt strangely heavy in the warm afternoon air. I rubbed one of the sleeves across my eyes.

"Where am I?"

"On the pavement."

I blinked my eyes a few more times, letting the sunlight filter through from large oaks above. "I mean... Wait? Is that the library?"

"Dunno, bro, I don't go to school here. I just came for the free lunch."

Thump.

The heavy book, bound in what certainly appeared to be human skin, tumbled out of my lap and onto the sidewalk.

"What? Yeah. Listen, did you see anything with me…"

How are you going to explain this one, Gene?

"Like an action figure. It was about this big," I said, holding up my ash-smeared hands. "And it would have been sort of greenish, with big wings and some really sharp-looking claws."

Mr. Free Lunch scratched at his head. "Nope. Sorry, bro."

Crap.

"Can you give me a hand?"

The stranger pulled me to my feet, and I wobbled briefly before getting my legs underneath me. I thanked him and started to leave, but then I noticed the folded-up newspaper under his arm.

Student Bike Tragedy.

"Is that today's Alligator?"

"Yeah."

"May I see it?"

Mop-top held up the front page and I took it from his hands.

Pictured below, Edwin Lovely, student and well-known community trouble-maker, lays unresponsive in ICU, tests indicate he may have suffered traumatic brain injury…

"I've gotta go!"

"Hey, that's my paper!"

I squeezed Ten Spins' unholy volume to my chest and ran for Morgan's dorm, my tired legs pumping hard in the humid air.

Brain dead my ass.

MORGAN'S ROOM.

I stopped at the door, my mind replaying the events of the last few hours—her face, her eyes, and the last flashes of Morgan's fists in the hailstorm of Death Shrouds.

Ten Spins' book lay heavy in my hands.

Was it worth it?

I shook off the doubt. She'd brought it on herself. Ed's life, or what remained of it, hung in the balance. I just hoped there was something between these pages that could reunite my roommate with his body.

I took a deep breath and let it out slowly, then turned the knob and entered to my girlfriend's room.

The Demon Hunter's disembodied head still floated, locked in an expression of torment in the center of The Jacobean Prefect. His eyes were closed and the frayed edges of his neck drifted like wispy hairs in the stillness of the room.

"Hang on, Ed," I said, pushing the rest of the junk off Morgan's tiny desk and dropping Ten Spins' volume on it. "There's got to be something in here."

I flipped through the pages, desperate for anything that might help us. However, unlike the movies I'd been raised on, there were no 'How to undo a Death Shroud's Soul-Sucking for Fun and Profit' sections in that stupid book.

I scrunched up my face and puzzled over the complex diagrams, and with each illustration my blood pressure rose just a little more. "Damn it."

Never was it more clear just how little knowledge I had compared to Morgan. She'd have figured this out in no time. I, on the other hand, could stare at this for months and not make sense of it.

"I'm not giving up, Ed," I said, tossing my Sojourner's Jacket on her bed.

"Hey, I was trying to sleep here," a familiar and devilish voice from within the heavy folds.

"What the—"

The Imp pushed the edges of my coat aside and unfurled his wings. "Yeah, it's way too damn early for me. I mean, heck, the sun's still up? Who's out and about at this hour? Idiots, that's who." The tiny Demon crawled under Morgan's bed sheets.

"I need your help."

The Imp made a noise that landed somewhere between anger and annoyance.

I ripped the sheets off the Minor Demon. "Damn it, I said I need your help."

The tiny green monster stretched out his arms and clicked a wicked-looking set of claws. "My help, eh? Well, isn't that just swell. What's in it for me?"

"What do you want?"

The Imp's tiny eyes snapped open wide. "What are you offering?"

I threw up my hands. "I don't know what things like you want?"

"Things?" The Imp's over-sized head tilted to one side. "Things?!"

"Listen, my roommate's soul has been eaten by a Death Shroud. All I have left is his head, and it's disintegrating." I pointed to Ed's gently bobbing head, still ensconced in the relative safety of the Jacobean Prefect.

"And you want me to do what?"

"Son of a…" I grabbed the evil book off Morgan's desk only to slam it back down again. "I want you to help me put what's left of his soul back in his body."

"I see… and what makes you think—"

Knock! Knock!

"Gene, are you in there? It's me, Porter."

"Crap!" I grabbed the edge of my jacket and threw it back over the Imp. "Don't move, and don't say anything."

"Who's that? She sounds sexy—" The tiny Demon's words were cut off by an ancient book of Deep Magick to the gut.

Oof!

"Yeah, hold on a second, Porter," I said, quickly scanning the room to make sure there was nothing overly strange sitting around.

Just this floating disembodied head.

I slid Morgan's desk chair over to partially block any view of my roommate's noggin and opened the door a crack. "Hey, Porter. What's up?"

Ed's girlfriend stood in the hall with bright red eyes. Small and almost helpless, a hint of tears glistened on her cheeks. "They're saying he's brain dead."

"I read the article—"

"You haven't come to the hospital! He's your friend, and you haven't even visited him. What kind of person does that?"

"I'm sorry, Porter. I've been busy and—"

"Don't tell me, tell him. He's the one that needs you now. I mean, the least you could do is go see him before…"

I turned back to check the Imp and my favorite floating soul-head—neither had moved. "I will. I just need to take a few minutes to finish something up here."

"His family is getting into town later today," Porter said, wiping the tears from her eyes. "It would be good for you to be there. I mean, it's the least you could do."

"I will."

Porter nodded and started to walk away, then stopped and turned back her face set like flint. "I don't know why, but I thought you were a better person. I was wrong. You're no better than Morgan. Whatever goodness there was in you, she destroyed it. Come to think of it, maybe there wasn't any there to begin with. Come for your friend, or don't. It doesn't matter to me anymore."

My heart sank as I watched Porter walk down the hall and out of the dorm. Was she right?

I closed Morgan's door and threw myself into her desk chair. It spun in the dim light of the room, turning slowly to bring me face to face with what remained of my roommate's soul.

"Ed, I'm sorry. This is all my fault."

My roommate's face was a macabre mask of pain.

"I'm going to fix this. I promise. I'll put you back."

"Huh, would you look at that, it *is* doable," the tiny Demon's voice said from beneath the crumpled sheets.

"What?!" I yanked the covers off Morgan's bed again.

The Imp held Ten Spins' Infernal Constructs in his lap. The dense work was comically larger than he was, but that hadn't stopped the diminutive green monster.

"So, yeah, it would appear you actually *can* do it. How long ago did the Death Shroud eat the rest of him?"

"Uh." I jumped out of Morgan's chair and grabbed the discarded Alligator on the floor, then skimmed the article. "Yesterday! It happened yesterday."

The Imp's tail flicked back and forth, then scratched at his head. "Hmm."

"What? What does that mean? Can we do it or can't we?"

The Imp turned a page, then turned back again. "Well…"

Ed Lovely's translucent head continued to bob gently in The Jacobean Prefect. It might have been my imagination, but the tattered edges of his neckline appeared to be smaller.

We're losing him.

"Damn it, tell me!"

The Imp's wide smiled reminded me of my old roommate's, except where Ed's was genial, the Imp's had more in common with an apex predator. I suddenly felt more like a bait-fish than a Magician.

"It can be done," the Demon said, gently closing the book and drumming his tiny claws along the cover.

"Well, then let's get to it!"

"No."

"What do you mean no?"

The Imp set the book aside. "No. First, I need to determine what exactly it'll cost you."

42

MINOR PROBLEMS

"Cost me?"

The Imp unfolded his wings. "Yes."

"I brought you out of the Gloom. Doesn't that buy me something?"

The tiny Demon examined his claws. "Are you breathing?"

"Yes."

"Then I would say you received a fair price for services rendered."

My Magick surged in my chest. I wasn't sure what would happen if I unleashed it, but I was pretty confident the Imp wouldn't like it.

"I highly recommend against doing that," the Minor Demon said, twisting his tail like a cobra. "You're new at this, aren't you?"

"What makes you say that?"

The Imp's toothy grin returned. He twisted the crumpled sheets in his tiny fingers. "Well, let's start with threatening an Imp with Magick. You don't do that if you enjoy living. See, we have a certain affinity for the stuff." The tiny Demon's tail swayed back and forth in mesmerizing fashion. "For instance, with the crack of my tail I could make things bad for your disappearing bobble-head—or worse."

"You're lying."

The Imp shook his head. "I lie about a lot of things, but I'm not lying about this. Here, let me show you."

The Imp's tail twitched and half the confining power of The Jacobean Prefect vanished like someone had flipped it off at the switch. Ed's scream returned, his face contorted in agony.

"Stop!" I cried, trying to will my Magick back into the faltering sigil.

The Imp giggled and spun in his seat. "And that was just a taste of the fun we could have."

I pumped Magick into the pattern and soon my roommate's face returned to its quiet yet painful contortions. "What is it you want? My soul?"

The Imp set the book aside and sprung into the air, his tiny wings holding him aloft expertly. "Your soul is tempting. Let me give it a sniff."

The green monster swooped down and ran a bulbous nose through my hair. "Nope. Not interested. Something else has already called dibs on it."

"What do you mean?"

The Imp landed on the bed post and folded his tiny arms. "Old power, primal, I'm not getting in the way of that. No, sir."

"What is it you do want?" I said, tabling these new concerns for the moment and brushing my hair back into place.

"Less boredom!"

Knock! Knock!

A couple of hard raps on Morgan's door caught me by surprise. "Who is it?"

"Jess. Where's Morgan?"

The Minor Demon took a deep breath. "Ah," he said, smiling at the latest distraction. "Now we're talking."

"I'll just tell her Morgan's out," I whispered.

"You're going to tell off a Reaver host? This I have to see."

"That's not a Reaver, that's Jess from down the hall, she's just here for more—"

"Special perfume?" the tiny Demon said, excitement creeping into his voice.

"How did you—."

"Where's Morgan?" Jess said again. This time, however, her voice had a much sharper tone to it.

"This's an old trick, Magician. There's a Reaver growing in that girl's body. I don't know that *she* knows it yet, but it's in there. Your old squeeze must have kept the monster under wraps with a bit of secret sauce, but given the fact that you appear to know absolutely nothing about Magick I'm guessing I shouldn't find that remotely surprising."

Boom! Boom!

"Let me in, Gene."

The door shook and my gut dropped out from under me. "What do I do?"

The Imp only smiled and let his wings flap gently. "You are really racking up the asks here. You've got a friend badly entangled in a barely functional Jacobean Prefect, and now an embryonic Reaver is about to violently molt on your doorstep. I'd say you've got quite a few problems now and no real solution for them."

"Can you help me?" I pleaded.

"Of course." The Imp unfolded his arms and placed his hands under his chin, giving him an almost cherubic impression. "But where would be the fun in that."

"Morgan had put a sigil on the door, do you think that'll stop her?"

Boom.

"Morgan!"

The Imp shrugged its tiny shoulders. "If that was your girl's sigil, then I would say it won't be doing much of anything until she comes back."

"Comes back?!" My gut and my heart sunk to the floor. "What do you mean comes back?"

The Imp laughed hard enough to tumble off the bed post. "Oh this is hysterical. I haven't had this much fun since the early eighteen-hundreds. You think any Phase Knot you trapped her in would continue to work once you left the Gloom?"

"Why wouldn't it?"

Boom! Boom!

"Well I don't know, did you set them up to be self-sustaining? Are you still there to power them?"

"No."

"Well, that answers that, doesn't it?"

My hands shook even as the door banged again.

"Morgan, let me in!" Jess shouted, her voice becoming more feral by the second.

Ed's head twisted uncomfortably in the air next to me, his eyes full of pain and I imagined more than a little judgement.

"So, what are you going to do, Magician?"

I tore open Morgan's drawers, tossing aside clothes and delicate underthings in search of those small vials I'd seen before. "Ah hah!"

I found one of the glass containers at the bottom of her dresser, gently wrapped in a heavy cloth.

"Well, look at you," the Imp said, one of Morgan's bras dangling from his large ears. "That ought to buy you some time. As long as you don't..."

I didn't stop to listen. I rolled the vial under the door and out into the hallway. The pounding stopped, and the dark shadow that filled the door seam vanished with it.

"...waste it all in one shot. Oh well."

I dropped into Morgan's desk chair, my heart racing and sweat beading up on my forehead. "She's gone."

"For now," the Imp nodded, "but she'll be back, and I'm betting there will be others."

Ed Lovely's head continued to drift in The Jacobean Prefect. Something was missing, my roommate's bottom jaw had vanished. The Imp noticed it as well.

"Even Jacobean had his shortcomings," he said, playing with his tail. "That Magician was sort of a jerk, far too conservative— and this was the fourteen hundreds, believe me that's saying something."

I ignored the Imp and paced narrow circles in the tiny dorm room.

"Ed's dying."

"Yep," the Imp said, picking up one of Morgan's bras and playing with the strap.

"I don't know how to put him back together."

The Imp fumbled with the tiny clasp. "Nope."

"I am going to have Reavers bursting out of people soon."

The small clasp clicked shut, and the Imp let out a happy giggle. "Yep."

"Porter hates me, and to top it all off, you're saying Morgan will find a way out of the Gloom and come after me?"

The Imp pulled the bra's elastic like a slingshot and tried to launch it across the room; instead it fell impotently on the hard floor. "I'd say any time now, actually."

"I'm screwed."

The Imp dug through the rest of Morgan's underwear. "That's a good way to look at it: accurate and on point. I'd say you are right screwed, yes."

I pulled Ten Spins' Infernal Constructs off the bed and shoved it in my backpack.

"Where are you going?" the tiny Demon said, springing to his feet.

"Ed's family is going to be at the hospital. I don't know if they're going to pull the plug on him or not, but I need to make sure they don't. At least not before I've found a way to put his soul back in his body."

"Good luck with that," the Imp said, flapping his wings and flying over to Morgan's window. "Might as well see the world before she gets out. Don't wait up!"

"Wait, I thought you were going to help me?"

The Imp landed on the narrow sill and pulled the window open with his tail. "I thought about it, but that wouldn't be much fun."

"Wait!"

The Imp's tail saluted me before he tumbled backwards out the window like a scuba instructor. I lunged for him, missing that little monster's legs by mere inches. I dangled over the edge of the sill while Kilgore's wings unfolded in the air. He waved, then caught an updraft and shot into the late afternoon sky.

Now you've done it, Gene.

I could almost hear Ed's laugh had he been here to watch this; instead, my roommate's disembodied head continued to turn like it was mounted on a diner's dessert case.

You're coming with me.

I grabbed a piece of paper off Morgan's desk and re-drew the Jacobean Prefect. I slid the paper over top of the same pattern we'd drawn on the floor earlier, willing just enough Magick into it to transfer Ed's head over like sliding a spatula. My roommate's ghostly noggin now floated gently above the scrap paper, none the worse for wear, but still fading fast.

Don't look at me like that. As if you'd have had a better idea.

I folded the paper and slipped it in my backpack; suddenly the thought of losing my roommate felt very real, and it turned my stomach.

Hang on, Ed.

43

SILENT PARTNER

$\mathscr{I}$ stood in front of Ed's hospital room with my hand on the knob, but couldn't seem to muster the courage to open it. My roommate's body lay on the other side, I just wasn't ready to see it, not yet. Doctors and nurses shuffled past, following paths to destinations unknown, and I couldn't help but want to join them. I wanted to get sucked up in the motion and pulled away—anywhere was better than here.

Come on, Gene. You can do this.

I took a deep breath and adjusted the straps of my backpack. Somewhere in that bag the tattered remnants of my roommate's soul sat like a butterfly pressed between the folds of cheap paper.

What's inside this room doesn't matter half as much as what's in your bag. It's just his body. You'll find a way to put the two pieces back together.

I shook my head and sighed. Sure, I had Ten Spins' Infernal Constructs with me, but that didn't mean I had a clue of what to do with it. I might as well be carrying around last year's tax code, for all the good it was doing me.

The door latch was cold in my fingers.

Ed's counting on you.

I closed my eyes and pulled. A rush of cool air greeted me, along with a chorus of beeps from imposing hospital equipment that lined the walls. Multi-colored lights popped on and off, while tiny needles bounced up and down in time with my roommate's labored breathing. At first it was difficult to find him behind the jungle of flowers. Ed may have been considered a polarizing character on campus, but he had admirers, many of which he'd saved from all manner of evil. Those people must have come out in droves and brought with them a florist's shop of well-wishes. Bright and cartoonish mylar balloons swayed gently in dense clusters above the hopeful scene.

Ed laid in his bed, a monitor above chirping out in time with his beating heart. I slid around a particularly large bouquet of yellow daisies and settled on an open spot beside him.

"I'm sorry."

My roommate didn't budge. He looked small in that bed, a far cry from the rockstar whose vocals had saved us only days earlier. It was my friend, but it wasn't. There was no vest, no Cheshire Cat grin, and no wild optimism in his closed eyes. To see him laying there was almost too much, and I blinked back the tears forming in the corner of my eyes.

"Morgan wasn't who I thought she was," I said, shoving my hands in my pockets, afraid to let my Magick anywhere near the complex machinery that was keeping Ed breathing. "You were right all along."

Beep. Beep.

Ed wasn't going to be answering me anytime soon—if ever.

I shook my head and started to pace a tight circle in the narrow room.

"I don't know what to do. I wish you were here. Morgan's AWOL and I'm certain she's coming for me."

The soft beep of Ed's monitors acted as a stand-in for my dearest friend.

Beep.

"Why? Well let's just say I left her in the Gloom, trapped in a Phase Knot and surrounded by Death Shrouds."

Beep.

I shook my head. "No, the Imp says the Knots won't last now that I'm not there to power it. Morgan will find a way out, and if she somehow survives the Death Shrouds, she's gonna be pissed."

Beep. Beep.

"Oh right," I said, making yet another right-hand turn. "The Imp. Yeah, so Morgan summoned an Imp." I paused for a second to watch his heartbeat, the bright line rising and falling on the crowded display. "You should have seen it, buddy. There were these spider-like things—Umbralings. They were everywhere. Honestly, I'm lucky I made it out alive."

The words were coming easier; there was something to talking them out, even when no one was there to hear them.

"I got this though," I said, placing my backpack on the only open chair in the room and unzipping the top flap. "It's a book. It's way too advanced for me, but if you were here I'm sure you could explain it. The Imp read through it, and he seemed to think there was a way to put your soul back together with your body."

Beep.

I shook my head. "No, I haven't figured that out yet. I did bring your soul though." I pulled the soul paper out of my bag and started to unfold it, but a soft knock on the door gave me reason to pause.

"Is someone in there?" a young woman's voice asked from outside.

Porter!

"Yeah, it's me. Gene. Come in," I said, tucking the soul sheet in my shirt pocket.

Porter pushed open the door gently. "Wow! That's a lot of flowers."

"They weren't here before?" I asked, carefully zipping up my backpack so she didn't see the Infernal Constructs, then setting it on the floor.

"What?"

"The flowers. I guess they weren't here when you came earlier?"

Porter shook her head. "No. How's Ed?"

I took a deep breath. "He's the quietest I've ever seen him."

That was stupid, Gene. She's already having a tough time as it is without your gallows humor.

She giggled. "That's funny."

Or not...

"How are you holding up?" Porter asked, stepping around a particularly large vase of tulips. "You feeling okay?"

"Me?" I said, dividing my attention between Ed and the backpack with its deeply Magickal contents. "I'm fine."

"Fine?" Porter stopped to twist one of the many balloon strings between her fingers. "You don't find it too *cold* in here?"

"Nah, I've felt worse."

"I bet." She let the mylar balloon bounce against the ceiling. "So, how long are you planning on staying?"

"Until his parents get here, I guess."

Porter tilted her head. "His parents are coming?"

"Yeah, you told me his parents were coming earlier, remember? In the hallway outside Morgan's room?"

At the mention of Morgan's name Porter's eyes flashed. "What were you doing in my room?"

That's not Porter.

"Morgan!"

Morgan, Porter, or whoever she was, lunged for my bag, grabbing it off the floor before I could clear Ed's bed.

"The illusion only shows you what you want to see, Eugene Law. So I guess I now know who you really care about."

"How did you—"

"Survive? Your Magick was enough to open the door just enough, so I made friends. It's what I do. I can be very persuasive when I want to be, but I'm sure you know that by now," the Porter-shaped Morgan said, flashing an oddly crooked grin.

"Wait, what about Ed?"

"What about him?" Porter said, throwing her hip to one side. "I got what I came here for. What happens now is none of my concern."

"But he'll die!"

"Gene," Morgan-Porter slung the bag over her shoulder, "you left me in the Gloom. Why should I care about him?"

"I..."

She pressed a finger to her lips. "Don't speak. I don't want to hear it anymore. I plan to take you apart one piece at a time, Eugene Law. Your roommate won't survive the night, and while nature is taking care of him, I've got a Reaver picked out with this girl's name on it," the illusion-covered Morgan said, pointing to her body.

"Like hell you will." I lunged for her, but she deftly avoided my clumsy attempt and yanked open the door.

We both froze, locked in the stern gaze of a much older couple standing just outside the door.

Ed's parents?

Morgan-Porter didn't waste time with idle chit-chat. She burst past them and headed down the narrow hallway, my backpack swinging wildly behind her.

"Are you Eugene Law?" the older man asked, his tightly buttoned plaid shirt straining to contain the round belly beneath it.

"Yes, sir."

My heart sank. I was going to have to tell them what

happened to their son, and with the book gone there was absolutely nothing I could do to save him.

The man I assumed was Ed's father stepped into the room, followed by a greying, curly haired woman with wide, horn-rimmed spectacles. "You're his roommate, right?"

"Yes, ma'am."

"Excellent. We have a number of questions for you," she said, moving past her husband to take a seat in the room's only chair.

Just answer their questions as fast as you can.

"What can I tell you? I know he fell in the street on his bike. I wasn't there at the time, but I—"

"We already know all that," the elder gentleman said, looking down rimless glasses at me, and adjusting a strained belt.

"I see, well I have to—"

"We want to know about how you two know Kevin Peterson."

"Who?"

The older man sighed and returned to the door, gently opening it to check the hallway, then closing it again.

"I'm afraid you've got the wrong room."

He bent the latch effortlessly—making sure we wouldn't be receiving anymore visitors—with the same effort it would have taken me to twist a bag-tie. "No, son, I assure you, we have *exactly* the right room. We're a tight-knit cluster, and when one of ours dies we investigate."

"Dies?"

The elderly woman's eyelids blinked vertically, a second membrane sliding out under the first.

Illickthids!

44

SOUL WEAVERS

The overweight man, who only moments ago had made it next to impossible to leave, advanced on me menacingly. "I say we rip him apart and divine what we can from his entrails."

I reached for my Magick and let the power rise in my chest like a swelling balloon.

"Magician, I've shit out turds more powerful than you."

"I don't want any trouble."

The old woman removed her glasses and rubbed her eyes gently. "Can we just talk, Harold? I told you to cool your jets. He might know what happened."

"You're Illickthids?" I asked, slowly stepping backward to put a rather large pot of blooming roses between me and Ed's aggressive visitors.

"We are," the woman said, folding her glasses neatly and laying them in her lap. "It's taken us a long time to track down you two—"

"I smell Reaver on him," Harold said, his fists tightening. "He's a Magician, and he smells like Reaver. What else is there to ask?"

Whrr! Click! Click! Whrr!

The woman let out a string of high-pitched clicking and popping sounds, and her partner seethed.

Click! Pop!

"I'm sorry, young man, but you have to understand there aren't a lot of us left. We are a dying race. Before long it'll just be Harold and me. That's why losing Kevin has been so distressing. Tell me, do you know what happened to him?"

The older man pulled up on his belt. "We know what happened to him! Reaver and the smell of burning chitin—what else is there to say? This Magician conjured a Reaver. Kevin must have tried to save the victim's soul, and he didn't survive."

"I didn't conjure any Reavers!" I said, my heart ramming against my rib cage.

"I believe him, Harold. Listen to his heartbeat." The elderly woman's second eyelid blinked rapidly.

"Agh!" Harold slammed his fists down on the table. "Then it was this one," he pointed to Ed's body, "he's got to be the conjurer. I remember his scent."

The elderly woman stood and adjusted the soft pleats of her skirt. "Perhaps you are right."

"No! Neither of you are right. Ed isn't the bad guy. The girl who just walked out that door is the Magician. *She's* the one bringing Reavers."

The woman ignored me. "Shall we?"

Harold nodded, removing his glasses and placing them in his shirt pocket.

"What are you doing?" I said, again letting my Magick bubble up in my chest. "I won't let you hurt him!"

Whrr! Click! Click!

The Magick roared in my body, hungry for a target and more than happy to be unleashed.

Moving far faster than I anticipated, Harold cleared Ed's hospital bed and pinned me against the far wall. He may have looked old and frail, yet in reality he was anything but. His second eyelids blinked a few times inches from my face.

My Magick surged down my arm, but the elder Illickthid was faster. His right hand no longer resembled a fist. It was now a serrated mantis claw pressed against my groin.

Whrr! Click! Click!

"Do it, Magician. Use your Magick and you'll be singing soprano from here on out," Harold said, then turned his attention back to the older woman. "The other one's soul is yours."

The elderly woman nodded, her body melting away like hot wax and revealing a large midnight-blue mantis. The Illickthid was old, her chitinous exoskeleton hazy like weathered paint. It held deep gouges, a battle map of scrapes and claw-strikes. Large and multi-faceted eyes sparkled a deep ruby red in the overhead light.

"No, stop!" I said, even as the sharp hook pressed against my man-bits. "He didn't do anything! Ed's innocent."

If the female Illickthid heard me, she didn't appear to care. She raised a hook-like claw over my roommate's body.

Whrr! Click! Click!

"Do it, Dorothy," Harold said.

For an instant her claw hovered in the air, and then she drove it down with a single furious burst of power.

"No!" I shouted, turning away. "Please, no!"

Whrr! Click! Clack! Clack!

I turned back to find Dorothy's claws slipping in and out of Ed's body without piercing it. Those razor-sharp hooks appeared to be digging for something.

Whrr! Clack! Click!

Harold and Dorothy continued to argue in their strange language of clicks and pops, but whatever she was looking for inside Ed's body she wasn't finding it. My captor's claw pressed harder against me. "Where is his soul?"

"In the gullet of a Death Shroud!" I shouted, tired of being pushed around by these two retirees.

Whrr! Click! Clack!

Harold pulled his claw back. "Did you say a Death Shroud?"

I placed a hand on my man-parts to confirm everything was still where it was supposed to be, and once I was content I was still a fully functioning member of society, I nodded. "Yes. His soul was eaten by a Death Shroud."

Click?

Clack.

Clack!

Clack...

"I'm sorry, young man," Harold said, stepping back to give me room to breathe. "We didn't mean to scare you, but we had to dig past your emotions to get deep enough to know the truth."

"You could have just asked! I told you what I knew."

Dorothy had returned to her elderly self, her claws replaced by soft and wrinkled hands that gently caressed Ed's body. "I see that now. I am so sorry for your friend. I wish there was something we could do for him, but without his soul there's nothing to weave."

"Weave?" I said, rubbing at the bruise Harold's claw had left on my hip.

"We are Soul Weavers," Harold said, joining Dorothy on the far side of Ed's bed. "You may call us Illickthids, but the direct translation is Soul Weaver."

The paper that held what remained of Ed's soul rested heavy against my chest.

Should I? Is it safe? Do you really have a choice?

"We'll let you be with your friend in his final hours. You can trust Harold and I won't rest until we find the girl that brought the Reavers." Dorothy placed a hand on her partner.

"And when we find her, we'll gut her like a fish," Harold added in a matter-of-fact tone that told me he meant it.

"Wait."

I slowly removed the paper, unfolding it gently on the body of my roommate. Jacobean's Prefect had held, its individual lines remaining un-smudged and the Magick I'd willed into it was still humming.

"Oh my," Dorothy said, retrieving her glasses from her pocket. "Jacobean's Prefect. You've saved his soul!"

The translucent top of Ed's head drifted above the hand-drawn sigil, his long hair all that remained—ironic given his intense love for that hair.

"No—it's all but gone. There's only a few inches left."

"Oh, sweetheart," Dorothy said, placing a warm hand on mine from across the bed. "You have all we need."

"What?!"

Harold smiled, the first time I'd seen him do such a thing since we'd met. "She's right. The soul expands, especially if it's resilient." He let his fingers pass through the tops of Ed's soul hair. "Oh yeah, that's got plenty of stretch to it. Check it out, Dorothy."

The elderly woman nodded, leaning in and taking a deep whiff of Ed's soul like she were checking a casserole. "Perfection. I can work with this. Harold, go get me some coffee. I think there was a vending machine near the end of the hall."

"On it," the old man said, snapping the bent latch like peanut-brittle. "Two creams?"

"Like I'd take it any other way."

"Yes Ma'am." The male Illickthid disappeared into the hospital hall.

"He's a good one, that Harold. A little rough around the edges, but you try being with me for a few hundred years."

"I…"

Dorothy grabbed one of the large vases and pulled the flowers out of it before shoving them in my hands.

"Huh?"

She then proceeded to pour the contents of the vase over Ed's body.

"Hey! What are you—"

"Oh, honey, you've got to get him good and wet if you ever expect to get the cables going."

"Cables?!"

Dorothy's hands returned to their mantis-claw shape. "Sugar, I've been sewing souls since I was a larvae. Your friend has great material to work with, so you run along now and let me do my thing. He'll be back and turning cartwheels in no time."

Ed's body lied soaking on the bedsheets in front of me, the last wisps of his soul-hair drifting gently above the wet paper.

"Now," Dorothy said, dipping the tips of her claws into the top of Ed's soul like the needle of a sewing machine. "You've got your own challenges. We'll come as soon we can. We may not look like much, but we were quite the Reaver slayers in our day."

"I don't know how to thank you..."

Dorothy winked a second eyelid at me. "Save a few of those bastards for me and we'll be right as rain, son."

MATCHBOX MEETINGS

y legs propelled me through yet another narrow gap between the buildings. I used every one of Ed's shortcuts to reach Morgan's dorm. In the twilight of the early evening, the brick building lay shrouded in twisting shadows . Oak tree branches swayed gently in the cool air, their leaves rustling in giddy anticipation for whatever the night would bring.

If Porter was in Morgan's crosshairs...

I shook aside those thoughts and raced up the steps.

The stairs were empty. My feet pounded on the steps in time with my heart. I didn't know what I'd find when I hit the floor, but I didn't care—this had to stop, and it had to stop now.

I burst through the door and stumbled out into an empty hall. There were no sounds of movement, and no voices behind closed doors, only the gentle hum of air conditioning filling the quiet floor.

I took a deep breath and tried to shake out the tension in my shoulders, then stalked the hall like a jungle cat. As I did, memories of the last few months filled my head.

It was all fake... all of it.

Morgan hadn't cared for me, she cared only for what I represented—a battery.

Magick rolled in my chest and tingled in my fists.

Let's see if she's ready for it.

I reached her door and grabbed the knob, surprised to find it unlocked. The cold metal twisted under my hand and I pushed my way inside. I wasn't prepared for what I discovered when I flicked the lights on.

Her room had been wrecked. There was no other way to put it. Torn sheets hung like tattered crepe paper from the bed. Morgan's dresser had been toppled over, its contents tossed across the floor like the entrails of a gutted beast. Her desk had been crushed, with empty gaps where drawers once sat.

What the hell?

I pushed aside the sheets and slumped on her bed. Morgan wasn't here, and neither was Porter. They were both out there, somewhere, and without Ed I had no idea how I'd find them, let alone what I would do if I did.

"Son of a bitch!"

I let my Magick expand, filling the room with cosmic frustration. It whipped the tiny space into a fury, sending broken shelves, ripped clothes, and just about anything else it could find swirling like the inside of a small tornado. The room became a maelstrom of anger and frustration, with me solidly in the center.

"Damn you, Morgan!" I shouted to no one in particular.

My Magick scraped at the walls and tore apart anything else that wasn't nailed down, but I didn't care. It felt good to let the power out; I was tired of being told what to do and how to do it. Jacobean could shove his Prefect where the sun didn't shine for all I cared.

She's outfoxed you at every turn.

The contents of Morgan's room continued to spin around me, and I let my Magick go further, giving into the frustration and anger I'd clamped down on for days. Drywall tore free from the walls, exposing wires that crackled and popped in the open air.

She expects this from you. She expects stupid displays of uncontrolled Magick.

The Yaga Doll's words came back to me in that moment.

'Your power will be your undoing.'

"Argh!"

I let my Magick go in a primal yell. The tiny cyclone dissipated, sending junk raining down on the formerly clean floor. I dropped to my knees in the center of that destruction.

None of this was getting me any closer to finding Morgan or Porter.

I wasn't a Magician. I was a mess.

Click. Click

The faint sound of something hitting the window got my attention.

"What the…"

A small moth-like bug whacked against the glass a few times, then stopped to crawl along the sill. I'd seen that insect before; it had a name, and lived in a matchbox—a matchbox I found sitting on that outside sill.

Tattlewing…

I climbed over the broken drywall and turned the window latch, letting the ancient glass and steel slowly swing open into the cool evening. The moth fluttered inside, dancing and darting in the hazy light of an overturned desk lamp.

"Bono," I said, trying to lure the moth away from the lamp and onto my hand. He twirled in the air a few times before coming to a stop on my palm. "Hey, did you see Morgan? Do you know what happened?"

The tiny moth raised up on its front legs and rubbed what looked like arms together.

I'm talking to a moth. No, I'm talking to Bono. I'm talking to a moth named Bono.

"Well? Can you tell me?"

The moth appeared to nod its angular head.

"Good God, man. Tell me!" I shouted at the tiny insect. "Ed's not coming. His soul is being embroidered by what might be your great, great grandmother, for all I know. It's just you and me, buddy. If you know something, you need to tell me."

The Tattlewing flapped his wings slowly.

"I'm sorry, I don't know what that means. Ed didn't teach me how to speak Tattlewing or whatever the hell it is you speak. I have to find Morgan, damn it. Porter is in danger if I don't. You remember Porter, don't you?"

The moth nodded again, this time flicking his wings in and out in a rapid pattern.

"Yes, Porter. You know Porter. Good. Can you find Porter? Wherever she is, Morgan won't be far away."

The insect bobbed his head, then rose up into the air, his tiny wings beating furiously.

"Wait, just a second." I scanned the room one last time. There was nothing here for me, nothing that would help me against Morgan or her Reavers, and nothing I could use to keep Porter safe.

"I'm on my own."

The moth landed on my nose, batting it a few times with his wings before rising off again.

"No, you're right. I have a moth named Bono. What's there to worry about?"

The Tattlewing slipped out the window and into the night air. Not being a moth myself, it left me to climb back through the piles of junk and out the dorm door.

Outside under the trees, Bono rested on Ed's bike, his wings beating in an almost irritated fashion. I grabbed the handlebars and climbed onboard. The tiny insect fluttered into the air and quickly crossed the sidewalk before heading toward the street. I paused for a second and let my fingers trace the scraped edges of the bike's handlebars. They brought back memories of Ed landing in that street, the Death Shroud, and all the darkness that lay ahead of me.

The Tattlewing drifted over the empty pavement and past the sidewalk on the other side.

"Wait up!" I shouted, dropping into a low gear. The scuffed-up bike groaned in protest. "I'm not as fast as you are."

Bono circled once, then drifted out of sight.

What are you doing, Gene?

The library's dark bricks glared down at me from beyond the distant trees.

Whatever I have to.

46

A WORLD ON FIRE

*T*he tiny moth faded in and out of view beneath the sodium-yellow streetlamps. I pedaled faster, ducking my head down to pick up speed, yet still keeping the diminutive Tattlewing in sight. Bono floated over the curb and turned off past the accounting building courtyard. We cut across the spot where I'd first met the tiny insect—the same place I had torn into my roommate, even when all he'd wanted to do was help me.

I should have listened to you, Ed.

Bono circled in the air a few times like an impatient child before fluttering back out and onto a side street. I pumped my legs and jumped the curb again, Ed's bike chain rattling.

Don't fail me now.

A hush lay over the street. The sun had already retreated behind the thick canopy of majestic oaks, and I found no other students in the narrow alley with me.

The Tattlewing kept flying, his little wings drawing me deeper into the heart of the campus. We hadn't gone more than a few more side streets when I confirmed exactly where we were going.

The library.

My roommate's moth circled back, brushing past my face before landing on the scuffed handlebars. Large oaks swayed gently in the faint breeze, their long moss beards wagging in the evening air. The library loomed large in front of us, its port-hole-like windows shining in the dark like a hungry panther stalking its prey.

"Is this it?"

The diminutive insect's wings opened and folded in rapid succession, not knowing much in the way of Tattlewing I had to assume that meant yes.

The plaza was empty. There were no students walking beneath those trees. No nighttime picnics and no one waiting on a park bench, no Morgan, and most of all, no Porter.

"Where are they?"

The moth paced back and forth on the knobby rubber grip of Ed's handlebars.

"I have no idea what that means."

Bono stopped and crossed his tiny front legs.

"I'm guessing the trail's gone cold?"

The moth's wings opened and closed.

Bingo.

I stepped off the bike and walked it to the curb. The library's soaring brick walls rose above the oak trees beneath it. I parked Ed's wheels against one of the racks, not bothering to lock it, and not sure I'd see it again.

"I made this mess, Bono," I said, letting the moth crawl up my hand and onto my shoulder. "I'm going to clean it up." I fished his tiny matchbox home out of my pocket. "Here you go buddy," I slide back the paper top. "You've done enough."

The insect crossed his little legs again.

"You sure?"

A gentle breeze caused the trees to stir and sent the dangling twists of spanish moss bobbing.

The insect's wings stayed closed.

"All right, little guy. I don't know if you can shoot laser beams out of your eyes or something. But whatever you can do, I'll take all the help I can get."

Bono's wings opened and closed in a rapid snapping motion.

"Right, I'm wasting time." I reached for the Magick in my chest and let it swell. "Let's do this."

I slipped Bono's box back in my pocket and took a deep breath.

One way or another it ends tonight, Morgan.

I APPROACHED THE LIBRARY CAUTIOUSLY; with each step, my furtive eyes kept tabs on the twisting moss or the rustle of branches. Bono, for his part, remained on high alert, his tiny front legs feeling the air and those multi-faceted eyes tracking any movement right along with me.

We had reached the inner sidewalk when I felt the first prickles of that dark place. Even from the Gloom, the power reached out into our world. It set my hairs on edge and my heart along with them.

"Come on, Morgan. Where are you?" I whispered, more to myself than anyone else. Had she gone back into the Gloom? Was she capable of that without me? Morgan had made it out on her own, but could she get back in?

I turned away from the main entrance, instead opting to return to the side door we'd used the first time. We hadn't finished rounding the corner before I found it, Ten Spins' Bent Key laying perfectly drawn in bright chalk along the sidewalk square.

Bono launched off my shoulder and circled in a violent and confusing pattern.

"I know, buddy, it's a trap."

The Tattlewing fluttered anxiously.

"I don't have the Sojourner's Jacket. I wouldn't survive more than a minute on the other side."

The moth opened its wings wide and glided on the gentle breeze.

"Wait, you want me to project myself."

A rapid wing snap told me as much.

"Brilliant!"

The tiny moth beamed.

"Now I just need to remember that sigil. How did it go?"

Bono landed on my shoulder and closed his little legs.

"Yeah, I'm guessing you don't know. I'll figure it out."

I searched the ground and found a small broken piece of chalk. It wasn't much.

Best get it right the first time then.

I crouched down to start, but Bono sprung off my shoulder and flew to a stretch of sidewalk behind some large oak trees.

"Oh, right, once I'm on the other side I don't want to pop up right next to them."

I swore the tiny moth rolled in the air like my roommate used to roll his eyes.

"I'm new at this, dude."

Am I really? I'm about to enter the Gloom for the third time. I practically get my mail delivered there.

I joined the Tattlewing, and once I was satisfied the moth wasn't going to have me relocate again, I started to trace the Seal of Ariadne from memory.

"What am I going to do once I get there?" I asked the tiny insect perched on the pavement just outside the design.

Bono shrugged his front legs.

"Yeah," I said, adding the complex whorls and swirls from memory. "I don't know either. I figure I'll know more once I'm there. I just hope the Umbralings aren't around."

The diminutive bug tucked his legs in.

"Yeah, I'm guessing you aren't a fan of them either. You stay here and keep an eye on me."

The moth snapped his wings in and out in rapid-fire succession.

"Great. If Porter is on the other side I can't waste any more time." I stepped into Ariadne's Seal and sank to my knees, checking the edges one more time against the best of my memory. "Bono, do you have any idea what happens if I get this wrong?"

The tiny insect paced back and forth just beyond the Seal's outer edge.

"Yeah, I don't either. Oh well, here goes nothing."

I closed my eyes and pressed my chalky palms against the damp concrete. Magick surged, running through my arms and down into the complex swirls of what I hoped was Ariadne's complete and accurate Seal, or at least something close enough to get me where I needed to go.

Just reach the other side. Find out what's happening and get a lay of the land. Keep an eye out for Porter, Jess, and anyone else caught up in Morgan's evil, and try not to get killed.

I took a deep breath and slowly let it go.

That's a tall order. How about just don't screw it up?

"Let's do this thing." I closed the Seal in my mind, letting the Magick twist and twirl through the complex patterns. I imagined the Gloom, its shadowy perpetual twilight, and the darkness that lay beyond.

The breeze shifted, and I opened my eyes. The Gloom I found myself floating in held little in common with the one I'd left scant hours ago.

This one was on fire.

LETTING GO

*T*he Gloom was burning.

I drifted above the soot and ash, gently tethered by Ariadne's thread. My body knelt quietly in the Seal of Ariadne, but something was off. The thread I'd remembered had been silvery, this one was not. It was black and twisted like the strands of an Umbraling's web.

I shook my head. I didn't have time to focus on that; the cord was still a tether, and it drifted softly in the burning twilight.

Don't get this cut...

Morgan's warning replayed in my mind, and I subconsciously twisted the thick thread in my hand, while in front of me the library burned.

"I promised you a way out, and I'll deliver it," Morgan's voice rang out from somewhere beyond the dense oaks I'd hidden behind.

The little insect had been right, to appear where I'd first planned would have been near-certain suicide.

Thank you, Bono!

My translucent body began to drift, and I had to focus to keep from floating out into the open. Movement in the Gloom was a challenge in this projected state, but I didn't have any other choice. I willed myself behind a particularly large oak that lined the outer edge of the plaza, giving me a bird's-eye view of Morgan and whomever she was talking to.

She paced in front of the library's main entrance. Her body language didn't display the confidence I had expected—instead it spoke of frustration. The Imp sat on her shoulder, his wings opening and closing in the gleaming fires of the library.

"The masters don't believe you," the Imp said, admiring his claws. "They think you have deceived them."

Morgan turned a sharp corner, and I noticed she carried Ten Spins' Infernal Constructs in her hands. "I have done no such thing. You know that. Why don't you convince them?"

The Imp shrugged his small rubbery shoulders. "Because it's boring. It'll be far more fun to watch you burn when you fail."

"And if I do fail, what happens to you?"

The Imp snapped his tail. "Damn it." He leapt off her shoulder and into the eternal twilight, flapping his wings and driving his body toward the library.

The Minor Demon landed on the ground before the fiery and imposing wooden doors. "She's telling the truth, wise ones. The young Magician she speaks of has tremendous talent. He's not very bright, but his Magick, pardon me. How did you describe it?"

Morgan shouted back to him. "He hits like a dump truck."

"Yes, a 'dump truck' of Magick."

The Imp leaned an ear into the fiery doors. "Right. Okay, so a 'dump truck' is a truck that delivers large quantities of—what? You missed most of the Industrial Revolution, and you expect me to catch you up on all of that now?"

Fire roared from the door seams, and the Imp slapped his forehead. "Let's just say it's like a stampede of wild horses."

He leaned in again.

"Yes, the big ones. Very large. I'd say giant horses. Lots and lots of them." The Imp's wings folded in gently and he appeared to be listening. "They want to know why he isn't here?"

Morgan dropped Ten Spins' Infernal Constructs on the ground and turned to face the fiery entrance. "He'll be here."

"Yes." The Imp nodded, then turned his attention to Morgan. "And how do you know this?"

Morgan pointed to the center of the plaza, where a slow shimmering of Magick took my breath away. Porter was on her side, bright-red blood on her cheeks, with her body pinned beneath the spinning Rubik's Cube. Something flickered in and out of sight above her prone form.

Her soul!

Porter's spirit was twisted and bent like a cubist's painting. Back in the real world bile rose up in my throat and it took all I had to hold it back.

"She's a ready receptacle," Morgan said, a wide smile on her face. "Sure, she hasn't been primed like the others, but with her spirit in knots there's no way a Reaver will have any problems climbing inside."

"Right, right," the Imp said, turning his attention back to the door. "Yes, she realizes the Reavers are under your control, but if you would provide another, that would be very much appreciated."

Morgan approached the door, turning her back to Porter. "Tell them I don't want another weak one either. The last Reaver didn't even survive a run-in with a Yaga Doll."

This was my chance. I took a deep breath and willed myself forward, pushing my mind to bring me to Porter.

Tips of flame licked at the door seams.

"What are they doing?" Morgan asked.

The Imp shrugged. "Thinking, is my guess."

I drifted closer to the Cube, my jet-black cord rolling out behind me like a streamer.

"Thinking!" Morgan cried, throwing her hands in the air.

"What is there to think about? They want out, and I promised them I'd get them out."

"Careful," the Imp said, his tail whipping dangerously. "You are not in a position to argue with them. The only reason you still draw breath is because of their great generosity and your foresight to bind me to you."

Morgan's Magick streamed from the Cube, filling the surrounding air with a complex series of interlocking sigils woven into the ash and soot of the Gloom.

"I'm so close," she said, wringing her hands at the diminutive Demon. "It's right there, just outside my grasp."

The Imp nodded. "And it'll stay that way unless you give them what they want."

"He'll be here."

I started to reach for my Magick, then stopped. Would she detect it?

Yes! You've got to think, Gene.

The Cube continued to spin, and with it, Porter's soul twisted tighter.

I'll figure a way out of this.

Something silvery flashed inside the twisted mess of Porter's soul, something I should have figured out much earlier.

Ariadne's Thread!

Porter wasn't in the Gloom—she was still outside. She was in the Plaza, somewhere hidden, and her spirit had been projected into the Gloom.

She's not here!

"Hold on, Porter," I whispered. "I'm coming."

I reached for my cord and gave it a tug, except instead of sliding back into my body, nothing happened.

I yanked again—still nothing.

"Having trouble, Gene?"

Morgan!

The cord burned in my fingers.

"You aren't going anywhere," she said as Ariadne's Thread encircled my hands with a mind of its own. "I told you, when you don't understand Magick you get things wrong, and getting things wrong has consequences."

My translucent body tumbled from the ashen sky, landing on the ground not far from Porter. Her twisted soul stared through me.

"Now," Morgan said, picking up the end of my thread and dragging me like a hooked fish toward the fiery doors. "Where were we? Oh, that's right. Tell them I've got their dump truck."

The Imp tented his fingers together and barely suppressed a giggle. "Actually, we were going with a stampede of horses, but they will be pleased either way."

I twisted in the soot-covered ground, but I couldn't stop her, Morgan was too strong in the Gloom. I kicked out with my translucent feet, but they only flapped like a flag in the breeze.

The Imp relayed her message and the flames of the door rose higher, burning with a brilliant fury. "Very good, I shall tell her."

"Tell me what?" Morgan pulled me onto the sidewalk while the thread quickly wrapped my feet.

"They want to know if you still would like the Reaver for the girl."

"No, don't do it, Morgan!" I shouted, fighting against the twisted steel-like thread.

"That depends, Gene. Will you do what I say?"

Porter's eyes looked at me from the twisted mass of soul locked beneath the Cube's Magick. Tears streaked down those ghostly cheeks.

"I… Yes."

"Prove it," Morgan said, placing a soft hand on my ghostly chest. "Give me your power. All of it."

"Morgan…"

"Do it, or what she's experiencing now will be bliss compared to what the Reaver will do to her."

"I can't, I don't know how. I—"

"Wrong answer, Gene!" Morgan turned to the Imp. "I'll take my Reaver now."

The Imp snapped his tail and placed a hand upon the fiery doors. "It's coming."

Somewhere in the distance an alien scream shattered the eternal twilight and shattered whatever feelings I had left for Morgan Crowley.

"I'll do it! Stop, don't hurt her."

"Better make it fast, Gene. Once the Reaver gets here I'm afraid there won't be much I can do."

Porter's eyes pleaded with me from the folds of her pinched face.

I'm sorry...

I reached into my chest and released the Magick locked inside those walls. It boiled and rumbled like the fires of the Gloom. Morgan's eyes sparkled in the flames of the library's door.

"All of it, Gene."

I closed my eyes and let go, setting fire to the barriers, the controls, and anything that stood between me and my Magick.

What have I done?

48

HELLFIRE

y Magick roared with the force of a tidal wave. Morgan's hand directed it toward the doors, and I felt the rumble before I saw it.

They're opening!

I wanted to scream out, but the pain was too great. My Magick raced down that blackened cord like a live wire, crackling and sparking in the infernal dark. Somewhere in the burning half-light of the Gloom, a Reaver screamed, and it was quickly answered by a second cry.

If you want to survive, don't cut the cord.

Morgan's words came back to me in that moment—it was barely a cohesive thought, but I didn't have much else to go on. I had to cut the cord. Without it my Magick would stay on the other side, safe in the real world, and attached to a body without a soul.

Morgan dug her sharp fingers into my chest and pulled even more Magick down that damnable thread.

Clack!

A metallic clank startled all of us. The Imp sprang into the air only to crash down against the ash-covered ground, his leg chained to something.

"What the—"

Morgan's question was interrupted by the translucent grin of the best roommate a guy could ever ask for. "Maxwell's Bind —I have all the best stuff." Ed shimmered into view, a strange patchwork of stitched-together soul. "The Imp is mine now."

Morgan's fingers tightened, pulling even more Magick from my collapsing spirit. "I have real power now. I don't need the Demon. Look," she pointed to the doors, "you're too late, they'll be open soon, and I will be rewarded!"

"Cut the cord, Ed!" I shouted.

My roommate's stitched-up soul turned to face me, even he continued to wrangle with the petulant Imp. "That's suicide!"

"That's how she's getting the power to open the doors. Cut it!"

My roommate's eyes traced the twisted thread; the realization sinking in and taking with it his signature grin.

My roommate held up the opposite end of the Imp's chain. "Do it."

The Imp shook his head. "She's bound and named me. I am Kilgore the—"

Ed yanked the chain as if he were dealing with a rabid dog. "I hold Maxwell's Bind. You're old enough to know what that means."

The Imp nodded, touching the clasp before snapping back his burnt fingers. "He was a jerk."

Ed smiled. "And he was also my great, great, great grandfather."

The bright green color drained from the Imp's face. "Crap."

The door rumbled open farther, sending bursts of flame into the Gloom along with wisps of something more malevolent.

"They're coming and there's nothing you can do to stop it!" Morgan cried.

"Maxwell's Bind commands you, do what I say or risk an unmaking!"

The Imp's tail cracked like a whip and sent the Magick curving away from the doors. It cut across my chest like a razorblade and sliced clean through Ariadne's Thread.

Boom!

Power no longer constrained by the manipulated thread tossed Morgan like a rag doll. She hit the ash-covered pavement with bone-jarring force, her head snapping against the hard ground. Morgan's spirit, with its own thread, rolled out of her body and up in the Gloom's twilight.

"Ed," I shouted, pulling the strands away. "Porter's back in the real-world. You've got to find her. She's trapped somewhere."

My roommate pulled the chain tight. "What about you?"

"I'll handle Morgan."

Ed's patchwork soul reached out to grab my own. "Gene, you have no thread. Your Magick is on the other side. You can't—"

"I can, and I will! Now go!" I ripped my hand away and launched myself at Morgan's drifting ghost.

"Come on," Ed said, pulling the Imp. "You're coming with me."

The Imp shook his tiny head. "We aren't going anywhere."

"Why?"

Multiple Reaver screams rocked through the Gloom.

It was Ed's turn to lose all color in his face. "Crap."

Bursts of fiery Chaos Magick filled the air from all sides. The twisted and macabre mis-match of appendages and organs shuffled into view. There had to be a dozen of them, their screams alien and terrifying.

Morgan's translucent eyes opened. "What have you done?"

"I'm putting things right," I said, grabbing Morgan's Thread.

The library's doors pushed open farther, sending the flames

and Magick rising higher. Dark and twisted shadows escaped from inside its infernal depths.

"You can't stop them, Gene. Why not join them?" Morgan said, her ghostly hands cupping my face. "Oh, Gene. I never wanted any of this to happen to us. I love you. I've always loved you. Why can't you see that?"

Morgan's eyes reflected the door's flames.

"You don't know what love is, Morgan, and whatever it is you *think* love is, it definitely isn't." I tossed the loops of her thread into the door's fire.

"Gene!" she screamed, her spirit yanked toward the yawning portal, twisting like a fish on the line. She clung to the door's edge as flames licked at her hands and set fire to the tips of her bright green hair. "Help me, Gene! You don't know what it's like on the other side. I can't survive that."

Morgan's Magick sputtered against the ceaseless pull of the library, Ariadne's Thread catching fire in the unquenchable flame. The door rumbled again, but this time it wasn't opening —it was closing. Without my Magick to keep it open, the door was pulling shut and taking Morgan with it.

I closed my eyes and turned away, grabbing tight to Morgan's Thread. "Goodbye, Morgan."

"Gene! I've always loved—"

I held the burning thread in my hands and pulled it taut.

"Please, Gene! No!"

I snapped it in two, condemning Morgan to whatever lay on the other side of those doors.

"No!" Her screams vanished in the library's flames.

What have I done?

"A little help, bro?" Ed's soul flickered in and out in the chaotic Magick of the twisted Reavers. He was surrounded, while above him the Imp continued to pull at Maxwell's Bind like an unruly toddler.

The Rubik's Cube that held Porter slowed to a stop,

tumbling to the ash-covered ground and releasing the young woman's soul to drift in the air like premium Reaver-feed.

"Ed, they're going after Porter!" The remaining monsters wasted little time in surrounding her unconscious spirit. Their misshapen mouthes screamed and gibbered in the burning twilight. "Ed?"

My roommate didn't respond, he couldn't. His patchwork soul had enough to do to just stay upright, the Imp's tether yanking his arm.

Porter or Ed...

I floated helplessly.

You can't save them both.

I reached for my Magick, but found it missing.

The cord!

No cord meant no Magick; I was about as useful as a plastic bag in the wind.

Whirr! Click! Click! Clack!

Larger-than-life mantises cut a path through the Gloom. Their chitinous shells sparkled in the fiery Magick. A voice echoed in my head, a deep and rumbling version of the sweet old woman I'd met in Ed's hospital room.

"I told you to leave some for me, Magician."

Reaver screams and the clicks and slashes of Illickthid claws filled the Gloom. Porter's eyes fluttered, and she winced.

"Gene?"

Porter?

"Gene? Is that you?" Her confused spirit reached out for me. "I can't... I can't breathe!" She clutched at her throat.

Ed fought to hold onto the angry Imp. "Pull her Thread!"

Porter's silvery thread drifted in the Gloom. I took a deep breath and grabbed her drifting spirit. The thread brushed against my hand and I looped my fingers around it, then put the entire mass into her hand.

"Pull!" I shouted.

Porter's short gasps sent my heart racing. "Pull it or we both die!"

Her fingers touched mine and the Gloom went white.

49

LOST AND FOUND

I blinked my eyes and found myself face first on the hard sidewalk with the scorched remains of Ariadne's Seal around me.

"Gene!"

Ed grabbed my arm and pulled me to my feet. My roommate looked more than a little worse for wear, his hospital gown still flapping in the light breeze. Mercifully, somewhere along the way he appeared to have stopped to acquire underpants.

"Where's Porter? She's running out of air," I asked, my legs wobbly.

"I don't know. I thought she came with you." Ed helped me steady myself.

"No, Morgan did something to her, but she has to be close by."

I leaned on Ed. Together we left the sidewalk and searched between the trees. We hadn't gone a dozen feet before we discovered Jess's unconscious body.

"She was one of the Reaver hosts." I let go of my roommate and pushed past the fallen girl. "See if she's okay; I've got to find Porter."

The rest of the plaza was a sea of unconscious women, along with a few men sprinkled in for good measure. Morgan must have been working hard to acquire an army of hosts.

I broke into a run, my legs finally working enough to propel me across the wide plaza.

She doesn't have much time! Where is she?

Each body I passed that wasn't Porter's made my heart beat faster. How long could she survive without air? And why did she need to?

I reached the center of the plaza and stopped. This had to be the spot, she couldn't be anywhere else, but there was nothing here.

"Porter!"

No response.

I leaned my hand against a large oak and tried to collect my thoughts. She had to be here. This was where I had seen her body.

Help...

Porter's voice drifted gently on the wind, bubbling up from inside the ancient tree. "The tree!"

"What?" Ed shouted from across the field. "Did you find her?"

Something wicked and dark twisted beneath the dense trunk.

The Witherings...

"It's a Withering, Ed. Porter's trapped inside it."

"How do you know?"

"Morgan talked about how many she'd found on campus," I said, running my hands along the bark. "Trust me."

Ed knocked on the tree. A hospital bracelet dangled from his narrow wrist. "How do we get her out?"

"Morgan knows, but she never taught me. I don't know the right Magick." I frantically circled the large tree looking for a clue, any clue that might help me free Porter.

"Gene, if she's trapped inside you've got to get her out before she becomes permanently part of the plaza"

"I know. I just… let me think."

Velcurses? No. What about the Gorbel? No! No! Damn it, the Eldero Seals aren't going to do it either. Why the hell is Magick so fucking complicated?

My gut seized and my lungs burned at the thought of Porter's tortured gasps.

"Porter!" I screamed, banging my fist against the trunk. "Hold on, just hold on!"

Ed grabbed my shoulder. "Don't just stand there. Do something."

"You don't understand, Magick is—"

My words vanished mid-sentence, everything I'd planned to say blowing away like smoke in the wind.

Why do humans make Magick so complicated?

"What, Gene? What don't I understand?"

I shook off Ed's hand. "Stand back."

Ed jumped away, giving me ample space in front of the mighty tree. I placed both hands solidly on the trunk and let my palms press up against the rough bark.

I don't know what I'm doing, Porter. But someone once told me that it didn't always matter. I hope they're right.

I reached for my Magick. It was tired and spent, a poor facsimile of what I'd wielded only moments ago in the heart of the Gloom, but it had to be enough. The Withering was angry and frustrated, but it was also strong, with deep roots and a beating heart.

Beating heart?

I reached deeper, and sure enough, there it was; a gently beating heart—quiet and soft, and barely alive in the depths of the ancient heartwood.

"She's in there," I said, willing what remained of my Magick deeper.

"Gene, your hands!" Ed's voice was laced with panic, but I didn't dare open my eyes.

"I can't reach her," I said, my fingers drifting through the thick and fibrous center.

"Stop, Gene. You're falling in!"

Ed's words faded into background noise in my pursuit of Porter's heartbeat.

Deeper. I have to go deeper.

I drew up the last bits of Magick from the well and pushed past the bark, past the pain, and deep into center of the old tree.

"Porter," I said, my voice broken and choked in the depths of the Withering.

Faint fingers brushed against mine, only briefly, but they were enough to draw out the last of my Magick.

Porter!

My hand grasped hers. I leaned forward, crashing my body against Porter's and throwing everything I had into one last push. She fell backward, slipping through the Withering's rough skin and landing against the soft grass of the plaza.

I landed with far less grace than she did, barreling into a hard knot of roots and knocking most of the sense out of my head.

Ed's face appeared above mine. "Gene!"

I tried to sit up, but a crushing wave of darkness rolled over me, and all I could do was lie back on the hard ground. I turned my head to find Porter's sparkling eyes shining at me.

"Hey, Gene," she said, her voice tired and clearly confused. "How you doing?"

"Better now."

Oblivion crept in around the edges of my vision, and I let it, because for the first time in a long time I wasn't lying to myself, or anyone else.

I was better now, a lot better.

50

CHEERS FOR FEARS

I twisted the wet mug slowly between my fingers.

"Another beer?" the waitress asked, swinging by our table.

Ed started to raise his hand, then stopped. "Actually, on second thought, I need to pass." He slid his empty mug across the table to her. She scooped it up by the handle then turned to me. "And you?"

"No, I'm waiting for someone."

The waitress nodded before returning to the bar.

Ed leaned back in the wide booth, stretching his hands behind his head. The Demon Hunter's fishing vest of trinkets jingled as he moved, a subtle nod to what Ed's evening was sure to be like. "You sure I can't talk you out of this?"

"Completely."

"I mean, you know this is a new one, right? Even for me. There's word on the street we've got an amorphous, globular, multi-entity Demon that calls itself 'The Sheen.'" Ed leaned over, presumably expecting to wow me with this new bit of information.

"Not interested. I told you before, I'm meeting someone."

My roommate frowned. "This is about Morgan, isn't it."

The hairs on the back of my neck stood up at the mere mention of my ex-girlfriend's name.

'I love you, Gene.'

You don't know what love is, Morgan...

That scene had been stuck on loop in my head for weeks, replaying again and again. Each time, it returned to the moment I had snapped her cord and left Morgan to burn in the fiery heart of the library.

Ed waved his hand slowly in front of my face, knocking me out of the unpleasant visual. "How many times am I going to have to tell you it's not your fault?"

"I know..."

My roommate shook his head. "No, you *don't* know, and that's the problem. How many people survived that night because of what you did?"

"A lot."

Ed banged his hand on the table. "Damn straight it was a lot. I know, I was there. There were a lot of really confused people on the grass. Your lie really sold it."

I frowned. It was my lie. I'd convinced them Morgan was cooking up some sort of psychotropic drug and they'd been exposed to it. The university ate it up. Kids were run through detox, Morgan was considered a fugitive, and everything went back to normal. Sort of.

I played with the condensation dripping down the sides of my glass. "They never found her body."

Ed waved me off. "And I doubt they ever will. I've done some digging. That library is bad news, Gene—very bad news. I can't imagine anyone surviving the other side. It was built to hold the likes of Ten Spins himself. There's no way Morgan lasts a day inside there."

A folded copy of the Alligator pressed up against my leg.

Police unable to locate fugitive Morgan Crowley...

My fingers crumpled up the paper and Ed immediately backpedaled. "But it doesn't matter. You didn't kill her, you understand me? You know me, do you think I'd live with a murderer?"

"No…"

Ed smiled and pulled my beer over to him, taking a sip and putting it back down. "Good. Now, let's get down to business. This mission is purely reconnaissance. The Sheen is way outside my weight class, but with you backing me up I think we can get some decent intel."

I took my glass back. "I told you, I'm off tonight."

Ed drummed his fingers on the table. "That's the fourth time in five weeks."

"And? Are you keeping track for my paystubs?"

"Gene," the Demon Hunter leaned forward, his elbows on the table, "this isn't a job. This is a *calling*."

"Good. Tell it I'm on sabbatical."

"But your Magick—"

It was my turn to frown. "Is mine. It's not yours, and it's not Morgan's. It is mine. Are you trying to argue otherwise?"

Ed backed off, the trinkets in his vest jingling quietly. "I'm not trying to take your Magick. I'm just—"

"Trying to use it to help your cause?"

My roommate blanched, but I didn't back down. "I'm tired, Ed. I'm tired of being used, of being made to do things I don't want to do just because of who I am."

Ed crossed his arms, but didn't respond. His eyes never wavered from my face. We sat that way in an uncomfortable silence until he broke into a wide grin. "It's okay, roomie. I understand. I've been pushing you way too hard to get back out there and get the Magick game going. You're right. You know yourself better than anyone, and you've been through a lot. The best thing for you to do right now is heal up." He tapped his fingers on the table in an excited little rhythm. "Besides, not everyone can move on quickly."

"It's over between you two, isn't it?" I asked, grateful for the opportunity to change the subject.

"Yeah." Ed slid my beer over and finished it. "She was a great person—really great—but in the end we just weren't compatible."

"Is this because of the mess?"

Ed waved me off. "One woman's mess is another man's organic filing system. Porter just didn't appreciate that."

"I can't imagine why not," I said under my breath.

Ed pushed the empty glass back to me. "Alright, this is your last chance, Gene. We've got an opportunity to make history here and track an extremely rare monster—amorphous blob Demons being some of the most difficult to pin down. You sure you don't want in?"

I frowned at the now empty mug, then glanced at my watch. "Positive."

"Raincheck?" Ed asked, extending a hand.

I accepted his callused fingers and we shook on it. "Sure, another time."

The Demon Hunter slid out of the booth and zipped up his vest, patting his pockets for something. "Damn, Gene. I think I left my wallet back at the room. Do you mind…"

It was my turn to wave my roommate off. "I'll put it on your tab. Don't stay out too late, okay?"

Ed was already gone, the Demon Hunter and his jingling trinkets disappearing into the cold evening air.

I sighed and glanced at my watch again, trying to remember when she said she'd be off. I waved for the waitress, but no sooner had I gotten her attention than the door swung open and my date arrived. Long jeans and heels, with a tight top that showed off the toned muscles of her arms, Porter slid into the booth opposite me. "Meghan, you're still working here?"

The waitress nodded. "At least until next semester. You want what he's having?"

Porter lifted up the empty glass and took a sniff. "Sure, this'll work—two please."

Meghan disappeared into the bustle of the restaurant.

"Please tell me we aren't eating here," Porter said, setting her purse down on the seat. "You know what they say about seeing how the sausage is made…"

"Hey, this is Ed's favorite place to eat."

No sooner had his name escaped my lips than I wanted to pull it back into my mouth and swallow it.

If hearing Ed's name had bothered her, Porter didn't show it. "Uh huh, and that should explain everything."

We shared a chuckle as our beers arrived. "Speaking of wild man Lovely, isn't this a mission night? Shouldn't you be out saving the world?"

"I asked for the night off," I said, before clinking glasses with her.

"Wow, and he didn't have a problem with it?"

"No."

Porter set her glass down and frowned at me. "You aren't doing this because of me, are you?"

"No, no. It's not that. I just needed some time off."

Porter's eyes told me she didn't quite believe my answer. "Okay, but next time I want you out there and in the rotation. You hear me? You have a gift and you should use it."

Her eyes caught the light and I found myself lost in them. She was everything Morgan wasn't. This woman cared, and not just about herself.

"Now, where do you want to go toni—"

Crash!

Somewhere in the kitchen glass shattered, sending Porter into a panic. She knocked over her beer and spilled it across the table, those shining eyes full of fear. I grabbed napkins and mopped up the spilled beer, while a clearly shaken Porter put her glass upright.

"So much for that," she said, eyeing the empty glass.

I dragged wadded-up napkins across the table, sopping up the last of the beer. "I can get you another one..."

"No, no. Let's pay the bill and get out of here. Can we eat off campus tonight?"

Porter put on a brave face, but I could tell she was still jumpy. It would be a while before either of us got past the memory of Morgan Crowley, but I knew right then and there it was a battle I wouldn't enter into alone.

I dropped a few bills on the table and took Porter's hand. She smiled and together we put the restaurant, and our fears, in the rear-view mirror—if only for the night.

MARTIN SHANNON'S WEIRD FLORIDA

Short Stories

0 - Danderous Delivery (Newsletter Subscribers Only)

1 - Hook, Line, and Slinker

2 - Ballroom and Chain

3 - Bahama Blues

4 - Plasma Pistols

5 - Lights Out

6 - Mourning Paper

7 - Ignorance and Unleaded

8 - Black Valentine

9 - Soulless

10 - Ten Turns (Coming Soon)

Novels

1 - Dead Set

2 - Gathering Gloom

3 - Beaten Path

4 - Bloody Deed

5 - No Fury (Coming Soon)

BEATEN PATH

TALES OF WEIRD FLORIDA

Florida isn't all beaches and sunshine. There are strange and hidden places in the center of the state, places where Wild Magick runs free and dark things lurk beneath the cypress.

A single dirty deed in a backwater bar for the House tips the scales and sets Gene on a collision course with Demon Hunters, Darklings, and the best in Animated Demin. In short order, Tampa's ex-Magician finds himself deep in the heart of the Green Swamp where bad decisions reign supreme.

For a broken Magician, sometimes the only way forward is to go back and take the beaten path. Available on Amazon.

Turn the page for a sneak peek at "Beaten Path."

STEEL-TOE SLUMBER

BEATEN PATH PREVIEW

*W*ater dripped from the dive bar's leaky faucet. It left a dark orange rust stain on the previously white sink before disappearing into the void of an open drain. I gripped that dingy porcelain and stared into a streak-filled mirror.

The locked bathroom door banged again. "Hurry up!"

"Screw you!" I shouted back, pounding my hand against the sink. "I'll be out when I'm out."

Whatever choice words the man on the other side of the door had for me, I wasn't paying attention to them; in fact, I wasn't paying attention to much of anything at that moment.

Even with a dead Imp laying on the dirty tile behind me like a lump of week-old Christmas pudding, my mind couldn't stop replaying the last conversation with my own Minor Demon.

They took her. No, it's not possible. Is it?

I had an iron-clad contract with the House, or that's what I'd been promised. In exchange for ten lifetimes of service, I had its assurances my daughter would be returned to me.

I'd seen it all with my own two eyes. She was Cathy, *my* Cathy. Wasn't she?

Stewart the Annoying couldn't lie to me, especially now that he'd been properly named in a fit of frustration and bound to servitude. He was as tied to me as stink on a dead rabbit, and he said they took her.

Who took her? Why do you care? You let her go. You condemned your own daughter to the fires of everlasting damnation.

I closed my eyes and was instantly greeted by the same nightmare that was my every night—the swirling Hellgate from all those months ago, my daughter clinging to the fiery edge, her screams echoing in my ears.

You weren't alone... The Defiler...

In my mind's eye, the many-tentacled Asaroth was there too. His corrupting arms reached for Cathy, and then beyond her, into our world. The inky monster was a primordial force of unchecked destruction and untold evil. On that night he'd been like a kid at Christmas, tentacles a flutter and ready to shuck our skin like discarded gift-wrap.

Not on my watch.

It was the impossible dilemma: stop the monster, or save the daughter.

I let her go. No, I commanded Stewart to protect her.

My eyes drifted to the dead Imp slowly decaying on the floor behind me.

Not exactly sending in the marines...

Stewart the Annoying, like the Imp whose body rotted on the floor, wasn't physically imposing. He was no Gillyfinkus Demon, or monstrous Thrull—frankly I'd seen raccoons around the trash cans more imposing than my Minor Demon. What could Stewart's rubbery little bat-winged body have done to keep her safe in the horrifying depths of the netherworld?

I turned the faucet on and let the water splash into the sink in broken bursts.

He was an Imp, which should have been exactly what she'd needed. They were the Jeopardy masters of the supernatural world. Monsters like Stewart knew the places, the players, and all their games. Those little rubbery bastards moved like rats in the underworld, always knowing exactly how to slip in and out unseen. He'd have found a way to hide her—I was sure of it.

But would she have let him?

I splashed the near-scalding water on my face, wiping at the dirt that had built up between unshaven bristles.

Cathy was as headstrong as her mother. Would she have fought him? Would she have tried to escape herself?

I shuddered. With Ariadne's Thread cut like a parade ribbon, Cathy would have been a lost balloon, drifting on the whims of the evil that prowled the shadows.

Please, for the love of God, please don't be like your mother just this once.

But Cathy was safe at home, I'd seen it myself. Those last two weeks after she'd been restored to us had been nigh Magickal in their own right. We'd done so many things together as a family: theme parks, restaurants, movies, the beach. But it wasn't one of those moments that stuck out, it was something simple.

'What ice cream do you want, Dad?'

'You know what I like.'

'Don't make me guess.'

The memory of Cathy's words hit me like a sucker punch to the gut. I had to catch my breath as the now scalding water sent a cloud of steam up to cover the mirror.

Don't make me guess.

She didn't know—why didn't she know?

Don't make me guess.

How had I missed that?

There was only one answer, and Stewart had told me just as much only moments ago—she wasn't Cathy.

'Not your daughter.'

How did you let this happen? What evil is living in Cathy's

skin? What is making its bed in the house your wife and son sleep in?

I turned off the water and wiped a hand across the dirty glass.

"It's time to get some answers."

My voice echoed in the empty bathroom and mixed with the live music worming its way through the thin walls.

"I can't leave your corpse here for someone to find. That's all I need, another urban legend springing up in the Strange Shine State."

The dive bar I'd tracked this Minor Demon to wasn't far outside Dade City, a tiny town in the center of the state and home to more than a few reclusive Bridge Trolls. Most of the time it was wise to steer clear of Bridge Trolls—I'd made that my mantra for many years—but the hunt had brought me here.

Sal's Bar.

You could practically smell the Bridge Troll in the air at Sal's. This made perfect sense given how close their territory was to the seedy watering hole. Still, I'd done my best to keep some distance between myself and those wrecking-ball-sized week-ruiners and had slipped into Sal's under the cover of darkness.

Window maybe?

I sized up the dead Imp versus the tight confines of the side window.

Working for the House had been a challenge to say the least. It took more than a little creativity to find a way to merge its directives with the other driving goal in my life—finding Tristan. It'd been tricky at first, but after a few weeks I'd gotten the hang of it.

I'm going on a Tristan hunt... I'm not afraid, but that bastard should be.

Tristan, Cathy's last boyfriend, the kid that had broken her heart, had snapped her Thread, and stolen the single most powerful book in my meager library. That teenager was a grade-A jerk as far as I was concerned, but he was also something else: damn tough to find.

I looped my fingers around the edge of the side windowsill and pulled my less-than-athletic body up far enough to see outside. It was dark, which limited my view, but the cross-breeze told me two things.

First, that side window was right over top a dumpster.

I'll take it.

And second, there was a little Bridge Troll scent in the air.

That's fine. I'm not hanging around.

I scooped up the gelatinous Imp carcass and maneuvered it under the window. Black and sticky Demon blood oozed down my hands and over my shirt.

Great.

One final heave got it up to the ledge and then over.

Splat!

The dead Imp's body landed in the dumpster with a sickening wet thump and effectively re-affirmed my desire to leave through the main door.

Honestly, I was somewhat surprised I'd heard the impact over the crowd of people drinking their troubles away at Sal's tonight. The converted bungalow served as a favorite watering hole for a unique cross-section of Florida.

Ladies night...

The band kicked it up a notch, and I wiped what I could of the Demon blood off on the last unused patches of paper towel scattered around the tiny bathroom.

Knock! Knock! Knock!

Someone banged against the door three times in rapid-fire succession. They weren't the petite raps of a gentleman keen to use the facilities, these impacts made the door rattle on its hinges.

"Yeah, listen. I said I'd be out when I was out and I'm wrapping up, so you just need to—"

I didn't get to finish my retort before the door to Sal's men's room blast inward right off its hinges. Two barrel-chested men that could have given Popeye a run for his money, and a young skinny kid not far into his twenties, poured into the tight confines of the tiny bathroom.

I raised my hands. "Right, so I'm all done. It's all yours—"

The fists came before I was ready for them. The first rammed into my gut with the force of a jackhammer, while the next caught the side of my skull.

Someone works with their hands...

For the second time that night I got to experience the unique displeasure of having all the air ejected from my lungs. Falling forward, I realized just how hard it was to use Magick without air.

Laying on the dingy tile, I didn't get much time to contemplate that challenge before a steel-toed boot ushered me into a deep and dreamless sleep.

AFTERWORD

Thank you for taking the time to follow the misadventures of West Florida's favorite Magician. You'll find parts of the Sunshine State represented in each story. I encourage you to pack up the family and come down to see the all the Weird in living color before it's gone.

But if you do, promise me you'll get one of those frilly drinks with the umbrellas in them and take a few moments to just be happy there's still a little mystery left in the world.

Martin
Somewhere under the Cypress
January 2020

ACKNOWLEDGMENTS

Books don't happen on their own, nor do they grow on trees—okay well, they sort of do—but you get the picture.

This book and all of its Magick could not have happened without the help of the following people:

Amber Townsend, my beta reader—thank you for being instrumental in keeping Weird Florida on track.

Jacob Faust, my supreme arc-master—thank you for watching my p's and q's, and helping me deliver a quality product.

Lonnie Mahoney, my proofreader—thank you for being my late stage grammar ninja.

Last but not least, thank you, reader. To know you've made it this far warms my heart more than you can imagine.

ABOUT THE AUTHOR

Martin Shannon's been using his imagination to avoid weeding since he was in short pants. His first series, *Tales of Weird Florida*, is an homage to the Sunshine State he knows and loves, and spent countless hours riding his bike through as a kid. It's got mystery, mayhem, and more than a little Magick. He hopes you enjoy the supernatural side of the upside down state, but if not, he's got a banjo, and he knows how to use it. You can find out more at www.martin-shannon.com.

ON NEWSLETTERS, WRITING, AND REVIEWS

Thank you for making it this far. It is my sincere hope you enjoyed the story, and the opportunity to slip into the sometimes too tight shoes of Eugene Law and company. If you did, please take a few seconds to help me spread the word, and in exchange I promise to send out free short stories as well as keep you up to date with each new novel in the Tales of Weird Florida world.

Writers live on reviews, newsletter sign-ups, and tiny scraps of praise. The writing life can get rather lonely, as evidenced by my social-media presence. So, drop by, say hello, sign up for the newsletter, and if you feel strongly enough, write a review or tell your friends. Remember, every time you write a review, an angel gets its wings.